I0767918

Cos-Player

The I, Player Series: Book One

David G. Martin

First Print Edition September 2025
ISBN: **979-8-9906024-5-8**

More Worlds
To Explore From

David G. Martin

The Magica Archives
How to Assassinate a Wizard

The Vex Duology
A Waking Nova
A Contest of Wills (Coming December 2025)

For Lindsey.

1

Earth.

Sure, its native species can be a pain. They aren't exactly the most evolved beings in the universe. But they do have some pretty cool hobbies and interests. These interests make doing business here a lot of fun. I mean, where else in the galaxy can I walk around in the open at a geek convention as almost my normal self, get compliments on my "costume," and make money all at the same time?

Oh, and speaking of money, humans are built for exploiting that, too. The collectibles market is insane, and the perfect cover for my real business. Nobody blinks twice at a vendor rolling in a few extra pallets of crates labeled Luke Skywalker Figures at a con, and the deals are easy money. The advanced tech market on a backwater place like Earth, away from the prying eyes of the galactic regulatory agencies, is booming, and that means that Earth is right where I want to be.

But I think I'm getting ahead of myself. Let me catch you up.

I'm Jarokin, but here on Earth I go by Jack. If you look up on a clear night, at the star that makes up the left point of what you call Orion's Belt. Well, where I'm from is just above that one. See that little star there? Yep, that's home. And guess what? That's about as close as I'll likely ever get to it again. Because I'm stranded here, on your planet. And that's just fine by me.

And so here we are, setting up another convention. This one is in Lexington, Kentucky. QUASITASTICON 9 is what this one is called, I think. I don't really know anymore. The names of these things keep getting more complicated as more of them pop up. The draw of this particular show is that the special guests are all from TV shows and movies before 2005, which if you're into those fandoms, is really cool. I, in particular, hope to grab one particular autograph from a certain cast member of *Firefly* that will complete my "Crew of Serenity" collection.

Hey, I'm allowed to like where I work, right?

And speaking of working, the vendor hall is all abustle right now. This particular hall is a nice one, too, not like the hotel ballrooms that the smaller shows sometimes shove us in. I do not usually go back to those unless there is a really pressing business matter to attend to. I always spring for a booth of at least forty feet long and forty feet wide if the venue offers it, making Jack's Menagerie of the Amazing Stuff pretty tough to miss. I'm what the serial attendees call a "staple" at these things, so I have to make sure there's always new stuff on the shelves.

That actually is not the hard part of all of this. The hard part is today—the dreaded load-in and set-up days at a con are the worst. Anyone who has worked at these kinds of shows will probably agree. The days with the people? Those are the best. And the after-hours entertainment and activities for us vendors can get pretty awesome, too.

But all that comes along in its own time. For now, I'm looking across the show floor, and I see some people that I just have to introduce you to.

The hall at this stage is a meandering mess of vendors, workers, teamsters, and other official people who probably have the right badge to be here all trying to cart in their wares, set up their stalls, and get them looking fine and dandy for all the shoppers that are totally here to see us and not the line-up of superstar actors, writers, and directors who bring all of their favorite worlds to life.

Two rows over from me, Bingo's Roleplaying Game Emporium is almost completely set up. The floor opened only two hours ago, and they are almost done. Nobody ever knows how they do it, but they are always on top of everything. I think they use magic, or some serious alien tech that folds time and space, in order to accomplish this, but I've never been able to prove it. The owner is always so coy when I try to figure out if they're really human.

Oh! Before we keep walking around, that's an important thing to point out. Not all of us vendors are human. Obviously, I am not, but some of the others are also from...out of town. We pretty much know each other and what we really sell behind the scenes, so we are kind of like a secondary vendor community operating in the shadows behind the main vendor community. It sounds way more complicated than it really is.

Trust me.

So yeah, three rows down from me, just on the other side of Bingo, is one of my fellow shadow vendors called Kinno. He is pretty lucky because he gets to use his real name in his human guise. Joquarons are not much smaller than humans either, and Kinno gets to just be mostly himself, with some minor *maccomp* adjustments. He probably could pass for human without it, as long as nobody looks too closely.

"Hey, Jack, my man!" Kinno calls over as he drops whatever box he has in his hands and comes over to greet me. We flail our hands around in our secret handshake before doing anything else.

"Yo, Kinno," I say after we have properly identified one another via the top-secret series of hand gestures, "so about those transistors you asked me for in Cleveland..."

"Shhhh!" Kinno whispers and looks around nervously.

"Dude! Not here!"

I look around at the other vendors, the nearest one being over twenty feet away. When I am done scanning, I look back to Kinno, who is nervously glancing around.

"Hey, man, what's got you bothered?" I ask.

"You never know who's listening, man," Kinno says, his voice even mousier than usual.

"What happened?" I ask again.

"Pshhh, nothing, dude," Kinno says, and a smile comes over his face, wiping away the previous moments of tension. "You know I hate talking about the real business when it's not business hours."

I raise an eyebrow and let the matter drop. That is, in fact, exactly the opposite of how Kinno is, and I have known him now for almost fifteen years. I would know. But, I don't have time to ask him about it right now, as I spot the booth I have been trying to find over his shoulder.

"Cool, cool, bro," I say, and sidestep to head down the next aisle. "Drinks tonight in that one place, right?" I say as I have already turned to walk away.

"Oh...yeah, bro, you got it!" Kinno calls after me. "You're buying, right?"

But I barely hear him as I walk down the row. As I walk toward the other booth I spotted, I feel the anger welling up. I march by two more vendors who wave and attempt to greet me, flashing them the best return greeting I can muster in the moment, which is a half smile and a quick, stilted wave that is much more of a brush-off than a greeting of any kind that a human might notice. I have been among them for a long time, but sometimes I still fall short on their more nuanced gestures and postures.

No time for that now, though, as I close in on the target of my growing wrath.

"Hey, there, Hal!" I say through gritted teeth as I march into the half-constructed booth that smells faintly of old grandma house and storage locker.

I have never understood the point of Hal's booth, Hal of a Good Deal. Yeah, the name is good, but this guy literally has the worst prices on everything that people already aren't buying. Pots and pans with wrong or parody fandom branding, high-end electronics that better fit in a Tokyo-based cutting-edge electronics showcase, and clothing trends that nobody ever picks back up, not even the retro cosplayers who think everything eventually comes back in style, and everything else in between can be found in Hal's booth.

Hal is another one of us, "shadow vendors," but when I say he is pretty much the most conspicuous of us, what I mean is that even the local Earth-based authorities have their eye on him. We all know what the problem is. We've all told him. He just says we don't know what we're talking about and keeps doing it, though.

I mean, how long can you really fly under the radar with a vendor booth that never makes any money, everyone knows it never makes any money, has no regular customers, is dead during the show beyond people demoing the latest VR technology on display, and yet con after con keeps coming back?

Yeah, that's right. He must be dealing in something else. He has to be. And yeah, sure, he is, cause of the whole alien thing and all. But that's beside the point. The Earthers think he's dealing drugs, or guns, or something. And that's potentially bad for business. And what's bad for business just can't be.

"Oh, hey, Jack!" Hal extends a hand to me, intent on partaking in the standard Earther greeting. I grab his hand and pull him close to me, wrapping my other arm around his shoulder. Any onlookers would assume that Hal and I are really good buddies.

We are not.

"I thought we discussed this at the last show," I say, talking into his ear at just above a whisper so none else can hear me. "Your sorry excuse for a booth is going to cause trouble for all of us. You better have something that sells this time, because I'm not sure how long I can convince the others not to force you out the violent way."

I release Hal from my grip and take a step back, my face now in a smile as he stares at me, bewildered, as if he has no idea what I'm talking about. I consider for a brief moment that maybe we're the ones who have misunderstood him this whole time. Maybe he really is incapable of understanding. I really don't want any harm to come to him, and not because I particularly like him, just because it's not my style. Wishing harm on others is bad cosmos, and I'm not about that.

Still, he's gotta stop it with the endangering of the rest of us.

"So good to see you, again! Hey, let's hammer those details on that deal this time, okay?" I say loud enough for any neighboring vendors to overhear.

"Uhh, yeah, sure," Hal manages to stammer out as I turn on my heel and exit the way I came.

I hope for his sake Hal manages to stop with his shenanigans. But in the end, it's not that big of a deal, I remind myself. He's annoying. Okay, I was mad. I admit it. He's angering. But things tend to work out, at least that's been my philosophy in life, and even though you've got no idea about where I've come from, that's a pretty bold philosophy for a someone like myself to have.

"Why do you act like you're Hal's friend loud enough for the rest of us to hear it?" This voice from behind me is disarming, and I turn to see her.

Yeah.

Her.

"Wha—?" is all I can get out after realizing that she has so deftly snuck up on me.

"Did you forget how to talk again, Jack?" Lyra says, the familiar half smile flashing across her face as she winks and steps up to walk with me.

I did for a moment, but Lyra always has that effect on me. I've known her for a few years now. She appeared on the con circuit a while back with her booth It's Just Crystals. Her smile and her wit immediately appealed to me. No other human had ever made me laugh as much as she did, and I think I lost money at a few cons that first year buying every crystal in her shop that I could. I'm not a hundred percent sure that they do everything she says they do, but hey, it's a big galaxy. Anything is possible, right?

Yeah, as humans go, Lyra is pretty cool.

"Why do you have to find this loser everywhere we go?"

Her little brother, Leo? Maybe not so much.

"Leo!" Lyra snaps at him as she looks sideways at me.

The teenager cocks his head to the side and flashes a grin that I am certain only blood relatives could find endearing in any way. "Aww, sis, don't be mad at me. Jack knows I'm only joking. Right, Jack?"

Lyra looks to me, unconvinced. What else is that in her expression? Is it worry? I don't really know. She might be hungry. She's known to skip breakfast for setup days, so she might be hungry.

"Yeah, of course," I say, brushing the whole thing off with a hand wave gesture that I am sure perfectly mimics the proper human gesture. "Leo and I are cool, right, dude?"

Lyra raises a dark eyebrow as she evaluates my response, but after a brief moment turns to her brother and shakes her head. "You're lucky Jack is cool with your stupid antics, Leo. Other people might not be so willing to put up with your stupidity."

Leo looks hurt for a moment, but then his smile returns. I still do not fully know if the expression progression in a human is genuine or part of what they call sarcasm. I mean, I get sarcasm and verbally it is easy to spot. But visually humans are tough to read, even with galactic-level bio-species interpretative software running on my maccomp.

"So are you almost done with setup?" Lyra asks me. I am not. I have barely got anything out of a box yet. Too busy shaking hands, setting up shadow deals, and making sure people like Hal don't wreck things for the rest of us.

"Uhh...no," I say, sighing. "I've been—"

"You've been talking to too many of the other vendors again," Lyra interjects. She pokes me in the midsection as she berates my bad vendor behavior. It's true, though. I am usually the last booth to get fully set up at these cons. Partially it's because I do not want many prying eyes to see what new stuff I might have for this weekend. I am more than just a shadow vendor, after all. Sometimes I get some pretty cool fandom collectibles in that I am dying to unveil on the opening day of a show. Dollars spend just as well in the shadow world as galactic coin, at least here on Earth, so it's not a big deal to actually participate in my cover business.

"You're already done?" I ask, knowing full well that despite her meticulous nature, Lyra has been finished for some time. She always finishes setting up completely before venturing away from her booth.

"You know it!" Leo interjects as we all three walk down the aisle toward my booth space.

I want to keep the conversation going, but I know that Lyra will only tell me that I need to finish before tonight.

"I can always come back later and finish it if you guys want to get something to eat," I say, still knowing the outcome.

Lyra tilts her head to the side and raises her eyebrow again, appraising me and the situation of my booth all in one devastating glance. I had to try, right?

"No," she says, her tone not open for negotiation. "Leo and I will bring you back something..." She pauses for a moment, waiting for my expression to turn from eager excitement to resignation at my fate. When it does, she continues.

"And," she says, already walking away, "you'll get whatever we bring you only if you're done."

I watch them walk away and turn the corner down another aisle without a reply. I don't need to reply. She's right, and I don't mind it, either. The game of our dialogue is fun, and I think she enjoys playing it out at every con, too.

Ah well, time to get this thing done.

Humans are funny creatures. Work first, then the rest. At least, that's how the better ones tend to be. Me? I don't like the work part much at all. I want to get to the selling part, both to the humans and to the shadow customers. That's the part that gets me out of bed in the morning. Oh, and it's not about the money, so don't get me wrong there.

Well, it's a little about the money.

The work is done in no time, perhaps in part thanks to my hidden alien physique making the job really light work. Earth's gravity is much lighter than it is on my home planet, and I have to work extra hard here to keep my increased strength compared to humans. It's not what you'd call super strength or anything like that. I doubt I'm even Captain America-level strong, but it's more of a total body thing. I process nitrogen-rich oxygen much better than they do, which is one reason I like this place so much more.

But enough about me. It's time for the con!

2

QUASITASTICON 9 opens up with the usual fanfare. In the hall next to ours, announcers are loudly introducing some of the celebrity guests, and the crowd cheers. It's a lot of energy that fortunately spills over into the vendor hall soon after.

And I'm ready for it all. I even have my "cosplay" on for opening day. Really it is just me with my maccomp setting turned down to almost non-existent. My true skin color, a cool grayish tint that is similar to a dark fog, is showing where I'm not covered with clothing, and my facial structure looks to humans as if it is a near-professionally applied set of prosthetics that elongates my nose slightly, bulges out along my jawline, and makes my ears scaly and forms the tips of them into sharp points that wrap around the back of my head and nearly touch.

So yeah, that is pretty much what I really look like underneath the maccomp. The only thing I have it keep is the bright blue human eyes "under the makeup," to keep me looking just a bit more human. Years ago I tried it with the maccomp completely off, but the realism of my "costume" upset some children and small animals. My species has eyes that look to humans like we are blind, and that tends to creep people out for some reason.

By the way, dogs know that I am not human. They're smarter than humans think they are. But they tend to only bark when my eyes are showing their true form.

"Hey, Jack!" the leader of a group of teenagers calls out to me as they rush over to the booth. The crowd is already in full swing, and the booths and aisles are starting to get packed. Looks to be a sell-out crowd, again, for this one.

"Heyo, Kielan, buddy! Good to see ya again. You lot get taller every year!"

I don't remember all their names. But this group is different. They have been coming to this con since before their parents were completely comfortable letting a group of young kids walk around the venue by themselves. Now they're around seventeen or so, I think, and they are probably driving themselves at this point. Human development is fascinating if you think about it. The more hormones flowing through their bodies, the more their parents let them do on their own. I may never understand that one.

"What all do you have this year, Jack?" the boy, says when the group enters my booth. They look around in awe, as usual. This is one of the fun parts for me that does not involve collecting money. Human children still have a little wonder in them. Keeps me hoping, at least.

"Well," I say, lowering my voice and stepping toward them, "this year I think you'll like what I have for you."

The five kids all exchange conspiratorial glances between themselves. I step behind a counter at the back of the booth and pull out a small case. I am careful about which case I grab because this one is next to the small crate of Kelaxion Death Batteries that I just got in for a shadow client. Those probably should not be in the hands of Earth teenagers.

"Now last we spoke," I say, resting my arms on the box in front of them, prolonging the reveal to ensure that they will empty out their wallets when they see what is inside, "you guys all said you were having trouble finding some of the Galaxy Adventures figures from the early '90s right?"

"Yeah!" Keilan says enthusiastically. "They're always sold out, like everywhere, and the ones that are for sale are way too expensive. We've pretty much given up on them at this point."

The nods and looks of disappointment among the group in front of me confirm that they are in the throes of giving up. Luckily, I am here to save their day, and take their money.

"Well, then," I say, sighing as if I was just put out by a major upset, "then I guess you won't be interested in...these!"

In one swift motion I lift the lid of the box, unveiling a treasure trove of Galaxy Adventures figures, all out of box, or "OOB" as the collectors say, but in very good condition, and with all their original parts.

Hey, I don't skimp when it comes to my customers.

The group goes wild, the cheers loud enough to draw the attention of those in nearby booths. Several heads, both human-faced and costumed, crane into the booth to see what the commotion is about. A couple even step inside when they see what I have on the shelves. Is that what they call word-of-mouth business? Probably. Kinda.

The group starts looking through what I have in a furious check of all that I managed to collect throughout the past year. After a few moments, they all look up to me as one unit, the reality of their situation hitting them.

"Hey, uhh, Jack," says Norra, who is currently cosplaying as an incredibly detailed and immaculately recreated fish warrior royal guard from the show *Atlantis' Keepers*. "So, how much are these?"

The rest of the group all stares me down, and I do not believe any of them are breathing as they wait for me to answer.

I could totally rip them off here. I have them in my grasp, and after seeing and touching these collectibles they will not be able to walk away. I know the look. I've seen it in humans and aliens alike for many years. My keen dealer senses have never failed me.

Ah, but these are good kids. And their cosplays are all spot on. That's really why I wanted them to come by. They always pay attention to the details. So I'm not going to rake them over the coals.

"For you guys? You know I like you all—been coming to see me for years now. And you have always bought from me. I don't forget that, you know. So, just for you, forty bucks per figure."

The price is a little below the worst of the price gougers, and I see Keilan frown. He doesn't have that much, and neither do his friends. But I can't just give these away. They did cost something to get, after all.

"Twe...Twenty-five, maybe?" Kik asks, his voice cracking at the attempt to haggle with me. I have to keep my face stoic, even though this was exactly what I wanted!

None of them have ever done much haggling with me before, and I said to myself that this was the year that I would help them learn to fight high prices. Maybe just not too well.

"Hmmm..." I say, making a show of being thoughtful about the price, "that is pretty close to what I paid for them myself."

This is when the panic starts to set in, and I have to wait and watch as they glance at each other and wait for a solution to come to one of them. One dark-haired kid frowns and chews his lip as he counts something on his fingers, while another begins frantically scrolling through banking apps on his phone, and yet another pulls out a wallet and begins to rifle through a short stack of bills.

And no, before I get judged for toying with their emotions, I am not doing this for my own amusement. They have to figure this out. I am helping them, trust me. I actually picked up these figures for about eight bucks each from an estate sale that I had to pretty much crash, but it was worth it. Don't judge me. I'm doing all this for them.

"Wh...what about as a lot?" Keilan asks, letting the question just hang in the air on its own. Not a bad move, kid.

"Well, as a lot, to get them all offloaded, not have to pack them up again, cart them to a new city, sell them to a bunch of other kids who I don't like as much at the next con..."

They chuckle a bit at my dry humor, which makes me lower the price in my head again.

"Five hundred for the box," I say.

"Four!" Kik bursts out before the others have a chance to confer, and they all look at him as if he has just ruined it all. They all groan and grimace, one throwing up his hands in defeat while another punches Kik lightly in the shoulder. Kik shrinks back a half step as they all look back to me, sure that their friend has spoiled my good mood by attempting to take advantage of my generosity.

I am smiling as they look at me, and it's almost my real smile. My true teeth are a little sharper than human teeth. Not really pointy, but a bit more rounded and thinner at the apex of the point. Stronger bones, 'cause of that gravity and all. But they don't see that. I've been told that my "prosthetic teeth" unsettle people even at cons.

"Done," I say, acting like they really raked me over the coals. I just made about two-hundred bucks. Not much in the grand scheme, but these kids just became kings for a day.

The cheers and whoops from the group again draw more attention to the booth, and they likely just made me more money for it.

I congratulate them on their newly found treasure as we process the transaction, and they run off into the crowd—to show one of their rival groups what they just scored, no doubt.

"Ah, another happy customer for you, I see," a voice behind me says.

Fortunately, my good mood is only slightly diminished as I turn to see a...man...standing in front of me. On Earth, he is known as Gorge, but I know his real name is Portabolia, and seeing his face during regular business hours is a rarity. He must really need something.

"Gorge," I say, nodding to him as I glance at the other con attendees currently browsing my shelves.

"Jack," he replies in kind. We do not exchange any more words until the few browsers make their purchases and leave. I note a lull in the traffic, which usually means that a popular panel is about to start, and people are lining up to try to get seats. Gorge's timing is good, even if unintended.

"So what can I do for you?" I ask, turning to Gorge, who is currently inspecting a collection of rare graded Topps cards.

Gorge takes a look around the booth before speaking. "I wouldn't have come to you now, but I need something," he says.

"Obviously," I say.

George either ignores or does not catch my sarcasm as he continues. "Hectaran Grunge Bolts," he says.

I suppress a wince.

"And I need them tonight," Gorge adds, stepping close to me, a look of insistence in his alien eyes, the only part of his true form showing through in his current disguise.

I sigh and let out a long breath. I have them. Of course I do. Nobody else in the state does. A Hectaran Grunge Bolt is a potentially nasty little bit of tech that instantly fuses with anything not carbon-based that it comes into contact with. Popular with the starship modders and builders, Grunge Bolts are incredibly rare on Earth due to the lack of abundant fiber steel materials commonly used in interstellar vessels.

"Planning a quick getaway?" I ask, trying to make light of the massive ask that he just made.

Gorge growls and steps even closer. I am beginning to feel my space being violated, so I smile and wait for him to say something. You never know what kinds of sensibilities or buttons anyone has. Like humans, right? Wow, are those things sensitive.

"That's none a' yer concern, Jack," Gorge says, his voice raised a bit too much for my comfort considering all the people about. Fortunately none of them have joined us in my booth just yet.

"Hey," I say, taking a step back from Gorge and smiling again, "of course I have what you need, Gorge. Don't I always?"

Gorge's posture changes as he processes what I tell him. "Uhh, yeah, okay Jack," he says. "You're right. I new I could count on you."

There is a relief in his voice that I do not understand, and I feel a tingle I usually get in my gallofornda gland when I feel like something is wrong. I do not feel like the problem is Gorge, though, at least not directly.

"Look," I say, stepping around my back table and grabbing a pad of paper. "I don't keep those with me on the floor, though. Too volatile, that stuff."

I motion for Gorge to join me at the back of the booth as a group of con attendees walks in the front and begins to browse. I scribble a number on a piece of paper and tear it off the sheet.

"Meet me here later tonight, after midnight," I say, handing him the paper.

"Uhh, midnight?" Gorge asks. "Can't you do it sooner?"

I shake my head. "I'm afraid not, my friend. Business runs on its own schedule, and I have much to attend to before I see you again."

"But I really need them," Gorge says with an urgency in his voice. The other people in the booth look up at him. He has attracted too much attention, and this conversation needs to end now.

"I've got ya covered, good buddy," I say, my voice raised in a reassuring tone. I move around the table and pat Gorge on the shoulder, nodding my head in the direction of the humans in the booth.

"Just let me look into it, and I'll get you that rare collectible. No sweat."

Gorge looks apprehensive to leave, but he understands the number one rule to our shadow business dealings: the humans can never suspect. No attention can be drawn to what we are really doing. He turns to leave and slowly walks out of the booth, but not before checking three times to make sure he still has the piece of paper I gave him. I see him check his watch as he walks out into the aisle. Eventually losing sight of him in the crowd, I turn to help my current customers find their next priceless artifact.

3

I was not lying to Gorge when I told him that I had business after the vendor hall shut down. I met with a few shadow clients, none of them looking for anything difficult. Nothing like Gorge, for sure. One of them did mention that they, too, were soon to be headed offworld, but I did not get the impression that they had the same urgency that Gorge had earlier.

But all that was not the reason I could not meet with Gorge until after midnight. There was another, much more socially rewarding reason for that. For a few years now, several of the regular vendors on the circuit, including myself, have been a part of an ongoing Dungeons & Dragons campaign, which we get together to play another session of after the first and last nights of every con where we are all present.

And since we are all convention circuit regulars, that happens about once a month and usually more. It is a good outlet for all of us. Dealing with the public at these events is not always a pleasant experience, though I have personally found fan-convention-going humans to be among the best in the lot.

"You ready for the Dungeon of St. Krongo?" Leo asks as I sit down at the table. We're in one of the executive suites of the hotel connected to the convention center. Our DM, Iris, always gets us this kind of room for gaming and parties. Most of us have no idea how she constantly affords to do this, and whenever any of us offer to help pay for the extravagance she provides, she acts offended and says that we are the only people who keep her sane, which is payment enough.

Eventually, we just stopped fighting it and decided to enjoy the perks of being one of "Iris' Chosen." At least that's what we've been called by vendors who are not part of the inner circle. Exactly what we would be the inner circle of, I have no idea, but here we are.

"Are we ever ready for a dungeon designed by Iris?" Herb asks, taking his seat directly opposite Leo.

"No, we aren't," I respond. "And that is what makes the experience so fascinating."

Leo just shakes his head at my response. "You are always fascinated by everything, Jack. That doesn't mean much."

"If only my little brother could still have some of Jack's childlike wonder, he'd be more tolerable to be around," Lyra adds as she takes a seat next to her brother. Leo is not happy with her entrance into the conversation and frowns at her.

"Well, maybe if my much older sister didn't drag me around the country where I see the kind of stuff that makes kids grow up too fast, I'd still have some of that childlike wonder you want me to have," Leo retorts.

"I've never heard you complain about it bef—" Lyra stops mid-sentence as her face suddenly gets serious. "Wait, what do you mean 'see the kind of stuff that makes kids grow up too fast?'"

The table is silent, all eyes on Leo as he visibly attempts to think his way out of the tight spot he dug himself into. Panic sets in as Lyra's gaze burns into him.

"Well, ah, ya know..." Leo stammers, his gaze darting around the room for help. None comes to him. "Just like, stuff. And things."

"No," Lyra says, "I don't know."

The door to the room opens, and in walks Iris and Kendra, the last two members of the group. Leo is saved by the bell as the greetings are exchanged, the snacks distributed, and a pizza order is compiled. You know, the usual pre-game session stuff that has to take place in order to get down to the business at hand.

Lyra flashes me a look of exasperation as the chaos unfolds. She was mostly grilling Leo just to make him fidget for saying something stupid, but I think the life she has them living sometimes gets to her from time to time. Leo did have to grow up pretty quickly, but we all know Lyra had no choice. When her brother came to live with her, there just wasn't any other option but to take him with her on the road and expose him to the life. She worries that she did the wrong thing.

I return her look with what I hope is a reassuring expression, and she drops her shoulders down to normal. Leo may be a handful, but he's practically grown now. And besides, Lyra hasn't been alone in helping to finish raising him. We have all, each one of us around the table, invested something into Leo's care and instruction, and Lyra knows that.

"Now," Iris says, calling the table to order, "when last we left our heroic adventurers, they had just accepted a quest from the Lady of..."

We all get into the ambiance of the game and lose track of time. When the knock comes to the door, Kendra gets up to get the pizza from the delivery guy. After a moment at the door, she turns around and walks back to the table, no pizza in hand.

"Uh, hey, Jack?" Kendra says with a confused frown. "There's a guy out here who says he needs to talk to you. Gorge? I think he said."

Everyone looks at me, and I check my watch. 10:42 p.m. Come on, Gorge, I told you after midnight.

And what was he doing here anyway? I wrote down my room number, not this one.

I sigh.

"I'm sorry, everyone," I say, getting up from the table. "He wasn't supposed to be here at all. Just give me a minute."

The questions and looks of puzzlement fly at me from the table as I hurry to the door, open it, and step out into the hallway.

"Jack!" Gorge yells, much too loudly for a hotel hallway, even one where a con is going on.

I put my finger up and motion for him to follow me down a few doors and into the stairwell. I check to make sure there is no one around before saying anything.

"What's the deal, Gorge? I told you after—"

"I know!" Gorge interrupts me. "But it can't wait, man. I gotta get those bolts now!"

I take a step back and look Gorge over. He is a mess compared to when I saw him earlier. And he is now really nervous. He is spooked, and that has me spooked.

"Listen, Gorge," I say, still looking around to make sure nobody could be listening. "You are damaging my calm right now, and that is putting our deal in jeopardy. Now, you tell me what has you so spooked, and..."

The creaking of a door on a floor below us tells me that we are not as alone as I would feel comfortable with. I grab Gorge by his jacket and pull him down a flight of stairs to the next floor, taking out my key card to open the door.

"And another thing," I say quietly. "How did you even find out where I was, let alone get access to that floor?"

"Hey, man, come on," Gorge bites back. "It's not like humans really understand security."

I nearly cuff him on the back of the back of his head. "Shut up with that! Dammit, are you trying to get us caught?"

Gorge is silent the rest of the way to my room. Once inside, Gorge stands nervously as I access the portable folding safe that I keep in my luggage.

Oh, yeah. A portable folding safe probably sounds weird, huh? Well, it is pretty easy to explain. Alien tech. That's the short answer. The slightly longer answer is that the neutronic power coupling that powers the safe allows it and the contents inside to be folded down into about the size of a notebook binder. I have mine masquerading as a 1990s-era Trapper Keeper. I missed the '90s here on Earth, but I have always thought I would have really liked living in them. Instead, I was busy being...Well, I was busy during the '90s. And not anywhere near Earth.

I set the Trapper Keeper on the bed and turn to Gorge.

"Okay, now before we do this, you're going to tell me what this is all about."

Gorge looks around the room as if checking the corners to make sure nobody is hiding in them.

"Are you..." he stammers as his eyes dart around again. "Are you sure nobody is...listening?"

"Yes, I'm sure," I say and gesture for him to continue.

"Look, I just need to get off this planet, like now, okay?" he says, clearly hoping that this will be enough.

"Got some heat on you for something?" I ask.

Gorge shakes his head. "Not me, just the planet in general. Word's out that there are some bad guys sniffing around the black market venues, looking for someone."

"Bad guys?" I ask.

"Yeah." He swallows, or whatever the equivalent thing his species does. "Word is they're looking for someone and some stuff."

I sigh. Galactic-level bounty hunters, repossessors, bill collectors, and everything in between are constantly passing through Earth, making sure all the right paperwork is in order in case they have an opportunity to make this fertile little commerce zone in the Milky Way into a chance for a big score.

"And that's it?" I ask as I move to the Trapper Keeper to start opening up the folding safe.

"Yeah," Gorge says, trying his best to regain his cool. "Yeah, that's it."

"Right..." I say as I bring out the box of Hectaran Grunge Bolts and set them on the table. "These aren't cheap, you know."

Gorge's eyes widen as he sees me produce the bolts, and a grin...a smile of relief?...flashes across his face.

"I know, man. I'm good for these. Here, look."

Gorge produces a payment pad that is disguised as an Earth tablet. He quickly touches a couple of buttons, and the account transfer screen comes up. I take a look at the amount he has entered and laugh.

"Hah! No way, Gorge!" I say. "Your price is about five hundred short for what I'm giving you."

"Five hundred? So you want three thousand kreds?" Gorge's smile has disappeared by now.

"You know anywhere else to get them?" I say, moving to take the box off the table.

Gorge places a hand out to stop me and says, "No! No...I mean, okay man. That's not cool. Three months ago I could find them in St. Louis for a thousand cheaper."

I look around and gesture to where we are, "I don't see us in St. Louis three months ago, Gorge. And nobody else has these right now, I guarantee it."

Gorge sighs. "I know, Jack, I know. Okay, how about twenty-seven hundred?"

I shake my head. "That's a funny way of pronouncing three thousand."

"Twenty-eight hundred?"

"Gorge..." I move to remove the box again.

"Okay! Okay! Okay! I...I was just going through the motions, Jack. Nothing personal."

I watch as Gorge changes the amount to three thousand.

"Okay," I say, nodding in approval.

Gorge deactivates his maccomp to let the payment pad read his bio-sig and hands the pad to me. I look everything over one more time before deactivating my own maccomp and doing the same.

I hand the pad back to Gorge after the confirmation screen verifies the transaction, and Gorge picks up the box of bolts from the table.

"So I guess I won't see you for a while, then, eh, Jack?" Gorge says.

"Not if you intend to use those to leave the planet. I'm just fine here. Earth is as good a home as any, and if you ask me—"

"WHOA!"

Gorge and I both jump at the exclamation and turn toward the door. Standing there is a human, staring at us, wide eyes and mouth agape at the sight of two aliens with completely deactivated maccomps staring back at him.

"Leo?"

4

"LEO!"

Leo just stands there, frozen in the moment, and I am thankful that Gorge does the same. The number of humans who know the truth about us can probably be counted on one hand, and the rest tend to not live long. It's a sad truth of the shadow markets, but humans who stumble into the knowledge of them tend to go missing on a permanent basis.

I see Gorge reaching for something in his pocket, and I turn toward him, jumping in between him and Leo. I reach for his hand which, as I suspected, is drawing a small pocket-sized las blaster. I grab for the blaster, and we struggle for a moment.

"He's seen us, Jack!"

"I...know...you idiot!" Wow! Gorge is stronger than I thought!

I feel a twinge of pain as Gorge's left fist connects with my abdomen. Fortunately for me, my species can't get the wind knocked out of us that way, but it still hurts. I let out a yell of pain and anger and jump on top of Gorge, driving him to the ground. He is a bit bulkier than I am, but he is clearly not a trained fighter.

But he proves to be a problem anyway. We struggle for a moment longer before we separate. Gorge grabs his box of bolts and darts for the doorway, which, thankfully, no longer has Leo standing in it.

I race after Gorge out into the hallway and see him bolting for the elevator. Leo is nowhere in sight, and I stop there to collect my wits. Breathing heavier than usual, I try to think about what Leo would do next.

Lyra. He would go to his sister.

I turn in the opposite direction of Gorge and head to the stairwell. If Leo followed us down here that way, he probably went back up that way, too. Gorge is already out of my mind as a problem as I head into the stairwell. He is leaving the planet anyway and will likely not consider one human knowing the truth on a planet he probably won't come back to as any kind of a problem. Or at the very least, as someone else's problem.

Like mine.

I don't have to go far before I find him. He's trying to get past the door leading into the top-floor hallway, and I remember that it was Lyra who mentioned she had their key to the RPG room and not him. I breathe a slight sigh of relief that is short-lived as Leo turns around and lets out a scream.

Oh crap! My maccomp has been off this whole time!

I decide to leave it off as I put up my hands and try to speak to the young Earther.

"Hey, Leo," I say, and he stops screaming for one moment as he recognizes my voice. The maccomp has little to do with my voice. Perhaps it is a bit more high-pitched than usual due to my biological makeup, but it's close enough that he definitely recognizes me.

"J-J-Jack?" he manages to mumble through the terror.

I can't blame him at all for his state. I likely look more like I have eaten Jack and put on his clothes and con badge.

"Yeah, buddy," I say, keeping my voice low and calm. "It's me. The *real* me. You...You know the truth now, I guess."

I sigh with the sudden realization that my life here on Earth is likely over. At least, it will not ever be the same again at the very least. Leo has seen the real me, and I can't take that back. I am not the sort of alien who kills humans just for knowing the truth. Don't very much like the ones who do, really. I tend to not do business with those types when I can help it. I did not know Gorge was one of the "Shoot Earthers First" crowd, but I'm not surprised either.

"You're...you...what..." I realize that Leo is beginning to hyperventilate and panic. I need to shock him out of this state, and I get an idea.

I reactivate my maccomp, and my human form instantly folds back into being, erasing all visual and auditory trace of my true form. Leo lets out a gasp, and I fear that he is getting worse, when he suddenly stops breathing altogether for a moment.

My fear quickly dissolves into amusement as I realize that Leo is smiling and staring at me once more with wide eyes.

"Jack? I really is you! How is this? What is that? Who was that other—? How long have you—?"

Leo is unable to finish one question before another pops out, and his string of questions relaxes me and gives me hope. Maybe this is not the disaster I thought it was. Well, not completely anyway.

"Yes, Leo," I start off as Leo takes a seat in the stairwell. I look around and down the stairs to make sure nobody is nearby who could hear us chat and sit down next to him. He looks up at me, but I can tell he is past the stage of running on me. Now he is trying to figure all this out, and I need to help him do so if I am going to have any hope of keeping my secret.

"I am an alien..."

"Like from outer space?"

"Yes, from outer space."

"Why are you here?"

"Well, that's complicated to answer, but the best way to put it is that I'm a merchant in an alien shadow market that hides in the shadows of the fandom convention circuit and deals in alien technology and goods that are smuggled onto and around Earth by others like me."

"The other one didn't look like you," Leo says, his face twisting into a look the combines a scrunched up nose with furrowed eyebrows and a wide-eyed stare that I think, if my human is correct, lands him somewhere in the neighborhood of concerned skepticism. Or a bowel obstruction. I am leaning toward the skepticism in this case.

"No, Gorge is a different species from me," I say.

"So, there are more of you?"

"There's whole galaxies full of us, Leo. Humans are far from the only species in the cosmos."

Leo gets a suddenly excited look on his face. "Who else knows about you? Does my sister know you're an alien?"

"No, Leo," I say, cutting off any further inquiry, "and I need you to help me keep it that way. It is very unsafe for you to know this. Telling anybody else, including your sister, might put her in danger, too."

"How do you look like us all the time?" Leo asks. I take out my maccomp and show it to him.

"With this," I say, de-activating and then re-activating it and resuming my human facade. Leo startles in momentary surprise at the shift in my appearance. One moment I am the alien sitting next to him, and in a blink I am the dorky shop owner he has known for years. I get it. I would jump, too.

"Whoa..." is all he manages to say before he raises a hand to poke my face. His finger pushes against my cheek, and he reels as he feels the skin of my altered appearance.

"It feels human," Leo says. "How?"

"The best answer is 'alien tech,'" I say. "It's just one of the things we all have to do to keep our secret and keep you humans safer. It's better if you don't all know that several thousand of us walk among you."

Leo is quiet for a moment as he takes in the reality of the

situation.

"So...I'm in danger now?"

"Not at the moment," I say. "Gorge is on his way off the planet, and I doubt he will speak to anyone of consequence before he leaves. For now, I believe you are safe, but the secret has to be kept. Do you understand?"

Leo is silent again as he thinks over the situation.

"So...does that mean I get some kind of cool alien communicator now, so we can keep in touch, and I can warn you of danger and you can keep an eye on me and all that?"

I laugh quietly at Leo's exuberance. Humans, especially teenagers, are incredibly resilient if you let them be. It doesn't matter what situation you put them in, they tend to roll with the punches and come out on top. It's part of why I like the native sentient species of Earth, and this young one in particular.

"Ah, no," I say, and I see the disappointment leak from his face. "It is much safer for you if you don't have any contact with the alien technologies that are here on Earth."

"Okay...well…" Leo stands, already in the moping stage of disappointment that this new secret is not turning out to be as exciting as he might have originally hoped. "I guess we had better get back to the game. They'll be wondering what happened to us."

I stand and follow Leo to the door, scanning my key card to let us onto the floor.

"You're being incredibly grown up about this, Leo. Most fully grown adults don't react this well or bounce back this quickly after learning the truth."

"Eh, it's not a big deal I guess."

"WHAT?!" It is my turn to be surprised.

"I mean, look at my life. I spend all my time around the craziest and strangest humans anyway. Why not aliens, too?"

Leo turns to walk to the room, and I am once more

impressed by the boy's ability to handle this. He still might freak out later, and is likely still in some level of shock at the whole business, but I have a good feeling about this.

"And besides," Leo adds just before opening the door to the RPG room, "my sister somehow *always* ends up liking the weird ones."

5

"I told you they would come back when they smelled the pizza!" Herb says as we walk back into the suite. The others cheer and welcome us back to the table.

Leo looks back at me, and I get the impression that he is checking to make sure my maccomp is still working. He looks at me with skepticism, as if now that he knows the secret behind the disguise, he is suddenly afraid that everyone else will be able to see past it, too.

And that also makes me afraid for reasons I cannot explain. The idea of the RPG group knowing the truth? All of them? The humans in the RPG group are my closest friends, as humans go anyway, and while I have often thought that I would like for some of them to know the truth, now that I am faced with Leo knowing, and the possibility that the others could just as easier find out, too, I become queasy at the thought of how complicated that would make everything. Maybe that really isn't what I want, after all.

"Who was that guy?" Lyra asks as Leo and I take our seats and help ourselves to some pizza.

I shrug. "Just another collector who doesn't understand the concepts of business hours and personal space. We won't be seeing him again."

"I hope Leo here did not cause you any trouble," Lyra says, glowering at her brother. "He got impatient with waiting and said he was going to try to find out where you went. He was up and out before I could grab his collar and wring his neck."

Lyra is scary sometimes. I am glad she is not my big sister. I actually have one of those, but she is nothing like Lyra. I cannot tell if Leo is lucky or unfortunate most of the time, and I think that means Lyra has been doing things right. But humans are pretty resilient that way. Even the most trying of circumstances can be overcome by their tenacity. If they ever joined the galactic stage, they would be a force to be reckoned with, for sure.

Well, Lyra would be, in any case.

"Nah," I say, casually waving off Lyra's apology for her brother. "He found me, and we were able to escape the crazy to get back up here in time for pizza and initiative rolls."

"And speaking of..." Iris uses my setup to perfectly segway back into the game. "The Dreaded Death Guardian of Kolvon is going first!"

We all groan in despair, and the rest of the night proceeds much like it should have in the first place. I catch Leo staring at me a few times during the night, but I am not worried by it. I push the issue out of my mind and continue to roll dice, letting tomorrow's problems belong there.

*　　　*　　　*

The next day, the crowds are bigger and more active, which keeps us all busy—busy enough for me not to have time to worry about Leo. I figure it is a good thing that he has less time to think about things, perhaps get to feeling more normal with the situation before we speak again. And we will have to speak again. He is my responsibility now, and that reality slowly sinks in throughout the day. Until I am sure he will be safe with all of this, I can't let him out of my sight.

The business is good, though. Most of it is human-based collectible business, and I make notes of items to replenish or attempt to acquire as the goods walk their way out of my booth, customers happy to have found what awaited them in the collection. This part of the job is fun. Humans love their collectibles, and I would be lying if I said that giving them that joy wasn't at least a little rewarding.

The shadow business had some action during the day as well. A few minor transactions for relatively minor goods that can easily masquerade as collectibles is the norm, and for the stuff that I can't pass around in sight of the humans, we make arrangements for after the show. All told, a normal day at a convention. I am relieved as we near the end of the day that nothing has gone amiss, but the warnings that Gorge passed along keep rattling their way bay to the front of my thoughts.

"Hey, Jack!" I turn to see one of my most consistent and longtime shadow customers, Warrin. He has his maccomp in full human mode today, blending in perfectly, as usual.

"Hello, Warrin," I say. "And what brings you to QUASITASTICON 9?"

He cringes as I say the name of the con. I do not blame him.

"Is that what they're calling this one?" Warrin says, looking up at the marketing banners in the hall.

"Yeah… So, Warrin, what can I do for you today?" I ask. Warrin likes to engage in small talk before he gets to the point, and while I don't usually mind it because it usually means he spends more, today I am in the mood to get to the point. The day is almost at an end here at the con, but I have a lot to do before I can properly consider the day to be over.

"I heard from Sid that you might be the only person who can help me with a particular need that one of my clients is asking for," Warrin answers. He does not appear to be affronted by my direct approach today. A relief.

"And what's that?" I ask.

"Prentian Nut Berries? I believe that's what they're called," Warrin answers.

"*Prentian*?" I ask. "Really? What client of yours would even have a taste for those?"

Warrin shrugs and shakes his head. "I have no idea. Sid was the one who remembered that *you* yourself are Prentian, maybe the only one on the planet. I had completely forgotten myself."

I blink a few times before saying anything else. Yeah, I have what Warrin is looking for, but they are pretty much my own personal snack, reserved for me because most alien species can't even metabolize one of the key base elements found in their seeds. To the human eye, a Prentian Nut Berry might look like some kind of modified grape, slightly off color from most red grapes and a little larger.

Because of my isolation from my home planet I usually have to hunt them down offworld and arrange for a shipment to be transported with a merchant who happens to be stopping by Luna before ferrying cargo down to Earth. The whole process is expensive, but they are a taste of home that I have been able to safely and regularly procure.

"Well," I say after a moment, "yeah, I have some. How much are they looking for?"

"One pound of them, to be precise," Warrin answers back.

I consider what he is asking and take a moment to mentally calculate what that amount should cost. I have the stock for it, but it means I will be out of them before the next shipment is due to arrive.

"Four hundred," I say.

Warrin snorts. It almost sounds human, and some of the people nearby look over toward us. I wave and point at Warrin. "Voice actors, eh?" They laugh with me and continue their browsing. I look back to Warrin with a serious look on my face.

"Oh, you were serious," Warrin says. "That is a lot for some fruit, Jack."

"I'm the only person on the planet who has them, Warrin," I say. "And they're my favorite snack, so this is putting me out just to consider meeting the needs of your client, whoever the mysterious person may be."

Warrin grunts quietly as he considers my price. I think he is smart enough to know I am not going to budge, but the price is astronomical. I know it is. I am annoyed by the ask, so I pumped up the price a bit. More than a bit. His client must really want these.

Warrin reluctantly hands over a data chip, and I walk behind my counter to grab the berries and process the shadow transaction. I expected more pushback, even a counter, but Warrin deals with some strange clients. There might be another Prentian on the planet that I did not know about. Unlikely, given how rare our species is in this part of the Milky Way, but anything is possible.

"There ya go, Warrin," I say, handing him a small cardboard shipping box outwardly marked with the labels of some collectible company. Keeping the transactions a secret is that game, after all.

Warrin takes the box from me, and I think I catch a look of relief on his face as he turns to leave.

"No goodbye?" I say after he has taken a few steps.

Warrin turns hastily and mutters a goodbye before wheeling around again and nearly knocking over some kids on his way out of the booth. The whole thing now strikes me as very odd. That's the second very strange transaction in two days now. One was weird enough, but after Warrin leaves I resolve to put some feelers of my own out later in tonight in order to figure out if there is something bigger going on that I am unaware of.

"ATTENTION QUASITASTICON ATTENDEES," the con's

announcer says over the loudspeakers, jarring me out of my thoughts. "THE VENDOR HALL IS CLOSING IN FIVE MINUTES. PLEASE PROCEED TO FINISH UP YOUR LAST PURCHASES OF THE DAY. THE VENDOR HALL WILL BE OPEN AGAIN TOMORROW AT 9 A.M."

There is a small rush of last-minute purchases that take my attention for the next several minutes as the collectors get the items they are sure will not be here tomorrow.

It is not long before the crowds disperse and I am finished with setting up for tomorrow and closing down the booth for the night. I walk out into the aisle and am greeted by just the young human I am on my way to see.

"Hey, Jack!" Leo says. "Still on for dinner?"

"Sure thing!" I say. Lyra is walking beside Leo, and she smiles as she looks up from her tablet. Likely she is already scrutinizing the sales numbers to make sure that they can afford dinner. I never get the impression that they have money troubles, at least not often, and it is likely because Lyra is so diligent about making every penny count. I admire her discipline.

"Where to?" I ask. Leo and I both look at Lyra, who puts away her tablet and makes a sigh of reserved happiness.

"I think we can do that pizza place that Leo really likes, if you both want to," she says.

"Leo?" I ask.

"Yeah! Let's go!"

6

Big Pete's Pie Palace is near the convention center hotel, which means that they are running a con special to attract all of the extra business in town. Fortunately for us, the owner, a sweet lady named Sally, made a connection with Lyra a few years ago while buying almost as many shiny rocks I have. So there is no problem getting a table, much to our collective relief.

"Was it just me," Lyra says as we take our seats, "or was today just brutal?"

"I was busy all day," I say, looking at the con specials. "This con keeps growing it, seems. Tomorrow is the big day, though, so it just gets better from here!"

Lyra kicks me under the table. "That's not helpful, Jack. I'm tired and ready to go home already. And Leo here was practically bouncing off the walls all day."

I wonder why.

But of course I do not have to wonder much. Leo knows a secret that he is, if I am honest with myself and about him, going to have trouble keeping. That boy may be about to pop.

"Hey," I say, hoping a change in subject will distract them both from their respective inner thoughts, "this one here. That's the one we should get."

I turn the Specials menu around for them to see and point to the pizza I am proposing.

Lyra lets out a low whistle.

Leo practically jumps out of his seat. "They can't be serious!"

"I think they are," I say.

An extra-large, hand-tossed pizza with extra cheese and up to fifteen toppings for thirty dollars.

"Fifteen toppings…" Leo says, a note of reverence in his voice. "Sally has lost her mind."

"How can she even cook that?" Lyra says.

I point to the back where the wood-burning pizza oven is roaring. "See that? She upgraded her pizza oven since last year. It's one of the old-fashioned wood-burning ones now. You can fit a dozen pizzas in that thing."

"Okay," Lyra says, pulling out a pencil. "Let's mark off fifteen toppings. This has absolutely no chance of turning out to be a disaster."

I chuckle as she looks up and me and winks. Leo does not notice the exchange and is instead reading over the list, calling out toppings he wants to add. After we get the list finalized, we put in our order and begin the anticipatory waiting period for what could be the most marvelous pizza disaster ever.

"Hey, uh, Jack?" Leo says, his eyes wide as he fidgets with the hem of his shirt. "Yeah?" I ask.

"Did you ever hear back from that guy who interrupted our game last night?" Leo's voice cracks slightly as he asks the question, and I catch sight of one of Lyra's eyebrows raising up at the question. Does she know something? Did Leo tell her anything? I am suddenly very aware that this could be its own kind of ambush, if Leo told Lyra, and they want to get the truth, or even more, out of me.

"Oh, no," I say, waving off the idea. "That guy is gone. Probably never see him again."

"Really?" Leo says, his voice quieter and with a cautious tone behind it. "Cause he's here."

I freeze. Leo's face only gets more serious when he sees my reaction. I have to play it cool, or there might be trouble. Gorge said he would be gone by now. What the hell is he doing here now?

"Oh yeah?" I say. "Well, that's a coincidence."

"Are you sure everything is okay with that?" Lyra asks. "Because he's with a couple other guys, and one of them keeps looking over this way. None of them look happy."

This cannot be happening. What kind of trouble has Gorge brought to me? I risk a glance in their direction, just casually moving in my seat hoping to make it look like I am not looking directly at them. They all see me look.

Crap.

"Ah, listen you two," I say. "I think I need to head out early. Like, right now."

Leo looks even more freaked out by the situation the more I speak, and Lyra's raised eyebrow returns, this time more severe. And this time directed at me.

"What kind of trouble are you *really* in, Jack?" Lyra asks, crossing her arms and setting her shoulders, a clear posture of expectation that her question *will* be answered promptly.

"Trouble?" I say. "No, not trouble. Just…forgot an appointment that I made. With a client. To buy a really expensive original movie prop that I have back at the hotel."

"Oh yeah, I remember you told me about that!" Leo says.

Props for trying to help me there, pal. Leo is a good kid. I hope this works.

I get up to leave, and I hand Leo some cash to cover my part of the dinner I will now not get to enjoy. These guys could be bad news, and Gorge has led them right to me. Hopefully, if I leave now, they will not consider the humans I am with a threat.

"I'll see you guys tomorrow at opening," I say. "Sorry to rush off!"

And with that, I rush off. I mean, I do not rush too quickly.

That would cause a stir. I do, however, hasten. My retreat from the pizza parlor is noticed, thankfully, and after a block I look back to see the two guys that Gorge was with following me. They are not trying to be inconspicuous, though, and that concerns me. I can probably beat them back to the hotel. Probably. But once I get them there, I am unsure of what to do.

My mind races as I think about why they could be after me. Gorge definitely talked about something, and from the way they followed me instead of Leo and Lyra, I guess that it has more to do with the shadow market than with Leo likely knowing the truth about me.

The pizza place is not far from the hotel, only a few blocks, and about a block away the after-con evening foot traffic starts picking up. More people finished with their day of fandom, collecting, and gaming, and ready to head out and get drunk for the second time this weekend. It won't be the last time for most of them.

I risk another glance back as I duck in and through lines of people waiting for their seats, and the two scruffy-looking, clearly alien guys who were following me are nowhere to be seen. I frown as I continue. Where did they go? I hope they did not peel off and decide to double back to the pizza place. No time to catch my breath in the crowd, though. Stick to the plan. The hotel is only half a block away now.

I rush through the automatic doors of the Downtown Marriott and into the cool and refreshing air-conditioned air—another of my favorite things that humans have become obsessed with. My home planet is a bit cooler than Earth naturally, so the really hot days still get to me. But I can always count on the expensive hotels to be a burst of cold air on my face. That and the produce cooler at a Costco.

As I enter the lobby I slow down my pace a bit and begin

fumbling around in my badge holder, which I am still wearing because I always forget to take it off after hours, for my room key. So I do not immediately notice the two people in secret-service-style suits get up from their seats and approach me.

"Prince Jarokin," one of them says, and I reflexively wave him off as I continue to fumble with my key card.

"*Prince Jarokin*," the man repeats, and what it saying finally clicks in my distracted brain. I drop my hotel room key card on the lobby floor and look up at the two men.

Ah. Not men. Good maccomp settings, sure, but I can tell these two individuals are not human.

"I'm sorry," I say, bending down to pick up my key card. "Did you just call me…"

"Prince Jarokin, yes," the other says. She is only marginally less physically built than the other one. Near miss on the blending in, but I do not think that was their primary goal anyway.

Oh boy.

If I have to guess, these are Prentian Royal Guards. But it is not much of a guess. I know who they are, and I never wanted to see them here, or anywhere, ever again. Were they the ones with Gorge in the pizza place? Why would they follow me from there just to intercept me here, in a hotel lobby? It's not like one is any less public than the other. This makes no sense to me as I attempt to puzzle out where I went wrong. I never wanted my family to find me. That was the point of being on Earth in the first place.

This weekend just got a whole lot worse. Like, end-of-the-world worse.

"Jack Linthon!" another voice from behind me yells out, and I turn to see the two burly ones from the pizza place.

Other people in the lobby are starting to take notice of what is happening. No alarming actions just yet, but I see a couple of phones get switched to video mode. I think they believe that they are about to see some kind of LARP play out here in the hotel lobby. That could be useful, actually.

"You will address Prince Jarokin in such a manner," the big royal guard moves to stand between me and the burly ones, while the other guard keeps her position next to me.

"Oh yeah?" says one of the burly ones. As the first one of the burly pair to speak, I mentally dub this one "Ugly One."

"Yeah," says the big man. I do not know this one personally, but if he is anything like the others, Ugly One will be the first to die.

"Well, that's gonna be a problem for you, see," Ugly Two pipes up, and I see that this is about to get really dangerous. There are so many humans standing around now, and I have got to try to avoid a shootout in the lobby. There's only so much the alien tech can suppress or modify before there's a containment breach.

There actually was a containment breach once. It was before I got here, though, during the Reagan years I think. Only top government officials were let in on it, though. I did lead to that defunct Star Wars defense program in the '80s. That is a fascinating read. But yeah, it was a mess on the shadow market's end, or so I have been told. Assassinations everywhere. So many people had to die.

Not this time. Not because of me.

"Whoa, now!" I say, and I squirrel my way past the guard to put myself between the Uglies and the guards. "Nobody needs to get hurt on my account. I'm sure that there's plenty of bounty to go around, right?"

The Uglies look confused for a moment, but I have not swayed the guards. I knew that would be a long-shot anyway, but I needed time to think of something else. Ugly One begins reaching into his coat pocket, followed quickly by Ugly Two.

"Yer comin' with us, Jack," Ugly Two says as they pull out

whatever blaster or energy-type weapon they happen to be using. So much tech in the universe. Categorizing all of it is kinda useless after a certain point.

The guards likewise reach for weapons, and I realize that this is about to reach the point of no return. My time here on Earth may be coming to an end, and I have no choice but to welcome it along I suppose. Time to save some humans.

I reach into my own coat and draw two Hotanthian Disintegraters. I've never had to actually use these before today, just a little in practice. But they do what the name suggests. Disintegration is the best way to keep secrets from the humans. I feel sorry for the guards, kind of. They are just doing their job I suppose. Returning a wayward prince back to his family is kinda noble. If you don't consider how the prince feels, I guess.

And yes, I know. I know. I'll have to explain the Prince Jarokin part later, though. Right now, I am a little busy.

Both groups pause as I hold out a blaster at each of them. Neither side wants me harmed, which is a relief coming from the Uglies' side. Some bounties don't care if you're dead or alive, so you can never be too sure. Good. They want me alive. At least I have that going for me.

And now, to use that to my advantage.

7

If there were not so many lives currently being endangered by this standoff, I would definitely have appreciated how cool it must have looked from the outside. All of the onlookers filming the very real, very dangerous alien encounter begin cheering us on, with some even wanting us to "start with the shooting already!" Well, this might end up as the best LARP any of them have ever seen.

"Again, Prince Jarokin is coming with us," the larger guard says, now holding his blaster out and pointing it past me and at the Uglies. The Uglies cannot decide if they should be pointing their weapons at me or at the guard, and they keep moving their attention between us.

Please let someone have a stun setting and actually be using it. Cause I don't.

"I say again, Whoa!" I yell, and both sides turn their attention to me. "I am *not* going anywhere with any of you! You'll have to shoot me to get me to do that, and I don't think that is what either side wants, now, is it?"

My guts nearly empty out onto the floor as I see both sides train their guns on me instead of each other.

"My bounty notice just says 'Alive,'" Ugly Two says. "Don't say nothin' about the condition of that life."

The smaller guard, who now that I have had time to study, reminds me of a royal guard I used to know named Grendia, which is the name I decide to call her in my head until I learn otherwise, says, "Our orders are likewise rather vague on condition, Prince Jarokin. As the saying goes on this planet, there's the easy way for you, or—" She clicks a button on her blaster that causes it to go through a charging sequence. "—the way I prefer it, to be honest."

Well, at least someone is being honest with me. I may be their prince, but I am sure they did not like the trip out here to this end of the Milky Way backwater swamp to come get me.

"Oh…" is all I manage to get out before the first shot is fired.

It misses me and slams into the wall across the room, sending sparks and charred building material flying. People scream, some in shock, some in delight, and I start my run. I have to get these maniacs away from people. They may not care about the lowly humans, but I do.

At first, the Uglies and the guards seem intent on trying to take each other out. Grendia shoots at me, and now I am almost certain that it really is her. I was, perhaps, not the best to her during my departure from the royal palace on Prentia. She may have been the guard on duty when I made my escape. In retrospect, she probably still holds a grudge. I doubt my parents were very nice to her after that.

Oh, the chaos!

I duck behind a column as the shots keep ringing out. There is a lot of confusion in the crowd, but a lot of laughter, too. Most of them still think they are being treated to a Hollywood-level special effects show, and I just have to hope that illusion holds for now. As long as no humans end up dead, we will be fine. I think.

The hotel staff may not think this is as fun as the con attendees. Most of them are hunkered down. I reach over to a device on my belt and flip a switch. It is a signal-blocking doo-dad that I picked up last year in San Diego. Never had a reason to use one before that, but I am really glad that guy who operates out of the South Pacific offered me a deal I could not refuse.

With the device active, no signals, data, or calls, mobile or landline, would be getting into or out of the area. It is an extreme measure, I suppose, but until I get this contained at a reasonable level, the humans are better off without their authorities present, believe it or not.

"Hey! Over here!" I shout, drawing the attention of both of the groups toward me. A shot flies my way and impacts the column just above my head.

"You idiot!" I shout back at whoever it was that shot at me. "You're either a terrible shot or don't have the brain cells to understand what 'alive' means!"

Several more shots fly past the column following my taunt. Good. Shoot not at the humans, check. Shoot at me instead. Yeah.

Aww, crap.

I swing an arm around the column and snap off a shot. It's a risky move. My weapons don't have a stun setting, but it isn't like any of them are using their stun settings either. I have that effect on people sometimes, I guess. Don't have a lot of stun bolts shot my way.

My disintegrator blast flies wide and shatters a window. *Oops.*

These things have a bit more kick than I remembered. And why do I have two of them? Oh, I remember now!

I flip a switch on the disintegrators, and connector ports open up on each one. I snap them together, and they interface with a quiet hiss.

"Hey!" I hear from across the lobby. "What are you doing over there?"

"Who cares what he's doing?" This voice I am sure belongs to Ugly Two. His maccomp gave him a tiny hint of a lisp that makes him sound a bit less intimidating—when you're not looking at him, that is.

The two groups exchange more insults, punctuated by a couple of shots and the sound of a body hitting the floor. I think it is one of the guards, but I cannot be sure. Truth be told, if I had to surrender to either group, I would prefer the guards. But let's not get to that point just yet.

My disintegrators stop their hissing and transform. Yes, they transform. This is why I bought them. I remember now.

The blaster handles on each of the disintegrators fold out into a slightly beefier handle good for gripping, and the beam emitters join to form a wide-form arc emitter. As I grip the handle, I feel the expected activation switch with my thumb and press it.

The shield pulses to life with a greenish-yellow power field emitting in a half circle covering my hand all the way to my shoulder.

Yeah. Now we're talkin'.

I round the corner at a full run. Years of formal weapons training in the Royal Court of Prentia have prepared me for this. That and a lot of lightsaber fencing lessons here on Earth. Lessons that maybe I took a bit more seriously than most of the other "combatants."

I was correct in thinking that one of the guards had been shot, and I see the body of the larger guard lying on the floor, a gaping chest wound still sputtering with blaster energy. Poor guy. He might not have deserved that. Maybe.

I do not slow my run as I barrel into the Uglies, using the shield to bash into Ugly Two, and punching out with my fist at Ugly One. They take the hits rather well, considering, but I am still strong enough to cause them to reel back and yell out in pain.

Ha! Still got it!

My victory almost comes to a short end as I wheel around and a blaster shot from Grendia deflects off my shield.

"Hey! That coulda killed someone! Maybe even Ugly Two!"

I yell and let my indignant rage sink into them, hoping the Uglies take a moment to decide which one of them I am talking about.

The humans have mostly come back to watch the show now, still recording as they please, but I know none of the footage is getting far, at least for now. One of them starts blasting some music out of a very powerful and loud but small bluetooth speaker. The beats cranks up, and the humans start to cheer me on. "Go, Prince Jerokin! Kick their asses!"

And suddenly I am in the middle of a firefight with bounty hunters, royal guards, and a soundtrack that belongs in a Deadpool movie.

All that done, I continue my tirade of violence on the Uglies. Grendia is rude, for sure, but I am not keen on turning my back on the Uglies. One and Two are both back up and leveling their blasters for another round of "Pin the blaster on the prince." Not my idea of a good time.

I deflect two more shots and slam the shield into Ugly Two. I feel something crack under the weight of the blow, and he shrieks. The sound is not human, and I wince as my likewise alien ears do not enjoy the wavelength of the bounty hunter's expression of pain. I continue my onslaught on Ugly Two, punching him in the throat to end the dreadful noise. He drops to the floor in a heap. I hope I haven't killed someone just now.

As I wheel around and attempt to shield myself from both sides again, I block two more shots, one from each remaining opponent. Grendia may now be the bigger threat. She really is trying not to kill me.

Another blur of motion that is more me acting on instinct than having any real plan for the moment, and I close the distance between Ugly One and myself. Before I get to him, he drops to the floor as a blaster bolt hits him in the head. I spin toward Grendia, out of breath and expecting an attack.

She is standing here, over the body of the fallen guard, breathing almost as heavily as I am. She frowns and shakes her head slightly, her upper lip tightening just a bit, as she notices, for what I think might be the first time, the crowd of human onlookers who are all paused quietly, waiting with bated breath to see the conclusion of our epic special effects LARP. Grendia likely has no idea that is what they think is happening, but I know I am running out of time. Things need to get contained quickly.

"Go, please," I say, lowering my shield.

"No, Princ—" Grendia begins to protest.

"Go now, and I will find you later," I say. "I promise."

"But..."

"*Grendia*, follow the command of your prince!" I yell, hoping that my voice of authority might still mean something to her.

She pauses for only a moment later and collects the fallen guard. He might still be alive, despite the injury. Prentians don't have many vital organs in the area he was shot.

I watch as Grendia walks in the direction of the kitchens and breathe a sigh of relief as the applause begins.

I bow, quickly adapting to the pressing need of having to clean this up before anybody outside of the containment range compromises my ability to clean it up. Believe it or not, I can still get out of this.

"Thank you, everyone!" I say and bow again. "I am sure you're wondering how all of this was accomplished. Well, we have a little magic behind us today. I pull out a small device that is a restricted item in almost every system of the modernized galaxy. Fortunately, Earth is not one of those places.

I set it on the floor in front of me, and press the button. The device does the rest. It's not magic by any means, but for the primitives on Earth, it at least looks like a pretty light show that "reverses" the "special effects" of the LARP. In short, little nano-light bots go out and fix stuff. I don't even know how it works, but it does. Mostly. It can't erase the digital files on people's phones. They have that footage. And as I turn off the signal device and people get their connections back, there it goes.

The LARP fight, which is how I hope it is received, will soon be everywhere. I sigh and separate my disintegrators again, sneaking low-power shots at the Uglies while the cover-up device does its work. Their bodies disintegrate with the lights, and I even hear a few people ask how we made them disappear.

"Thank you all again," I say as the device finishes up. "I'm glad you enjoyed the show!"

With that, I collect the device, now all but spent as they are one-use objects, and head to the elevators. As I do, the reality slowly begins to sink in that this problem will not be going away on its own, and I have no idea how to fix any of it.

8

"PRINCE?!"

Leo is sitting in my hotel room, watching one of the many videos of the "Epic Lobby Alien LARP Fight at QUASITASTICON 9" currently going semi-viral on all the platforms. His eyes get wider with every repeated viewing.

"I wouldn't make a big deal out of that," I say, attempting to pass it off as nothing to be concerned with.

"But…like…this is..this was," I fear that Leo may be on the verge of hyperventilating. This may be too much for him to take.

After the incident, I took some time to make sure everything was cleaned up. I searched briefly for Grendia, but she was long gone. I am sure I will see her again. She does not give up so easily, and with her standing orders from one, or maybe both, of my parents to take me back to Prentia, I am sure that this is far from over.

The Uglies found me through Gorge. That part is clear. I am not sure how Grendia found me. When I arrived on Earth, the first thing I did was sell my ship. The thing is, I sold it in pieces, pieces that I thought were too small to track to any one place. I was pretty sure it was a good idea, and it means I was telling the truth earlier when I said that I was stranded on Earth. I have no ship, no backup plan to flee the planet. Earth is my hiding spot. I like it here. In the end I guess it does not matter how she found me, though.

Grendia is not what worries me.

There is a bounty on my head. My parents are serious about getting me back home, but why now, after all this time? And is my location something known to the galaxy at large? This could get really dicey very fast, and I need a lot of answers to questions that go beyond just wanting to stay hidden. My parents are looking for me again, and I was sure they had given up on that years ago. Something has changed. But what?

"This was a *real* fight, wasn't it?!"

Can't get much past Leo. Nope, not that one.

"It was, yes," I say.

"Why did you let the other ones go?" Leo asks.

"Because they weren't really trying to cause me harm. At least, the one who didn't get shot wasn't. The other one might, now that I think of it. He did not seem to be a very happy one." Leo sits and listens, trying to understand everything that I am saying.

"Lyra will be starting to wonder where I am," Leo says. "It's getting kinda late, and she's not all that happy that I told her I was going to go find you after you ditched us at dinner. She's seen the video, you know."

I wince at the news. Leo is right, but I had no choice. I was, at the time, just trying to make sure that they would be safe. I had no idea that those Prentian Guards would be waiting for me in the hotel lobby. That was when dealing with the problem quietly became impossible, and, well, the rest happened as it did.

"I am so sorry for that, Leo, but you know why I did it."

"Yeah. *I* do," Leo says, putting an extra teenage emphasis on his reflexive pronoun.

The message is clear. Lyra is not happy with me. Not the position I want to be in. Have to think of a way to make that right.

"I'll take you both out to dinner tomorrow night," I say, hoping this might be a step in the right direction.

Leo frowns. "I don't think that's going to cut it with Lyra, *Prince* Jarokin, or whatever your real name is."

I know he's right, but what else can I do?

"Okay," I say, sitting down in the chair across from Leo and folding my arms in front of me. "Then why doesn't the great Leo, with infinite insight into the mind of his independent and willful sister, tell me what I should do?"

Leo looks at me like I have just said the dumbest thing on Earth. A pretty tall order, considering that, well, *this is Earth.*

"I can't believe I have to explain this to you, alien man," Leo says, setting his phone down and squarely facing me. "Lyra *likes* you, dude. And I'm pretty sure you like her. Now, I'm doing my best right now to get over the fact that you're an alien, and that's been a lot to do, believe me. But Lyra, Jack, Lyra still thinks you're a human. Don't you see how this might get a little complicated? And like, not just for you or her, but especially for me."

Leo's words paused my brain for a moment. He had a point. I had not yet acted on any feelings I may have for Lyra because of that one big thing that separates us. I *am* an alien, at least here I am. And that poses all kinds of problems if I am going to get emotionally involved with someone. Leo didn't say it to spare me, but where he's going with this is right. I have to decide if I am going to take the next step with his sister. If not, I need to back out of their lives and let her have a chance with a human.

"So, are you saying that you want me to just stop talking to your sister?" I ask.

Leo rolls his eyes at me.

"Okay, aliens are dumber than humans, got it," he says, and leans forward, holding his hand up, his fingers pressed together to a point and making them look somewhat like they would if they were on the inside of a sock puppet.

"I'll say this next part slowly, to make sure you understand," Leo says. I am beginning to not appreciate his tone, but I let the boy express himself. He has had a rough couple of days after all.

"You need to take her out on a date, Jack," Leo says and leans back in the chair, his arms landing on the arm rests as if he just did an epic mic drop.

I am stunned. That was not at all what I expected him to say. Do I want to take Lyra on a date? Yeah. Yeah, I do. But it's just…

It's just.

"Don't you think I have bigger issues to worry about at the moment, Leo?" I ask, trying to change the subject.

"No. I don't," Leo said. "You ditched us last night because you were trying to protect us. And only I know why. I won't tell her, Jack, but maybe you should."

I shake my head at his statement. "No, Leo. That's not how this works. Humans aren't supposed to know anything at all about aliens on Earth, the shadow market, or anything else extraterrestrial that goes on here. You're in the dark for a reason. There are powers out there in the universe, great and terrible powers, who believe that humanity has not yet proven that they are ready to know what is really out there."

"Okay, but what about me?"

"The intergalactic community says I should kill you, Leo."

Concern flashes in Leo's face, but it is quickly replaced by a stern look, eyes narrowing to focus in on me.

"Buuuuuttttt," he says slowly, "you have *not* killed me. You *won't* kill me, will you?"

I sigh. I really don't know what I am doing anymore. The rules are there for a reason, and I have followed them all up to this point. I have also never personally brought any human into the crosshairs before, either, and that changes things. I can't do it. I won't do it. All of the laws of the galaxy say that I should, in order to protect humanity's natural progression, but I won't do it. *Star Trek*'s Prime Directive didn't rule Picard's life and won't rule mine either.

But with Lyra, if I tell her, then there would definitely be others who would want to cause her harm if they ever find out. Leo is in terrible danger now anyway, and I think I have done a bad job of stating exactly how much. Perhaps that is for the better. There are some aliens who do not follow the kill orders, but Gorge is likely not one of them. I need to find him first, I think, if he is still on the planet after the Uglies' attempt on me went sideways. I hope he is gone.

"Well," I say, resolved in my course of action, "it's getting a bit late. You need to go back to Lyra and tell her…" I pause and look at Leo, my brow furrowing. "…tell her whatever she needs to hear. Except for, you know, what she needs to not hear."

Leo rolls his eyes again and gets up from the chair. "You're gonna chicken out, aren't you? Yeah, I knew it."

Leo crosses the room and pauses with his hand on the door handle.

"Look, you're a cool guy, and I still want to be your friend, but you need to figure out how me and Lyra fit into this problem you've dragged us into. Lyra might not know what I know, but she's in it now, too, because of me."

I nod as he looks back at me with a blank stare meant to let his words sink in. I keep underestimating that kid's maturity, for sure. Without another word, Leo opens the door and walks out into the hallway. The door closes softly, the latch clicking as it shuts. And I am left alone with only my thoughts.

I am not left long with my thoughts as I hear a soft knock on the door.

"Forget to chide me about something else?" I say, albeit in a good-natured tone, and freeze when I see who is on the other side.

My blood runs cold as I prepare for another fight, but the person on the other side of the door simply stands, waiting for me to act first.

"Grendia."

9

"Is the other one okay?" I ask.

We are walking down the sidewalk near the hotel. When she knocked on the door, Grendia simply stood there, waiting to be acknowledged, and I suggested that we take a walk out in the nighttime air. She simply nodded and walked quietly along with me. A few people in the lobby recognized us on the way out, and we got a few shouts of praise and whoops of excitement as the con attendees expressed their enjoyment of *the show* from earlier.

"He will be, my prince," Grendia says quietly. "His wound was bad, but he will heal eventually. I have him in a *hepostatic shell* back on our ship."

"And then you came to see me alone," I add.

"I was not sure before that you would recognize me," Grendia says, "but I realized that you did. And I thought that if I came just to talk you would—"

"That I would go with you back to Prentia without a fight this time?" I interrupt her, my voice losing its even temper. She recoils slightly, and I instantly regret snapping at her. Grendia was always kind to me. We might have even been what humans consider friends, but our statuses within our culture kept us apart from any significant social interaction.

"*No*," she bites back. "I wanted to make sure that you knew that the way we approached you, the actions we took. That…that wasn't me. That was *him*. That was Niolen."

Ah, Niolen. I remembered the name now that she said it. Never liked him. I always thought he was a spy for my mother. I still do.

"So, my mother sent you?" I ask.

Grendia shakes her head. "No. Your father did. I tried to tell him that Niolan was not the man for the job, but in your absence your mother's influence has become more powerful in the court. It is perhaps even more so than your father's now."

While that is not good news to hear, the troubles of my homeworld are no longer mine. I left that life decades ago, and nobody, not Grendia, not my father, and certainly not my mother, is going to drag me back into it.

"I am sorry to hear that, but it does not change the decision I made," I say. We keep walking at a casual pace.

"I said as much," Grendia says. "But nobody cares to listen to me. They never have."

"Do they know you tracked me to Earth?" I ask.

Grendia shakes her head slightly. "I do not believe so. Niolan wanted to bring you home as a prize and parade you into the palace for all to see. I do not think he would have risked one of the other guard hunter teams finding you first when he reported our progress."

That is a slight comfort. Niolan's ambition might have saved me, and not just me.

"So what do you plan to do?" I remember Grendia as someone who does not follow the pull of ambition, but her sense of duty is still in play. If she is loyal to my father, then she could still be planning to take me home somehow.

"I..." she stops talking and walking and looks up at the sky. Even in the city, on a clear night like this, the stars are somewhat visible. The humans really don't understand what they have done with their light pollution. They are missing the grandness of the sky lit by the galaxies. And no, they do not corner the market on pollution of any kind, environmental or light. Plenty of planets in the galactic community are even far worse off than Earth. But the night sky was always sacred to my people, even when *we* were the primitives, and we went to great lengths to preserve it.

I wait for Grendia to finish her thought. Her next words are vital to how I am going to treat her from here on out, as a threat, or as something else.

"I am tired of Prentian…*everything*," she says, her voice breaking a little as she speaks. I see the exhaustion in her posture as she drops her pretense and lets me see the real her for a moment. Well, the "real" her that is currently being concealed by her maccomp anyway.

A wave of relief washes over me as I begin to gain the first hope that Grendia may not be my enemy after all. I could use an ally. I really could. It has been just me for so long. A friend might be nice. But I am getting ahead of myself. Grendia simply said she is tired. That could mean a lot of things.

"I understand," I say, waiting for her to speak again. The night is calm. It is near midnight now, and the traffic is next to nothing, getting more sparse the farther we walk away from the convention center.

"Do you, Jarokin?" she asks, looking up at me and tilting her head to the side. "When you left, it was so sudden, and I was held responsible for it.."

I wince once more as I am reminded that my departure had likely caused her a lot of trouble. It was unavoidable. A last-minute change to the guard schedule had made it Grendia's fault instead of someone else's that I had escaped the leash my parents had me on in the palace.

"I'm sorry for that," I say, but Grendia frowns and shakes her head.

"I am *not* looking for your apology, Jarokin," she says. "I was mad at you for a long time. Years. *Many* years. But you were right."

Those words, all of her words, were a lot to take in at once.

"But," Grendia continues, "you also left. And that was a wrong of its own kind. One that you will have to pay for, somehow, someday."

"And today?" I ask, suddenly aware that we are alone and Grendia is still a highly trained and capable Prentian Royal Guard. This could have been a trap.

"Today," Grendia says as she turns and keeps walking. "Today I'm just out on a walk on an alien planet, remarking to the only person in earshot about how dim our star is from here."

I start to walk alongside her again. This has already been a really weird con, and it's only Friday night. Leo, Lyra, now Grendia. I used to think I was going through life completely alone, and that I liked it. But now I am not so sure. Leo is right. I need to make a decision about Lyra, a full decision. Is it safer for both her *and* Leo to know the truth? How much longer can I reasonably expect Leo to keep the secret anyway?

And now Grendia is in the mix. I have no idea what kind of trouble she may yet pose. For tonight, though, we are not enemies. She is not hunting me, and I am not Prince of Prentia. I am just Jarokin. And I am Jack. And I need to figure out what that means now.

"Yeah," I say, "it's pretty dim here."

10

We get back to the hotel late. Grendia and I part down in the lobby, and I think she is not going to turn me in. At least not yet. I get back to my room and close the door behind me. I really hope there aren't any more unexpected guests tonight. My phone beeps at me as I am sitting down with a drink, and I take it out to see what outside force needs my attention now.

It is a text from Leo, with a video file attached, titled LARP Aliens on the Town. I open the video and see Grendia and myself walking through the hotel lobby and out into the night. The video follows us for a few steps outside and then cuts out. The comments section is not mean, but not helpful either.

"Oooo! Where are those two going? To settle their differences over some dinner, and more…?"

"Oh hey! That dude has some moves. Is it true he's just a vendor at the con? Where's his LARP panel at @QUASITASTICON?"

"Aliens in love!"

And my personal favorite.

"I guess he decided who he wants to take him to the stars tonight!"

I can't tell if Leo is trying to help me or is upset with me. Sending me this is a clear message that the trouble I am in with Lyra has likely just got more complicated. I look at the clock. Nearly 3 a.m. Too late to do anything about it until the morning. I'll be running on little enough sleep as it is, and tomorrow is the con's biggest day.

I sip on my drink and browse social media, looking at the comments sections in the LARP video posts. Before long I have watched the fight from every available angle. The Uglies really didn't care who they were shooting at, and it is not a small miracle—if those do exist—that no humans were harmed in the making of this film. Some of the comments question how the rubble looked so real and how I "disposed" of the Uglies' bodies, but none of the theories come close to the truth. I am sure the crazies and conspiracy nuts will eventually get a hold of this and could cause some trouble.

This whole situation is brand new territory for me in a lot of ways. Any of us being in the spotlight is potential trouble. My brain hurts from all of the possibilities running through it. I glance up at the window and see the first vestiges of daylight peeking through the bottom of the curtains. I need to at least try to get a couple of hours of sleep before I have to be back at the vendor hall.

As I collapse on the bed, I think briefly before losing consciousness that it is possible this could just all blow over on its own anyway.

*   *   *

Observing the crowd gathered at the entrance to the vendor hall two hours before it opens tells me that it has, in fact, not blown over. They are all on their phones, which is not abnormal these days. But I can see it on their faces and hear it in their voices. They are talking about the LARP video. Maybe not all of them. But yeah, there's a buzz today.

I am able to sneak into the vendor's entrance without attracting too much attention. It helps that I altered my maccomp before leaving my room this morning to go with my Full Human settings. No attempt to cosplay today from me. I need to be as unrecognizable as possible.

"Hey, Jack!" I hear from a few rows over as I walk into the

hall. "Great video, my man!"

Well. Shit.

So much for hoping that going full human today would help me. I wave in the direction of the greeting and walk on past. I have to get the booth set up and try to make it over to see Lyra before we open up. Have to try to get some kind of damage control going this morning.

I round the last corner between me and my booth, and my heart sinks. No hope of normal today. Grendia is standing there, waiting for me. I recognize her first from her posture more than anything, but her appearance is still close enough to what she looked like at the hotel that she will likely be recognized by others. She, too, was smart enough to realize that changing her maccomp appearance would likely be a good idea, but she has yet to learn that humans are much more clever than we give them credit for. All that taken into account, I still did not expect her to show up in the vendor hall today, much less before the hall even opens. I glance at the badge she is wearing and am unsurprised to see, even from a distance, that it is clearly a vendor badge. How she got one, I don't want to know. I just hope however she obtained it, the fine people working for QUASITASTICON 9 won't take offense to it.

Oh, and great. She's talking to Lyra. Well, so they've met now. Grendia is the first to spot my approach, and she turns from Lyra to address me.

"Good, morning, Jar…uh…Jack," she says, stammering. She's new to this game, so I don't wholly fault her for the slip. Still, kind of inconvenient there.

"Yeah…" Lyra says as she also turns toward me, "*good morning.*"

Uh oh.

Lyra is the first to break the silent tension as I walk up to the pair of them.

"So I was just chatting with…uhh…what did you say your name was?" Lyra asks, looking at Grendia.

"Gia," Grendia says, preempting any attempt by me to intercede. I am impressed. She already thought of that.

"Right…Gia," Lyra continues. "And she says that after your little LARP display last night, you brought her on to help you at the booth for the rest of the weekend."

I do my best to roll with the rapidly unfolding situation and nod my agreement with the statement, letting the gesture buy a few seconds for my mouth to catch up with the rest of me.

"Yeah," I manage to get out, "that's right. Gia here is my temporary help for the rest of the con."

Lyra's eyebrow raises. I'm in trouble. Need to get out of this situation quickly.

"In fact," I continue, "Gia, why don't you go ahead and start up the register equipment and familiarize yourself with how it works. I'll follow in just a sec to answer any questions you might have."

Grendia nods. "Yes, my prince." Her eyes get wide as she turns away quickly and walks into the booth.

I look at Lyra. That eyebrow is not going anywhere. I am becoming concerned that it might get stuck there if I don't give her a reason to lower it soon.

"*My prince?*" she asks, once Grendia is a fair distance away.

I do my best to wave off the slip.

"Oh, she's just really into that LARP thing from last night," I say.

Lie one.

"Yeah," Lyra says, "I bet she's *real into* roleplay."

"No!" I blurt out, and people look over at us. Lyra looks around uncomfortably as I wave to people and just shrug.

"I mean, no, it's not like that," I say.

"Not like what?" Lyra asks.

"Look," I begin, "I met Gia and her friends at a con last year, and we got to talking about how cool it would be to do a really high-tech kind of LARP flash mob kinda thing. It took on a life of its own, and, well, you saw the videos, I'm sure."

Lie two.

"Uh huh," Lyra says.

"And I'm sorry," I say. "I'm sorry about ditching you last night. You and Leo. That was my fault, and I'm sorry that it happened."

Lyra looks more and more impatient as I talk. This is not going well. She knows that I'm not telling her everything, and I can see the frustration behind her expression. Perhaps I can't read humanity in general all that well, even after all these years, but I can read Lyra. I know her. I trust her.

Do I?

"But I want to make it up to you," I say. "I want to take you to dinner. Tonight."

Lyra sighs.

"And no," I say, stepping a little closer, "I don't mean you and Leo. I mean just you. I want to take you out to dinner. On a date. Tonight."

"A…date?" Lyra's voice wavers when she speaks.

I have no idea where this sudden boldness and directness is coming from, but I decide to take advantage. I look her in the eyes, locking her gaze onto my own, and nod slowly.

"Yes, Lyra," I say, realizing as I speak that we're having this moment on the vendor floor of QUASITASTICON 9, just out in the open. "I want to take you out on a date. I have for some time, and someone finally convinced me it was time I act."

Lyra's eyes flicker in the direction of Grendia, and I move my head to gain her attention again.

"No, not her. Like I said, she's just a friend. Nothing more."

Lyra is stoic. I am losing her. This was a terrible idea. She was mad, and I made it worse. I said all the wrong things. Should never have listened to Leo. What does that boy know about anything, anyway? Where are the exits? Should I just get on a spaceship and leave?

"Okay," she says, after an agonizing eternity of my own thoughts gouging into my psyche.

"Okay?" I ask, making sure I heard what I thought.

"Yeah, Jack," Lyra says, and a smile creeps into the corner of her lips. "You *can* make it up to me. And yes, I want to go on a date with you. A real one. Just us."

I smile. I can't help it. Something finally went right! I can't believe I did this. Lyra is smiling and looks as unsure of herself as I feel about myself. But I asked her out! Go me!

"Well, uhh," I say, not sure how to exit the conversation now it has reached what I thought to be the least likely conclusion of it.

"Yeah, uhh," Lyra says back to me.

"Meet up after?" I ask.

Lyra frowns, and my heart sinks again.

I blew it!

"No," she says. "You have to do this right, Jack. Pick me up at my door, dress up a bit—if you can, that is. Take me out for real. If we're finally going to do this, I want it done right."

Fair enough. I owe her that, and so much more.

"Okay," I say, now sporting a sly grin of my own, "a proper date. Just like in the movies."

Lyra nods her approval and turns to leave.

"And don't expect to get away with the surface-level conversations we always have, either," Lyra warns me. "I want *real* talk tonight, Jack."

And then she is gone. I watch her as far as I can and stand there like a fool frozen in place by a gloop grenade for a while longer.

I am only jolted out of my stupor by the sound of someone clearing their throat behind me. I jump and almost reach for one of my disintegrators. I guess I'm still on edge, too. I whirl around to find Grendia standing a few feet behind me.

"So," she says, her face bearing a semblance of amusement, "that seemed to go well."

I frown and motion for her to step into the booth in front of me. I follow her as she walks to the back where I find everything has been set up correctly and just how I like it for the start of a day. There is even new inventory placed out on shelves and properly tagged, just how I would have done it.

How long was she observing me before she and Niolan made their move?

"I like her, I think," Grendia says, ignoring my inspection of her work. "She seems to have you figured out."

"Figured out?" I ask. "Me?"

"What?" Grendia asks, her eyes widening in mock surprise. "Like it's hard?"

11

I decide not to ask Grendia why she is here, fearing that the answer will be something I don't want to hear yet. She is obviously keeping an eye on me, but for what purpose? Based on the size and demeanor of the crowd that comes through the doors when the halls open, I am thankful for the help regardless of her reasons for being here.

We receive a lot of requests for selfies, which Grendia immediately begins charging for, so many that a line forms that stretches out into the aisle. That is a big violation at cons like this, and I have to shut it down quickly before I get a visit, and a fine, from convention staff. I promise the crowds that I will figure out a time and place for them to get their selfies, and that I will post on social media when we have it figured out. My phone blows up with new followers on all of the platforms, and soon "Jack's Menagerie" is trending again.

The business doesn't hate the attention. We are very busy for a couple of hours, me doing the selling and the finding of rare items that only I, of course, have, and Grendia taking their money. She seems to be a natural with the whole process, and I am impressed that such a formal Prentian Royal Guard can so easily adapt to this new situation on an alien world where hours before this her only goal was to kidnap a guy and forcefully abscond offworld with him.

The crowd dies down again as the majority of the autograph lines start to form, and we are able to take a small break from the action.

"So," Grendia says, sipping on a fountain drink. I think she likes Sunkist. A lot. She has had six of them so far today. How she has been able to procure them all, though, I have not figured out.

"So?" I respond.

"This is what you do now, huh?" Grendia asks. "You spend your days among the humans, pretending to like what they like, and selling them whatever it is that strikes their fancy?"

"Well," I say, raising a finger that I start to waggle as I speak, "first off, I am not pretending. I like the same stuff they do. Sci-fi is freaking cool."

"You know the only reason their so-called science fiction exists in the first place is because some aliens were reckless in visiting Earth, and the humans just went with it, right? Most of their fiction isn't anywhere near what it's really like." Grendia looks around as she speaks. I think she wants to know about all of this, but she is skeptical that it is worth her time and energy.

"But that's the coolest part of it all!" I say. "They dream much bigger than we do, Gia."

I am careful to use her chosen human name to get into the habit for when we are in earshot of humans.

"They have such imaginations, you have no idea. Humanity isn't bound by the rules of the reality of what's really out there yet, and they still get to think it's all about them."

Grendia shrugs, "I suppose there's a certain appeal to that, considering where *you* come from."

"Hey, you come from there, too," I say.

Just as Grendia is about to object to my interpretation of her meaning, a tall human walks into the booth. He is not dressed like a con attendee, and I suppress a look of surprise when I notice that the badge he is wearing is not the kind that grants him access to the convention's many panels and attractions. It is a police badge.

"Hello there, sir," I say quickly. "What search for a fine collectible brings you into Jack's Menagerie of Amazing Stuff today?"

The man regards me silently for a moment and looks at Grendia as well. She is silent and sips on her soda, doing her best to look nonchalant. I still don't know if we're doing that right or not. Humans never adequately explain what it actually means to be *nonchalant*. Their dictionaries lose something in the effort, I think.

The man reaches into his coat pocket, and I have to make a waving motion with my hand behind my back to keep Grendia from taking the action as a possible threat. I am not completely sure it is not a threat. It could be another bounty hunter masquerading as a human law enforcement officer, after all, but I believe this one is actually human. Still not a good sign, but at least I'm fairly certain he's human.

I contain a sigh of relief as he pulls out a phone and taps on it for a moment before answering me. Humans do love their dramatic pauses.

"I am Detective Sergeant Collins," he says, holding the phone up, so I can see the screen, "and I need you to tell me what exactly happened in the events in this video from last night."

12

"Well, Detective," I say, "I would be glad to tell you all about it, but as you can see, I'm working right now. Is there another time we can meet?"

Human authorities sticking their noses into things. Great. Just what I didn't need today. I suppose I shouldn't be surprised. They do like to try to control things on their planet.

Detective Collins frowns at my offer. He wants to question me now.

"If it's at all possible, Mr. Grant," Collins says, "I would really like to get this case closed out by the end of the day."

"What is it exactly that you're investigating?" I ask.

Collins glances around the booth. He is as uncomfortable discussing anything in this place as I am. I notice some sweat beads on his forehead. Perhaps not uncommon, considering he is wearing a suit and tie and it is over ninety degrees outside. But I am in a mood to close this out as well.

"Just making sure that everyone involved is okay," he says. "Consider it a wellness check. Some of the things in this video are quite convincing, especially how the fallen actors pull off their disappearing act right in the middle of everyone."

So at least one human is questioning what they see. That's not the best for me, or for them. Best to go along with him for now and see what he knows. If I'm lucky, I can help steer his investigation to a swift close without raising any more questions.

"Okay," I say. "I understand that. These kinds of flash-mob performance-arts things can be pretty realistic, huh?"

Collins lets out a nervous laugh. "Uhh, well, yeah. That's what I told my boss. My son is into this kind of thing, and they actually showed me the video first before I was put on the case. I was really impressed with the special effects, like most people, I see."

I look around the booth, and Gia is helping several customers find what they are looking for. I nod to her and motion that I am going to go with Collins. She nods back and taps on her ear to let me know that she has a comm device just in case I need to get in touch with her.

"Let's go find that quiet place, Detective," I say, turning back to meet his gaze.

Collins nods, and we walk to the front of the vendor hall, exiting out a door far from the crowds and lines, and proceed through one of the back tunnels of the convention center. I have not been back here before, but Collins seems to know where he is going well enough for the both of us.

"I used to work security here back when the convention center first opened," he says as we turn a corner. "It was back when I was a beat cop, and the pay wasn't all that good. Not that it's all that good now, but at least I don't need a second job to make it work."

I let him talk, keeping an eye on how many turns we make and how far we walk. We are somewhere near the other side of the convention center before he stops at a door with a plaque that reads Meeting Room 6A and opens it, allowing me to go in first.

As I walk into the room, something hits me hard in the back of the head, and I tumble forward. I try to reach for a disintegrator, but I have fallen on them, making it impossible to draw either of them. My head feels like it is in shambles, and my vision is blurred. The room is suddenly darker. Someone turned out the lights.

"Sorry about this," I hear Collins say.

Another impact to my head.

Is he seriously pistol-whipping me?

And then it all goes black.

Light. Some light, at least, shining through my eyelids. I am not dead.

Mistake one.

"Hey, that wasn't what we discussed," I hear Collins say. We might still be in the same room where he jumped me, but I have no idea.

"I don't care what we discussed before," another voice responds to Collins. This voice is more gravelly and less human. I think I am starting to put it together.

More bounty hunters, most likely. And they somehow got to a local cop, got him to come after me. He mentioned a son earlier, right? If I was betting on this round of "Bad Guy Methodology Practices" I'd put the credits on the son being leverage here. Poor Collins. They are so gonna kill him. He's probably a good dude, too.

"I can't have a death, even the death of an alien who shouldn't be here, on my conscience," Collins says.

Yay! Moral fortitude! You go, Collins!

"How about the death of your son, eh?" says a third voice. This one is a bit lighter in tone and easier on the ears. So, three to one, at least.

I hear Collins sigh. "No, you know where I draw the line. I have to protect my son. They are all I have."

Boo! Family values getting in the way of saving the innocent alien tied to a chair in front of you!

"You say he's a war criminal?" Collins asks.

"Oh yeah," the softer voice says, "one of the worst ever.

Blowed up a whole galaxy once."

"Holy crap!" Collins yells. "That's possible!"

As far as you know.

"We're just trying to do the right thing here," the gravelly voice says. "Last night was no special effects display. He straight up murdered people to cover up his secret."

They sure are wasting a lot of time talking. Do kidnappings usually go like this? I always imagined they would be more business, less jabbering. They're gonna kill Collins anyway, so why waste the time?

I hear a door open and the sounds of a fourth person enter the room. Ah, so they were waiting for someone else. That makes sense. Gravelly and Softy have a boss. Most people do. And Collins is about to get it to the face.

"Why is he still here?" the new voice chimes into the conversation as soon as the door closes. This voice has some authority behind it. Definitely the leader, and probably the brains. I'm thinking Gravelly and Softy haven't exactly been following the plan. And as long as the plan involves keeping me alive until I can figure a way out of this mess, I can work with that.

"Oh, uhh, hey, bossy," Gravelly says.

Bossy sighs. "I *hate* it when you call me that."

"Oh! Right. Yeah, sorry bosse—err…boss." Gravelly sounds like Bossy has just taken his lunch money. He thought he had been doing a good job up until that point. Such a letdown. Morale might be the biggest of Bossy's problems if this interaction is any indicator.

"Well…" Bossy says, "I'm waiting."

I hear the sound of what I would guess are blasters being drawn from under coats.

"Hey, what's this now?" Collins asks. There is a note of surprise in his voice. I'm not sure why. These guys were *always* gonna double-cross him. They probably left the "no humans can know" part out of their sales pitch when they recruited him.

This pains me to admit, but there is little I can do to help Collins. Poor, soon-to-be-dead bastard. Not much of a detective, though, for not seeing this coming.

I hear the sounds of a struggle ensue. Collins isn't going down without a fight. This could get good real soon, and I'm missing out on all of it. I have been trying to get out of my restraints since I woke up, but I'm not there yet. Maybe in another minute or…

SNAP

The restraints suddenly break, and I spring into action.

I pull the hood off my head and take a split second to take stock of the situation. Collins is tussling with Gravelly, going for his gun, while Softy trains her gun on them both, looking like she is really confused about which one she should shoot. Bossy is more removed from the action, still by the door. She is the only one who has noticed me so far, her eyes becoming wide with surprise. They should have restrained me better.

Mistake two.

I draw a disintegrator and point it at Softy, pulling the trigger without a second thought. The bolt hits Softy with a sharp scorch as it goes to work on her insides, quickly eating away at the bonds between her cells and causing them to rip apart from one another in an exponential cascade of cellular-level destruction.

Ever seen an old movie reel stop in the wrong place as the projector light burns the film cell? Yeah, it's pretty much that. Just to a person.

But I have no time to waste. I continue moving across the room and make a grab at Bossy. She is too quick for me, though, and she back steps toward the door, opening it in one fluid motion and darting out of the room. A quick glance out the door shows me that we are still in the convention center.

BANG

I cringe as the gun goes off behind me. I whirl around to see Gravelly standing over Collins, blood beginning to soak out of the human's chest and into his clothes. That's a lot of blood.

"Hey, you!" Gravelly says, just now catching up with the rest of the action. "Did you kill Fleone?!"

Ah, so that was her name. Well, she'll always be Softy to me.

I point my disintegrator at Gravelly. "Yeah, I did. And unless you want to follow along, I wouldn't try…"

The warning is useless. The brute just has rage in his vision at this point. I can't say I don't get it. I *did* probably just kill his best, maybe even only, friend. Gravelly rushes toward me, and I pull my trigger again. He makes no move to attempt to avoid the shot.

I step through the remnants of Gravelly as they burn their last and kneel down next to Collins. He is a goner. I have no way to help him. The bullet is in his liver most likely and probably tore through something else on its way out.

"Oh, come on." Collins coughs as he speaks, blood trickling from his mouth. "You're not supposed to look at a dying man like that, ya know. Got a lot to learn about being human if you want to keep blending in."

"I'm not what they said I am," I say, taking Collins' hand and holding it as he fades.

"Got that idea, yeah," Collins says, an attempt at a chuckle causing a coughing fit that lasts a few moments.

"My son," he says, his voice getting lower. "They can't get to them. Has to be kept safe. Please."

A truly vindictive person might kill Collins' son just because things went wrong. And I have no idea if Bossy has just threatened his son or was actually holding him in a location to use as random. In the case of the latter, it is almost certain that these types would kill the son on their way out.

I nod. "Yes. I will find them. They will be kept safe. I promise."

That's what you tell a dying father, right? I have no idea if I can make good on the promise, but I make it anyway. Collins says no more after I assure him his son will be safe. A few moments later, his eyes lose their luster, and I am alone in the room.

I sigh heavily as I stand up. This next part is necessary, but I am very aware that I am robbing Collins' son of their ability to properly grieve. The disintegrator will leave nothing to bury, and there will be no evidence that Collins was here, or died, or how he died.

But it had to be done.

I leave the room a few minutes later, cleaned of all evidence of what happened. I look around and see the hallway off to my right. Bossy ran in that direction. She has a five-minute head start, but I doubt she has gone far. It is very unlikely that such a person is willing to come so close to their prize and then just run away. More likely Bossy went to get reinforcements.

It's time I go get some of my own.

13

Instead of going directly after Bossy, I head back into the vendor hall. The crowds are back to their mob-level strength, but I see a calm and cool Grendia handling everything with the dedicated poise of a royal guard. Overwhelmed, sure, but she would never let the humans see it.

The look of relief on her face is evident as she sees me walk back into the booth. I shake my head to let her know that things did not go well, and we work hard for the next half hour to clear out most of the crowds before they disperse a bit again. For the first time, I am really glad that panels and autograph signings happen on a regular schedule. I used to hate the ebb and flow of the foot traffic, but today it is a boon that I will never complain about again.

When we can finally speak, I quickly update Grendia on all that happened. She curses that she was not there to protect me, but I assure her that I am just fine. Collins' son, however, might not be so lucky. And Bossy is still out there. Grendia agrees that it is unlikely that the threat is over.

"What do you want to do?" Grendia asks.

"We need to get out of here, find Bossy, and make sure Collins' son is safe," I say. None of that sounds at all as easy as I said it.

"But the booth," Grendia says. "I doubt we are allowed to just leave it here without some kind of attention being drawn. And attention is the last thing we need right now."

I nod. I cannot leave the booth unattended. That's like, Things Not to Do at a Con 101.

"I could handle the booth," Leo says.

Grendia whirls around on the boy, and I catch on a moment too late that it is Leo who joined the conversation. How long has he been standing there?

I hold up a hand to stop Grendia from completing her take-down maneuver on Leo. The boy looks suitably frightened by the speed of Grendia's reaction to him butting into the conversation, and I have to reassure him that she will not harm him.

"Leo," I say, shaking my head. "Where did you come from?"

Leo shrugs and pops another handful of popcorn from the bag he is holding into his mouth. This kid. He has literally popped some popcorn and is watching the drama unfold in front of him.

"Who is this?" Grendia says.

"Who is *this*?" Leo responds.

"Gia, Leo. Leo, Gia," I say quickly. "Gia is…"

"Oh yeah!" Leo says as he points to Gia. "I know you! From last night in the hotel video. Wow. Good disguise today. Wait…is that who you went out with last night, Jack? Lyra was really unhappy about that, you know, and—"

I cut off what he is about to say next. "I spoke to your sister this morning, Leo. We're going out on a date tonight."

It was Leo's turn to be surprised. "Wow! Like, really, a real date?"

"You should have seen it," Gia chimes in. "Jarokin was incredibly sweet. Nervous, timid, afraid even. To think that an Earth woman could do all that to the pr—"

"*Jack*," I forcefully remind Grendia of my human name, and I see a wink of mischief pass between Leo and Grendia.

Did those two just become instant friends or something? I certainly don't like that. Nope.

"Look," I say, attempting to get us back on course, "Gia and

I need to go do something important."

"Alien stuff?" Leo asks, as if the whole concept has now become a casual weekly occurrence to him, a regular part of his life.

"Uhh…yeah," I say.

Leo shrugs. "Okay. I got ya covered. I know your passwords and all that from helping you out last year."

Gia looks at me and shrugs. I think she is impressed with this particular human. He is nothing like what she would expect, I imagine.

"Just one thing," Leo says as we are leaving.

"What's that?" I turn around and ask.

"Don't be late to your date with my sister," Leo says with a wink and a finger gun pointed at me.

The message is clear. If I somehow miss our date, I'm gonna wish I was dead. And not from anything Leo would do to me, either.

*   *   *

We head out of the vendor hall at a brisk pace. Grendia has a device in her hands that looks like an Earth phone, but I know it is a bio-sig capture device. She is scanning for non-human presence.

"Do you think they are holding the son here?" she asks.

"I have no idea," I say as I look around in a useless attempt to spot Bossy in the crowd. Saturday is the worst possible day for a hunt like this. The cosplay parade and competition is today, and everyone who brought an outfit has it on. It's the best time and place to hide a bunch of aliens. That has always been my favorite thing about cons, but today I hate it.

"Anything?" I ask.

"Nothing yet," Grendia says.

"They would not have left, not without me. I was the target," I say, and Grendia nods her agreement.

I look around at the crowds for a few more minutes, and an idea hits me. I take out my phone and open up an app. I start typing in a message and motion for Grendia to follow me. We are walking in the direction of the panel rooms, and I keep going until I find one that is empty. The sign on the door says that this room will not be used for another couple of hours.

Perfect.

I hold up my phone and take a picture of the room number. Grendia follows me into the empty room and looks around.

"Why are we here?" she asks.

I finish what I am typing and hit send before I respond to her.

"I just told social media that the people who made the Epic Lobby Alien LARP Fight at QUASITASTICON 9 video are doing an impromptu signing session in this room in fifteen minutes."

Grendia looks confused for only a moment before catching on to the plan. She smiles the same mischievous smile I saw from her earlier when she and Leo were having fun making a fool of me, and then she is off. We are both off. The room does not need much prep, but we want to make sure that we can see everyone who comes into the room from the dais where the signing table is. Some slight rearranging, and in moments we are done.

I hear the telltale sounds of a crowd gathering outside the door. Hopefully nobody from the con will attempt to interfere. That would make things more complicated, yes, but not impossible.

"You know," Grendia says after she is finished prepping the room, "this could put a lot of people in danger."

I shake my head and shrug. "They are already in danger.

They just don't know it. At least this way, we can concentrate the danger on me, and together we can come up with a plan to neutralize the threat without any more Collinses happening."

Grendia nods. Nothing is ideal about this situation. But when you can't find the needle, sometimes what you need is a really big magnet.

"You ready?" I ask.

"I am not," Grendia says, and I look over at her. She is smiling back at me.

"Was that…sarcasm?" I ask.

"Sarcasm?" she says as she walks toward the door to let in the gathered masses. "I don't think I've been on Earth long enough to try doing that."

14

The phrase "took on a life of its own" applies to what happens next. When the doors open, the crowds flood in, and so, too, do matching polo shirt convention organizers who corral the people, form them into lines, and bring the whole thing into an ordered procession in a scene unlike anything I have ever witnessed. I do not know if the people are pliable, the con workers are really good at their jobs, or if there is a higher power at work containing the chaos, but I am equally impressed and grateful that it happens.

Before I am fully aware of all of this, a con worker comes up to me and begins handling me, too.

"Hello, Mr. Grant," she says, a bubbly personality bursting forth from her bright face full of fantasy elf makeup, ears and all. The detail is impressive, and the contacts she is wearing make her eyes appear like starfields. I could not be more impressed if the look was actually achieved with a maccomp.

"Uhh, hello," I say.

"I'm Jessica, from the QT9 Pop-Up and Requisition Team," she continues. I think her caffeine levels are dangerously high for a human to be sustaining. "We were on standby awaiting word of where your signing would be today, and we have come prepared."

I look around at all of the barely contained commotion. Are Pop-Up and Requisition Teams even a thing? I don't think they are. What is going on here? I watch as one of Jessica's team members attempts to guide Grendia to a table on the stage. Grendia looks to me for guidance on what to do. I just shrug and start walking over to the table and chair that Jessica has begun indicating is where I will be signing autographs.

As I take my seat, my eyes land on the pile of printed photos on the table in front of me. They are pictures of stills, really good quality ones, from the hotel lobby during last night's "show." A box of pens is next to the stack, and I look up at Jessica. She is there with a smile of encouragement and gives me a thumbs-up. She must have taken me looking at her as the sign that I am ready to start the line because a few moments later the con staff starts letting them up to me in small groups.

The next hour is a blur of "Hi, there" and "Wow! That was so awesome, dude!" and "I'm already planning my next cosplay based on her!" and so many more faces and exchanges that I cannot possibly remember them all. I am able to look over a few times to see that Grendia appears to be doing just fine and actually has a longer line than I do, and I hear the compliments from the people as she meets them, praising her performance as the best in the act. I try not to let that sting my pride as I remember that these fans, while pretty cool to witness in action, are not the real reason we are doing this.

If my hunch is right, Bossy and whatever other crew she has lurking around won't want to pass up the opportunity to keep me in their sites. I do my best to scan the lines and the crowd to see if I can spot anybody who looks suspicious, anyone paying a little too much attention to either Grendia or myself, but it is difficult to tell anything for sure. There are a lot of phones and devices out, snapping selfies, doing lives. They are probably hoping to catch another LARP flash mob, and part of me—the fun part of me that still exists underneath all of the seriousness of the past few days— kinda wants to give that to them.

Grendia and I actually could pull it off if we prepared ahead of time. It would be expensive, and we would have to come up with another way to do the special effects in order to make sure we didn't run the risk of hurting anybody, but it might be possible to do this, and…

NO, Jack!

The all too annoying voice of reason butts back into my head as I sign another picture and tell more fans that I am so appreciative that they enjoyed the show. This isn't what I do. I'm a shadow vendor in the alien market. That's my job, and I would really like to get back to it when all of this blows over.

My eyes are suddenly drawn to a small group standing in the back corner. They are clustered around a central figure. It *could* be Bossy and some new cronies. Even if it is not, I hope that they are here, waiting for it to wind down and take their chance on grabbing me again. I wonder what they know about Grendia? Even if they know that she is also an alien, it is unlikely that they are aware that she is Prentian like me.

I spend the rest of the hour looking at other groups that hang around in the area for too long, suspecting each one in turn of being the dastardly and nefarious hunters responsible for Collins' death. And each one in turn gets cleared of that suspicion as they eventually leave, having finished their vigil of waiting for their last party member standing in one of the lines.

At the end of the hour, the con team makes the announcement that the signing is over, and they will notify everyone via social media should another pop-up event happen over the rest of the weekend. I am relieved that it is over, at least the performance part. I do not envy all those actors, writers, and famous-for-whatever people who do this every weekend on the regular in between their actual jobs. Perhaps I don't feel too badly for them, though. *They* signed up for it, after all.

"Did you see anything?" Grendia asks as she meets me off the stage.

I shake my head. "Nothing concrete, but my gut tells me

they are close by. I made my presence known, and any good hunter would want to watch and take advantage of it."

"Okay!" Jessica pops up next to the both of us, still bubbly and exuberant. I really wish caffeine worked on me like it does on them. "So that was fun, right?"

"It was something, yeah," I say. Grendia opens her mouth to contribute, but Jessica is too quick.

"Okay, so we have to go over some ground rules for next time to make sure that some of the close calls don't happen again," Jessica says, raising her tablet up to check it for reference.

"The standard fee of 60 percent of proceeds collected for a pop-up autograph signing are pretty easy to understand, but in order to not incur a fine next time, we require at least two hours' notice prior to the event."

"Not much of a pop-up if there is advance notice," Grendia says. Jessica gives Grendia some major side-eye, and I have to shake my head slightly to keep Grendia from escalating the situation. Side-eye can be a very easily misunderstood expression for an alien. On some planets, it is more like walking down the center road of an old western town at high noon, spurs clanking as you walk, hand ready to draw out your pistol and shoot the person in front of you. On others, it is a sign of bad intestinal gas build up. Based on Grendia's reaction to Jessica doing it, I did not have to guess which way her interpretation was leaning.

"That all sounds fine," I say, wanting to end the conversation and get on with our hunter hunting.

"Great!" Jessica says, once more giving Grendia a side-eye glance as she darts away and starts issuing orders to the con crew who has to get the room back in shape in time for the actually scheduled events that will happen here soon.

"So what do we do now?" Grendia asks.

"I'm not surprised that they didn't try anything while there were so many people around, but now that the crowd is dispersing and they know where I am, they will likely just wait for me to be alone," I say.

"Are you…" Grendia starts in, and I already know what she wants to say.

"It's the only way," I say. "You can keep a safe distance if you want, but they must not know you are there."

Grendia looks unhappy with the idea of me purposely putting myself out there as bait, but I have to bring this to a close before it gets out of hand. Well, before it gets any more out of hand than it already is. I don't want to spend the rest of forever looking over my shoulder, and stopping Bossy's crew is step one to getting there.

"What's your plan?" Grendia asks, sounding unconvinced that anything I tell her will be acceptable.

"I think I want some lunch," I say.

"Food? Now?" Grendia asks. She was obviously not expecting me to say that.

"Food."

15

Some cons are better known for it than QUASITASTICON 9, but almost every convention in the fandom and gaming genres attracts a greater or lesser presence of food trucks to the downtown area. I hardly ever have occasion to make it out to the food trucks during these events, and I am enjoying this rare pleasure of the culinary variety in spite of the circumstances that allow me to partake of it.

I walk down the lane of food trucks trying to figure out what I want to try today. Ultimately it is unimportant for the plan, but if I am going to wait around to be probably kidnapped and possibly killed, well, I want to do it while eating something truly delicious. I walk around for a few more minutes before I stop in my tracks.

There it is.

The sight of it starts my mouth watering like I have seldom experienced before. I take a few more steps, and the smell hits me. Perfectly seasoned meats, fresh ingredients, and the sizzle of tortillas being warmed for the making. I have found it. The truck I've always wanted to try.

Logan's Shocking Taco Truck.

I join the line and post a picture of me waiting to place my order on social media. It doesn't hurt to sell the whole ruse, but I'm actually excited about this one. I have heard about this food truck and its amazing delicacies for years.

Tacos. Whenever it is destined to be that humanity does finally join the galactic community, I would guess that a significant portion of the planet's tourism will be because of the taco. Is there a greater human food? I just don't know if there is. At least, I haven't had it yet. And humans are really good cooks, too. Pizza, steak, potatoes, chili, whatever calamari really is. It's all good. The taco has stiff competition and still manages to come out on the top of the food heap.

"The three taco sample plate, please, extra hot," I say when I get up to the window. I pay and move over to the waiting area where other taco-eating hopefuls await their plates.

It is a few moments before I become aware of two people standing next to me, one to each side. The one on my left leans in close.

"Don't make any moves, *Jack*," he says. I am unclear on whether he is attempting to use my name or repeating the oft-used generic Earth colloquialism that makes it into gangster movies and the like.

"Yeah," says the one on the right, quietly enough that only I can hear him, "wouldn't want anything to happen to all these people 'round here, would ya?"

Seriously, the group of hunters needs to watch better *How to Talk Like a Human* videos on YouTube. This actual gangster routine is getting old.

But they have a point. I don't want them pulling an Ugly and shooting up the area.

"Can I at least wait for my tacos?" I ask, looking to the one on my left. He is pointing a small hold-out-style blaster at me that is thankfully concealed enough for no one around us to notice.

"I think your lunch is canceled," he says and motions for me to turn and follow the other one.

They quietly lead me around a corner and down a service alleyway behind the convention center. It's interesting to note that these kinds of downtown buildings really have a lot of nooks and side alleys where all kinds of terrible things might happen to anybody who stumbles by. I bet it was worse before cameras became a thing. I am not worried about those, though. It is likely that one or both of them is carrying some kind of visual jamming device to confuse any nearby surveillance equipment. At least, I would if I was doing their job. I suppose that doesn't mean they are smart enough to do it, though.

We stop short of a door, and I am surprised that we make no move to go inside it. Instead, we wait for a few minutes. Both of them say nothing beyond telling me to stand still. They pat me down and take my disintegrators but thankfully leave my maccomp alone. At least they are following some of the rules.

"So are we waiting for someone, then?" I ask.

"Shut up," one responds. I get a clap to the side of my head to punctuate the order, which causes me to take a half step to keep my balance. The other one grabs me by my collar to steady me and put me back in my place.

Ah, Clappy and Grabby. So nice to meet you both.

A few more minutes of waiting, and the double doors in front of us swing open. I smile as Bossy and two more yet to be named walk out to meet us. The doors close behind us before anyone talks.

Bossy sighs and shakes her head. "You're troublesome and expensive. That puts me in a bad mood."

On cue, to punctuate her bad mood, Grabby punches me in the gut. I double over and drop to one knee.

"Rude," I cough out as Clappy infringes on Grabby's territory and yanks me back to my feet.

"Oh yes," Bossy says, her eyes darting up and down me as if inspecting some livestock that she has just acquired. "Manners *are* important on this world, aren't they?"

This time it is Clappy who punches me in the stomach, and I drop to both knees. The may not knock the wind out of me, but I still feel pain there well enough to make me react as if it does. This unfortunately makes it easier for galactic ruffian types to cause general pain and suffering just by punching most species in a somewhat central bodily location.

After I am back on my feet, thanks to Grabby this time, I look Bossy in the eyes.

"So what will it be," I say, "the old 'we're gonna make you wish the contract wanted you dead' speech? Or no, maybe you'll try to figure out if I'm more valuable to someone else *before* you turn me in. Or—"

Another nod from Bossy, and both Clappy and Grabby punch me in the stomach. No dropping to my knees this time. I fall backward on the asphalt, hard. My head explodes in pain as it takes the brunt of the impact. They let me lie there for a moment, I'm not sure how long. Sucking in wind, clutching my ribs, trying like hell to shake my head enough to allow me to see less than sixteen of them standing around, just leaning over me and laughing their asses off.

I think it is time to turn the tables.

They get me back on my feet again before Bossy moves closer to me and stares into my eyes.

"No," Bossy says, "I think for all the trouble you've caused me I might just sell you to the Joraxyan Slavers Union and leave it at that. They always find such creative uses for Prentians, I hear."

I laugh in response to her threat.

"Ha!" I belt out, and Bossy jumps back at my yell. "Clearly you've never met my mother. The Joraxyans study her abridged book on how to make other people suffer."

Bossy looks amused at my rambling. I hope she is. I plan to do more of it until help arrives. Why it isn't here yet already, I have no idea.

"And another thing, if..." I start sucking in wind again at

this point. It is no affectation, either. I really am out of breath just from this little amount of talking, but I have to keep stalling.

"...If you plan on staying alive, you're probably better off just selling me instead of actually turning in the bounty. I mean, if you know I'm Prentian, then you must know who I really am, right? Do you want to mess with my mother? Do you really think she would deal with you on the level? Ha! She's screwed over everyone she's ever done business with, including my father! Oh yeah, don't think I'm some spoiled love child, either. I'm a business transaction, lady, so you can't intimidate me by telling me I'm gonna be someone's servant again. Why do you think I left that hell hole in the first place?"

Seriously? What is she waiting for?

Bossy is nearing the end of her patience, but I also think she is intrigued by my monologue. I think she's used to more fear from the people she hunts down. Well, then *this* lady has another thing coming.

"And what's more," I continue, looking to each of the henchmen as they begin to nervously shift from foot to foot waiting on Bossy's next order, "you know who else is on this planet? A Prentian Royal Guard unit."

I nod profusely as I let that sink in.

"Yeah, I'm not joking. And neither do they. In fact, I'm pretty damn sure that one of them should be showing up to kick all your asses back to the Tractarii Nebula RIGHT...ABOUT...NOW..."

I look around, expecting Grendia to make a dramatic entrance and save me from having to stall these fools with my face bones next. The goons are on edge. At least I had them convinced. Bossy even looks a little concerned that I might be right. The clock ticks on, and only the distant sound of traffic and the con goers walking by several feet away can be heard. I even think I hear a slight wind blowing through the alleyway, punctuating that no one else is there with us.

"Huh…" I say.

When nothing happens, Bossy's look of apprehension fades away, and she utters a slight chuckle. Shaking her head, she motions for Clappy and Grabby to bring me with them, and she turns toward the door. The other two goons, who have still not done enough to warrant internal names, open a door each. When the doors open, Bossy stops and lets out a yell of surprise.

Grendia stands on the other side of the door, a bladed weapon in each hand, each pulsing with macro cellular energy.

And she looks pissed.

16

Grendia is breathing heavily, and I notice that her blonde hair, which had been tied neatly behind her in a bun the last time I saw her, was now coming loose, several locks hanging down in front of her face. The overall effect, added to her lightly blood-spattered vest and leggings, make for a very fearsome sight, and I almost feel sorry for Bossy and her crew for what is about to happen to them. She has already been fighting. That much is clear, and I spare a thought to imagine the poor goons that Bossy must have sent to deal with Grendia, counting on them to handle her and leave Bossy free to take me away.

Third and final mistake.

The first few moments of the fight unravel in slow motion for me. I am pretty sure that's because of my still fairly recent head injury, but it's still pretty cool to experience. Grendia flies into action, jumping toward one of the unnamed goons and burying her blade in his chest. Poor, unnamed bastard. Oh well.

Next she leaps at the other unnamed goon. He fares a little bit better, but not much. That one loses an arm in a brave but useless defense against Grendia-powered blades. His yell of equal parts terror and pain is what shocks me out of the slow-motion vision stupor. I frown. I was enjoying "cinema mode."

Bossy brandishes a blade of her own and meets Grendia's attack as the royal guard switches her attention from the incredibly recently dubbed "Lefty" to a new target. The two begin exchanging blows, and I am enthralled by the flashing series of blade strikes and parries as Bossy shows off that she is no slouch in the hand-fighting department.

I can't tell who is winning the fight. Grendia attacks, and Bossy parries, only to leave herself open for an impossibly swift kick from Grendia. The kick is in turn blocked by an elbow, and the two reset and circle one another to try again. Each time one of them attacks, the other counters perfectly. I am more than a little scared at this display from Grendia. She is *way* more dangerous than I gave her credit for. If she had really wanted to take me into custody in the hotel lobby, she absolutely could have. A few more exchanges end with both combatants suffering superficial wounds, little more than scratches and bruises.

I look up to my left and right to see Clappy and Grabby equally engrossed in the titanic fight playing out in front of them. Taking advantage of their inattentiveness, I make a grab for one of my disintegrators in Grabby's belt. I am almost fast enough, but the bigger alien catches on just in time.

"Hey!" he yells and attempts to kick me. I roll forward to dodge, the top of his boot only slightly catching me. It is not enough to hurt me, but it is enough to add momentum to my acrobatic maneuver and sends me back to the asphalt, this time on my face. I roll over, spitting out the accumulated grit and blood now in my mouth, and raise my hands just in time to block a second kick from the now very aggravated Grabby. I grab his foot instead of blocking the kick and pull hard.

The unexpected move pulls him off balance, and I roll to the side to avoid him landing on top of me. I lash out with an elbow and feel a satisfying crunch as the strike connects with Grabby's face, followed by a muffled curse that I'm pretty sure has something to do with accusing me of engaging in sexual misconduct with a space duck. Clappy has now caught on to the fact that his prisoner has decided to try to escape, and he is drawing his blaster.

I fumble behind me with my still extended arm, hoping to

grab a weapon out of Grabby's belt. I am rewarded with the feeling of a pistol grip in my hand, and I yank it out of the belt, swinging it widely in front of me. I squeeze the trigger to see a disintegrator bolt fly just past Clappy's cheek, leaving a scorch mark, but not making a direct hit.

Clappy drops his blaster and puts his hand to his face, a look of astonishment plastered on his mug. I am surprised he is still alive, too, but at least he is not armed for now. I take the lull in my fight to get to my feet and see that Lefty has gathered himself enough to engage Grendia as well. Despite the loss of his arm, he appears to be a solid hand fighter.

I can give no more attention to Grendia as I see the hulking form of Grabby rise up in front of me, blocking my view.

"Yer gonna pay for that, runt," he says, but his nose is smashed enough that it sounds like he's all stuffed up, and his voice now sounds like a cartoon character that has just been smacked in the face with a giant mallet. I am unable to stifle a chuckle at the sound, which enrages the larger alien enough that he charges me.

My eyes widen as I perceive my increased danger level, and I am unable to move out of the way this time as Grabby tackles me to the ground, slamming my already tender noggin on the asphalt once more. The flurry of blows that he rains down on me over the next several seconds make me question every snarky thing I've ever done in life, as if taking them all back would change the fact that I've got nearly three hundred pounds of enraged alien muscle pinning me to the ground and pummeling me senseless.

"Yeah! Beat 'im good, Hookedan!" I hear Clappy cheer on.

Hookedan? Yeah, Grabby is a way better name.

Through all this currently being done to me, I hear someone I can't see cry out in pain. I can't tell if it was Grendia or Bossy, and I begin to panic that I might soon be alone in this fight. As my mind races to find a way out, I realize that I've somehow managed to keep hold of the disintegrator. I can't move the hand that grips the weapons, and I definitely can't see it, either, what with all the fists repeatedly interjecting themselves into my field of vision. I have no choice. I pull the trigger. What have I got to lose at this point, right?

The pop of the muffled disintegrator blast sounds far too distant to be a thing happening literally right next to me, and I wait for the searing pain of disintegration to begin taking over my body. Grabby stops punching me and pulls back a bit, clearly confused and incapable of understanding.

The next few seconds pass with Grabby progressively feeling lighter, and I finally see the disintegration reaction trail up his body, taking its time as it works through the massive alien's enhanced musculature and survival implant systems, which I am able to clearly see once the outer layers of his anatomy flake away. Some aliens are resistant to the disintegration process, but very few are outright immune to it. Grabby must be one of the ones that it takes a moment to set in.

I slowly get to my feet, my head throbbing harder than ever, and I see that Grendia is still fighting both Lefty and Bossy. Bossy has a nasty gash wound on her side that is glowing, pulsing even, with the residual energy of Grendia's energy blades. Clappy has overcome the shock of the last few moments and managed to recover his blaster.

Before I can do anything about him, he raises his weapon and pulls the trigger. I feel the impact of the shot hit me hard on my left side, and I go down again, clutching the spot where it hit. I just cannot stay off the ground today. I yell out in pain, but the yell is cut short with the realization that I am in nowhere near the amount of pain I should be in after getting shot with a blaster bolt.

Clappy is still aiming his blaster at me, and I snap off another shot in his direction, still trying to figure out exactly what is going on with my wound. The shot misses again, but Clappy is spooked once more by the near miss, enough so that he shakes his head, gives Grendia and Bossy a quick look, and bolts into the still-open doorway. I sigh.

You have got to be kidding me. I am not in the mood for a chase sequence right now.

I pull my hand away from the wound, and I squint to make sure I am seeing what I am seeing. There is some blood, but not near as much as I was expecting. Small bits and parts are mixed in with what blood is there. Electronic parts. Maccomp parts.

I look over the rest of me. Yep. It was the maccomp that saved me. Well, kinda. Saved me in the sense that I'm not dead just yet. But in the sense that I now *look* like the full-blown alien that I actually am, I'm not so sure yet.

I look up to see Clappy running farther down the hallway. Yep, he's gonna keep going. I summon the strength to drag myself to my feet for what I hope will be the last time for now, and I take a few woozy steps toward the door.

"Jarokin!" Grendia yells as she parries another blow from Bossy's blade. "You're…*YOU!*"

"No time for that now!" I yell back as I take a few quicker steps. Clappy is almost out of sight now. Can't let him escape.

"Jarokin, wait!" Grendia yells after me, and I hear her struggle again with Bossy. I can't wait around to see how that ends, but I trust that Grendia has it handled. Lefty is again on the ground, hopefully for good this time, so at least I am not leaving her to fight outnumbered.

Not that I think she would care about that.

I speed up to a quick jog as I run into the convention center in pursuit of Clappy. No communicator. No phone. No maccomp.

Just a disintegrator in one hand and a singular mission to stop a bad guy.

17

"Why is this place such a maze!" I yell out as I round yet another corner and find nothing but another endless set of doors and corners.

Seriously. What is the purpose of all of this? What do they keep down here? And who could even find it once they do? I have been pursuing Clappy through the back halls of the convention center for a few minutes, and I have managed to catch sight of him a couple of times. I am trying to find the way up to the main levels. If I was Clappy, that's where I would be heading.

I decide instead to look for stairs. That's also how I would try to get to another level if I was being chased. Too much to risk using an elevator. After another turn, I find a wall map of the floor. I am closer to the stairs than I thought, and as I turn in the right direction, I hear another set of footsteps running down an intersecting hallway.

Stopping short of the junction between the hallways, I hold my disintegrator up and try my best to focus my eyes down the barrel. I think I have a concussion. No naps for me any time soon.

The rapid footsteps reach the junction, and Clappy rounds the corner, turning away from me toward the stairs. I wait a moment to make sure that I have him in my sights and pull the trigger. The blast goes wide again.

I can't hit anything today!

Clappy spins around and holds out his weapon, sending three shots flying down the corridor at me. Thankfully, Clappy is as bad a shot as I am today, and I only need to stand still to avoid getting hit. Which I do, because my reaction time is terrible right now. Hmm. Maybe more like a "concussion plus."

Fortunately, Clappy is still too much in the mood to run and doesn't notice that I am really in no good shape for a gun battle. He turns and bolts for the stairs. I run after him, having no other choice than to keep trying to find a way to stop him from escaping and possibly coming back with even more trouble.

When I reach the stairs, Clappy is opening the door one flight above, which leads out into the main convention halls. There will be lots of people up there. Too many people. I don't have a maccomp anymore, and I halt at the door, wondering if this is the right call.

No choice. Cosplay it, Jack.

With no idea how or why that short internal pep talk changes anything about the situation, I fling the door open and run out into the QUASITASTICON 9 crowd.

I get a few looks at first, people perhaps a little taken aback by the authentic-looking alien cosplayer who just burst out onto the floor. But the attention is short-lived as I push my way through the crowds, trying desperately to keep Clappy in sight. Clappy is much less delicate with the humans who get in his way, shoving and pushing as he needs in order to keep expanding the distance between us. Ironically this makes him easier to keep track of. I just have to follow the string of con attendees still cursing at him by the time I move past them.

I have no idea where Clappy is trying to go, and perhaps he does not really know, either. They had to have a plan for getting me out of here, and even if that plan has now been blown to shreds, the escape route itself may still be there. A vehicle, perhaps? I really hope they didn't land a spaceship on the convention center's roof. Please don't let them have landed a spaceship on the roof. I don't know if I can handle that today.

Clappy looks back to see if I have managed to keep up with

him, and his eyes narrow as he sees that I am gaining on his position. He stops and looks around at the people nearest to him.

No. Don't you do it, you scummy coward.

I see Clappy make a move toward a group of humans that are nearby, and he stretches out a hand to try to grab at one of the kids standing with them. As he steps closer, another child dressed as a Jedi youngling, swings their toy lightsaber, hitting Clappy's hand away from the child he was grabbing for.

"No you don't!" the lightsaber-wielding youngling yells. "We don't like bounty hunters here!"

The kid has no idea how accurate they are as Clappy utters a curse in a language thankfully none of the humans can understand and flees toward a nearby door. That kid will never know how much of a hero they really are.

Clappy pulls open the door and dashes inside. I quickly move after him and pull open the door before it closes, darting inside. The door is a side entrance to a dim ballroom-sized hall that is unfortunately packed full of people. I cannot immediately tell what is going on exactly, but I do see strong stage lights pointing at Clappy, who has run up the side stairs in front of me and made it halfway across the stage before skidding to a stop and raising his hand to shade his eyes as he desperately tries to look around and get his bearings.

Knowing this is my chance to catch up to him, I bound up the stairs and run onto the stage. It is only then that I am able to see where we are, and what we have run into the middle of. The crowd is almost all cosplayers. Costumes and outfits of every kind, shape, fandom, and corner of the imagination are in front of me. There is a judges' station down in front of the stage and seven VIP judges staring at us in wide-eyed wonder, trying to figure out if this is part of the planned event or not. A few contestants wait in the wings, off stage on the far side of Clappy, and an announcer who has frozen in mid-sentence is glued to their podium at the extreme other end of the stage.

It's the freakin' cosplay contest!

The crowd is silent, probably as stunned as Clappy and I are now that we have realized where we have chosen to work out our intergalactic beef. Nobody is sure what to do next, including me. The idiot in the middle of the stage solves the problem for me.

Clappy turns and points his blaster at me. "I'm not going out this like. Not without taking a whole mess of your precious humans with me!"

He points his blaster out into the crowd, and I raise my disintegrator, leveling it at what I hope is his chest. Clappy reaches into his pocket and pulls out a small spherical device. It is shiny and has a few blinking indicator lights on it alongside an activation switch. I know immediately that it is a…

"He's got a thermal detonator!" someone in the crowd yells, and the crowd begins shouting a mix of cheers, boos, and not a few calls of encouragement for Clappy to use the device.

They think this is another show!

The phones are out and recording, just like before, and I know I'm never going to hear the end of this from Leo, from Lyra, and most especially from Grendia. Do humans *ever* know when they're in mortal danger? Is life just a game to them? Well, it seems like it is for this crowd.

But I happen to know that the device that Clappy is holding is, in fact, *not* a thermal detonator. It's a CSDT, or Contained Singularity Diminishing Translator sphere. Not exactly a grenade, more like a gravity enhancement device. It increases the pull of gravity within its effect radius by almost a thousand times, violently smashing the atoms of anything caught such that the remains of any organic material could be better classified as an adhesive. Not a pleasant way to go, I hear, as the effect is not instantaneous.

"Put down the thermo-gravitic enhancement device," I say in the strongest tone I can muster. "There's still a way out of this for you, you know. We can help one another."

I mean what I am saying. He probably can provide me with valuable information, but at this point I'm just trying to get him to stop pointing a blaster at the crowd and put the gravity grenade away.

Clappy looks out into the crowd, then back at me. He is going to do it. I can tell. I have one shot to get this right.

"No!" he screams, and his fingers tighten on the grenade, moving the switch to activate it.

I pull my trigger one more time. The disintegrator bolt flies out and hits the gravity grenade instead of Clappy. The device begins pulsing rapidly, and I am prepared for the consequences of my failures. It's all over now. I will soon be paste, along with half the people in this room.

We all wait, all of us. Clappy, me, every human. I close my eyes tight, waiting for the excruciating pain of a million planets pulling me into the ground, slowly crushing my very essence into space goo. It feels like our collective breathing halts in anticipation as the grenade pulses more rapidly and then fizzles, making a sad de-powering sound as it crumbles to dust in Clappy's hands. He looks up at me, confusion and terror on his face.

That…should not have worked like that.

I had been aiming for Clappy's chest. The grenade was *not* my target. The disintegrator should have set it off. Clappy and I exchange confused looks. We are the only two beings in that room who know that something went really weird just now.

Clappy obviously decides that this is his chance to kill more humans anyway and raises his blaster to the crowd. I snap off a shot at him. This one hits him in the leg. He falls backward, his shot going into the ceiling. I walk across the stage and kneel next to him on the lesser injured of my two knees as the disintegrator reaction works its way up his body. The look of hatred on his face changes to complete confusion as I speak the last words he will ever hear.

"You really should have let me have my tacos."

18

The ballroom explodes in thunderous applause and cheering. I look around to see what they are cheering at before I realize it is me. I stand and squint as a second spotlight hits me, illuminating every inch of my true alien form. The panic in my chest rises as the adrenaline of the last several minutes begins to level off. I am going to crash hard soon, and I need to not be here when it happens. Where is Grendia?

I try to walk off the stage, but by now both sets of stairs are blocked by cheering fans. A chant begins in the crowd, faint at first, but it quickly builds to the point that I can understand it.

"Lobby Guy!"

"Lobby Guy!"

"Lobby Guy!"

Okay, well, I guess I'm Lobby Guy now. There are worse names they could have given me, I suppose. I look out into the crowd and raise my hand to shield my eyes from the worst of the spotlights. The crowd takes this as a signal to them, and acknowledgment of their chanting, and they get even louder.

I look across the stage to the cosplay contest announcer, who is conferring with a representative from the judges' table. This cannot be good. They both nod and look at me, and I just sigh. My various body pains are starting to sink in. I look around to see if there is any way to escape from the room, but the backstage area doesn't lead anywhere, being just a curtained-off partition between the front of the stage and the back of it. No doors or stairs that I can see.

"QUASITASTICON 9 COSPLAY CONTEST ATTENDEES!"

The judges' voice somehow manages to blast over the rambunctious crowd, and after a few more blaring attempts to get their attention, the noise begins to die down.

"The judges have made their choices!" When this announcement hits them, the crowd quickly hushes down. We all wait to see what the judge will say next, and the spotlights shift from me to the announcer. The room is not dark enough for me to slip away unnoticed, and I quietly curse the situation. How long can I be out in the open like this without questions? I mean, even for the most realistic cosplay makeup, it's a tough stretch to be able to replicate some of my true anatomy with prosthetics.

"The judges of QUASITASTICON 9 have made their decision concerning the winners," the announcer finally continues, "and despite the very dramatic, visually spectacular, and late entry from Hotel Lobby Alien Guy, they have decided that this year's winner will be the very impressive double costume team entry titled 'Goro and the Man in the five-hundred-dollar Sunglasses!'"

The crowd erupts in fervor again, this time with a slightly different tone. Fortunately most of the noise is cheering, but there are some who feel the result should have gone differently. I am relieved not to have crashed the event entirely by having my intergalactic family drama spilling out onto their stage, and I make for the door.

Before I make it down the stairs, I am swamped by people wanting my autograph or to ask me about the show they just saw, if there's another one coming up, and so forth. I try to be polite, but my vision is getting hazy. I take a few more steps, attempting to make it back out the side door that I came in through, but I am unsuccessful. The last thing I am aware of is that cinema mode is back, and I am slowly pitching forward, my face on its way to a meeting of destiny with the ballroom floor.

I wake up in a bed, covered mostly by a sheet and a few immodest undergarments that I was definitely *not* wearing before. Before. Before…I passed out. In the ballroom. Without a maccomp! I look around nervously and attempt to sit up more. That is a terrible mistake, as I am instantly woozy. The room begins to spin on an axis that is not consistent with the orientation of the Earth in general, and I immediately lie back into the propped-up position I woke up in. I let out an involuntary sound of pain as not only my head but also my side where my maccomp got shot to pieces begins to throb.

I hear footsteps from out in the suite, and a few moments later the still visually rotating image of Grendia fills the doorway. She quickly crosses the distance to the bed and sits down next to me, placing a cold towel on my forehead. The world begins to stabilize a little bit as I attempt to blink away the dizziness.

"You're lucky I found you before the paramedics got to you," Grendia says.

And I know I am. Paramedics would have been one of the worst possible encounters I could have had.

I only manage a slight nod in response. My mouth seems to not be working just yet past uttering small, pathetic sounds of hurt and discomfort. After a few more seconds of the towel helping me clear my vision and my thoughts, I am able to speak a bit.

"Thank you," I say, and place my hand on Grendia's hand. "I owe you a lot, you know."

Grendia smiles and nods. "Oh, yeah. I know. That was incredibly reckless what you did, Jarokin. If I hadn't found you already unconscious, you soon would have been."

She's not mad, that much I can tell. She's concerned. I am a wreck, and all she has seen of me so far is the actions of a Prentian Prince who acts before he thinks. So in her mind, nothing has changed since I left our home planet.

I glance at the window. The blackout shades are drawn, but I can still see some light leaking in through the bottom of them.

"It's late afternoon," Grendia says. "The vendor hall is about to close, in case you are wondering. Your phone has been blowing up since I recovered it from the bounty hunters."

Grendia indicates my phone on the table beside the bed. Next to it is a new maccomp that I am very grateful to see. She likely picked it up off one of the hunters before she, I assume, disposed of the bodies. She gets up off the bed and goes into the bathroom to place the wet towel on the sink and dry her hands. When she returns, she stops a few feet away and looks down at me.

"That shouldn't have worked, you know," she says. Her tone has shifted from the one of concern she had while beside me to one of stern censure.

"What?" I ask. I have clearly not caught up to her in this conversation, and I reach for my phone to take a look at what all I have missed in the world. I look at the time. I must have been out for a couple of hours at least.

"The gravity device he had," Grendia says. "Your shot should have set it off. Disintegrator energy is anti-matter based, and that grenade is gravity-matter activated. It should have—"

"I know," I cut off Grendia's lecture before it can gain any more steam. I should not have used my weapon in the presence of that device, and I knew it then, too. But what choice did I have?

"Are you suicidal?" Grendia asks, and I can tell that this is not a casual conversation continuation.

"No," I say, opening my phone.

"Then *what* exactly *the hell* was that?" Grendia yells at me.

I put down my phone before I can see any of the messages that are waiting for me. I don't feel like I have the time for this, but Grendia clearly believes that I do. And since I currently owe her my life, again, I decide that I am not up for fighting her.

"I don't know," is all I can muster. Because the truth is, I really don't. "Ever since Leo walked in on Gorge and me the other night, I have had absolutely no idea what I am doing. Life was simple, it was easy. Buy stuff, sell stuff. Talk to humans. Talk to aliens. Nobody knows about me or what or *who* I am. I liked it. It was great. But now…now everything is trash. People are trying to kill me. I have a maybe-could-be girlfriend whose brother knows I'm an alien. My best friend just shows up out of nowhere and tries to kidnap me and take me back to see my evil mother. Yeah, I don't even get an evil stepmother. Nope. I get to actually share blood with the evil one. I am now also apparently the star of some kind of close-up special-effects magic cosplay drama action movie playing out an intergalactic beef at the dumbest named fandom con I've ever heard of!"

I am out of breath after this rant. Grendia just stands there, looking at me. I think her eyes are tearing up. Did I say something to upset her? Great. Now I have to deal with this.

"Am I really your best friend?" Grendia says, her voice uncharacteristically quiet and calm.

"I was obviously talking about Niolan," I say.

Grendia responds by throwing the towel she is holding into my face. She balled it up inhumanly tight as well, so it hits like a softball. I reel back and clutch my sore nose, letting out a cry of pain as this acute strike adds to the list of injuries.

"Okay," I say, moving my hand away from my face to check for blood. There is none, for the first time today. "I deserved that."

"You deserved worse!" Grendia says, but she has a smile on her face, and she winks slightly as she moves across the room to the dresser.

This is the first time that I notice that we are not in my hotel room, but most of my stuff appears to be here. Grendia obviously also managed to get us a new room during the time I was out. She's absolutely amazing, and I can't believe I have gone so long without her in my life. Grendia was the only thing I liked about my life in the palace, but she would not have come with me back then, and I think she knows that, too. She was still too dedicated to the cause. I think she still is, in her own way, but I no longer have any reservations about having her with me. I hope she is here to stay.

"What are you getting?" I ask. I am risking movement now, and thankfully I find that I can move fairly well. The majority of my severe injury is centered on my head and blaster wound. Other than a few scrapes and lingering bruises, I might be able to walk mostly normal.

"A change of clothes for you," she says. "We have something else to take care of before your date tonight."

"And what's that?" I ask. I get to my feet and am relieved that I don't immediately fall back onto the bed. Grendia must have hit me with some pretty good stuff. I will need more of it.

"We have to ditch the hunters' ship and finish cleaning up their presence here on the planet," Grendia says as she sets a change of clothes out for me and turns to walk out of the room.

"Ah, right," I say. "Where is their ship?"

"Oh, it's nearby," Grendia says as she exits to let me get changed.

"The idiots parked it on the roof."

19

"Ya know, this doesn't even get to me at this point," I say.

We are standing on the roof of the convention center, staring at Bossy's ship. It's just sitting here, out in the open. Nothing to see, nope, not here. And it's not like this is the tallest building around, either. There are plenty of buildings and hotels towering over the convention center that have been able to look down upon this blatantly out-in-the-open starship all day long. And nothing. Well, we did see a helicopter fly by shortly after we came up here, but it was a news chopper that obviously was more interested in traffic than in the alien craft on top of the nerd convention.

"Has no one said anything?" I ask Grendia.

"I monitored a few calls to the local authorities, but the radio chatter wrote them all off as being some kind of promotional or marketing stunt for the convention," Grendia says.

"We could invade tomorrow, and they wouldn't believe it," I say, shaking my head. Humanity really has a problem with being able to differentiate reality from fiction, and I'm beginning to get concerned. Is it our fault? Do they just see too many weird things they can't process because of us, so their still-developing brains just write it off? And then they continue along with their day, I guess. Wow.

"Security?" I ask.

"Looks minimal," Grendia says as she plugs her tablet into the ship's door panel.

"We will need to move it somewhere we can stash it for a couple of days until we can get back to it, after the con," I say.

Grendia nods in agreement. "Niolan and I parked our ship a few miles away, in the warehouse district. Surprisingly easy, actually. We thought we would have to walk for miles or find a transport of some kind. Instead…"

She pauses and cranes her neck to the east, looking in the distance for a moment before she points in a general direction. "…I can see where we parked from here!"

"Think there's enough room to park this one, too?" I ask.

In response, the door to the ship hisses and slides open. Grendia unplugs her tablet and motions for me to follow her up the short ramp into the ship.

"Yeah, there should be," she says. "When was the last time you were in one of these anyway?"

I slowly walk up the ramp and look around. It's been almost two decades since I was on one of these, not since I sold the last parts of the ship that brought me here. The familiar smells of duraplas resin and fibosteel coupled with the almost imperceptible hum of the transcore engine make me feel like I have been missing something I never knew was gone.

"A really long time," I say.

We walk through the ship and give it as good of an inspection as we can in the short amount of time we have. Weapons drawn, we look for any stragglers that might have been left to guard the ship and might have decided to hide when we came along. No life signs on board, so we head up to the cockpit.

"A long enough time that you have forgotten how to fly?" Grendia asks, indicating the pilot's seat.

I smile and move to take it before she can. "Not at all, Gren. Not. At. All."

There are thousands of makes and models of space-going vessels across the known galaxies. Most of them that accommodate lifeforms compatible with Prentians and humans are laid out in a somewhat standard fashion. Occasionally one might come across a ship build by a species that thinks *nothing* like anybody else, and anyone not specifically familiar with how to operate it is about as helpless as a baby that's been thrown out with bath water. That should make sense, I think.

I begin toggling switches and pressing buttons, and within moments the ship is going through its start-up sequence. Screens come to life, indicating what I can already tell just by listening: this is one very special ship. Not stock by any means. As terrible as this group of hunters might have been on the personal level, it is clear that at least someone on that crew loved this ship.

Grendia and I exchange a smile as the last indicator lights flicker to green. We both secure our crash webbing, Grendia sitting in the navigator station beside the pilot seat. I engage the cloaking field and place my hands on the controls.

"You ready for this?" I ask.

"Go ahead, Jarokin," Grendia says. "Have some *fuuuuu—*"

Grendia's sentence is cut off as I punch the repulsor throttle to maximum while simultaneously opening up the main thrusters to full. Gravity pins us both to our seats as the ship blasts off the convention center roof, reaching an altitude of a few thousand feet in just a few seconds. I continue to climb and increase speed as I execute several barrel rolls and banking turns.

Grendia stoically endures my enthusiastic maneuvers and finally lets out a breath when I level off at fifty thousand feet and take a look around. We both look out the viewports to see the Earth several miles below us.

"And I'm spoiled for airplane travel for a while, I think," I say, looking out at the blue and green planet below us. The Rocky Mountains are in the far distance, which puts us somewhere above Kansas City, I believe. I didn't really pay attention to which way I was heading while I was having my fun, and I maybe flew a little farther than I intended to.

"It is a beautiful planet," Grendia says. "Is that why you chose it?"

"Partially," I say. "But humans really are a good people overall. They remind me of us, at their best and at their worst. But I think they have some things figured out that we don't, too. It's hard to explain until you really interact with them, get to know them. They dream, Grendia, unlike any other species. They dream like we used to. And I envy them for that. I think I really chose them as much as I chose their planet."

Grendia takes in my words and nods. There is really nothing for her to respond to, so we both look back out the viewports for a few more minutes before I bank north and begin a slow, lazy circle back toward Lexington. Grendia continues to look out the viewport for a few more seconds before turning back to look at me.

"They've changed you," she says, "these humans. You're not the same. I think that is good."

Now it is my turn to not know how to respond. Have I really changed that much since I first arrived on Earth? Prentians live on average a couple of centuries longer than humans, so I've pretty much spent the first part of my young adult life here. To put it into human terms, the past two decades on Earth have been like my early twenties. I guess it's possible that I've changed. I shouldn't be surprised by this realization, but it took Grendia saying it for me to really notice. I am not the same Prince Jarokin who arrived on this planet in 2003, according to the Earth calendar. I hope how I have changed is, as Grendia says, for the better.

"We're coming up on Lexington," I say.

Grendia highlights the abandoned warehouse where her ship is parked, and I begin an approach to land. There is a wide double door on the side of the warehouse, more than large enough for a ship of this size, and Grendia presses a button on her tablet as we approach. The doors slide back wide enough for me to ease the ship past them and close quickly after we are in.

The royal guard ship is on the extreme north end of the warehouse, and I decide to park the hunters' ship on the opposite end, keeping the cloaking field on in order to add a little extra layer of protection from any unwanted window gazers. A starship might be written off as a marketing gimmick at the convention center, but a few miles away there might be a few more serious questions should it be spotted.

We exit the ship, and I take the command codes with me in case we need the ship again. I meet Grendia over on the other side of the warehouse where she is seated at a salvaged conference table and flipping through status screens on her tablet.

"How is Niolan?" I ask.

"Stable," Grendia says. "I still have not decided what we should do when he wakes up."

"Well, we can't kill him," I say.

Grendia looks up at me, a genuine look of pleading disappointment on her face. I think she is joking, but I still cannot tell with her yet. She's probably joking. Maybe. I don't know. No?

"Well, we have to do *something*," with him, she responds. "He knows you're here, obviously, and he's loyal to your mother. *And* he was sent by your father."

"I know," I say, holding up a hand to stop Grendia's next additional fact. "But it still feels wrong to just kill him when he's injured, especially after you saved his life."

"We could strand him somewhere," Grendia offers.

I frown. The idea is not the worst, but I still would feel bad about it. As much as I may not like Niolan, he is a very loyal and mostly decent soldier in service to my family's royal house. Exiling him somewhere does not seem like a just reward for his decades of service.

My phone beeps, and I casually glance at the notification.

HOLY CRAP!

I jump to my feet and head for the door without saying a word. Grendia follows me quickly.

"What is it?" she asks.

"I'm going to be late for my date!"

20

Leo has been slowly shaking his head at me for the last several minutes. Grendia and I got back from stashing the hunters' ship only to find Leo waiting for us outside our new room. How he knew the location of our new room, I didn't ask. He brought donuts, so I decided to let him "help" me get ready for the date.

"Are you planning to take her dumpster diving?" Leo says, rifling through one of my bags.

"Hey, that's not nice," I say. "It's not like I packed for this trip with the assumption, or even the hope, that I might get to go out on an actual date while I was here."

"That is obvious," Leo says, giving up looking through my spare clothes and sitting down in a chair.

"He was never that sharp a dresser anyway!" Grendia yells in from the other room.

"You're not helping!" I yell back, and I hear a cackle of delight that her comment elicited such a response.

"Where were you guys all day, anyway?" Leo asks.

"Yeah, I'm sorry," I say. "I really owe you one, Leo."

"No you don't," Leo says casually. "My commission is more than enough compensation for covering for you, both in your booth and with the other vendors. Oh, and my sister, too. You know, she actually started thinking that you'd become nervous about your date and decided to just abandon your responsibilities as a vendor and dump them on her kid brother while you went and got drunk somewhere to buck up the courage to follow through with it."

"She did not!" I protest.

Leo shrugs. "Not that you were actually there to know any different."

Leo is just upset that he wasn't included in all the day's action. I suppose from the parts of my exploits that were public, it might have looked like I had an exciting day. Having a second fight video go viral in as many days has helped to sell the lifestyle, I guess.

Next on Lifestyles of the Galactically Hunted!

"Okay," I say, standing up straight and patting myself down one more time. "How do I look?"

Leo resumes shaking his head from side to side, this time accompanied by a long, slow whistle of disapproval. The reaction is enough to cause Grendia to make an appearance at the door.

"Is this Earth fashion?" Grendia asks.

"No," Leo says before I can respond to her. "No, it is not."

I look at myself in the mirror. It's appalling, and I know it. I'm trying everything I can to dress up a scuffed pair of jeans, and I have selected the only shirt I have with a collar, which is a printed pattern New Hope polo shirt with the Millennium Falcon flying out of my chest. It's literally the nicest that I brought with me.

I sigh and shake my head, turning back to Leo and Grendia.

"Well, this is what it is. Lyra either likes me and will look past it, or she doesn't. And I end up back here in a few minutes ordering pizza with you guys."

Leo frowns at my declaration. "Uhh, no."

"What do you mean *no*?" I ask.

"I mean I am not going to waste my Saturday night just sitting here waiting to see if your date with my sister gets past the door reveal. I have *better* things to do, Jack." Leo's words sting, but they are fair. It's not all about me. The past couple of days sure have got me feeling like it, though, and maybe that's a good enough reason for me to focus on someone else for a few hours.

"And what about you?" I ask, my eyes now landing on Grendia.

"Oh, I'm going with Leo," Grendia says. "He's offered to show me what a roleplaying game actually is, and after that introduce me to pizza and video games. All standard young people activities here on Earth, he assures me."

When did they have time to plan all of this?

I blink a couple of times to allow myself to take all this in. Grendia is finding her way here quite easily, and she could do worse than Leo as a guide for her intro to human behavior.

"You be careful, then," I say. They both look at one another, clearly unsure which of them I was talking to.

I grab my personal items off the dresser, my hand pausing at my disintegrators. I don't think I will need them while out on a date, but I thought the same thing up until last night in the hotel lobby, too. Leo and Grendia both see me pause.

"Do you really think you will run into trouble while on a date?" Leo asks.

"Trouble seems to know where Jarokin is," Grendia says. "Have you not been paying attention?"

"Still," I say, pulling my sport coat over my shoulders, "I am *just* going on a date."

It is Grendia's turn to shake her head slowly, and Leo joins in the gesture out of solidarity. I grab one of the disintegrators and hook it to the adaptive holster belt at my waist. The belt forms a concealment holster around the disintegrator, camouflaging it into my jeans and shirt. It's not a true concealment, but casual viewers hardly ever see through the device's functional cloak.

"I'll take one, just to make you both happy," I say. "I will leave the other one with you."

I hand the second disintegrator to Grendia, who takes it and disappears the weapon under her own jacket. She seems pleased with the arrangement. I turn to Leo, who seems strangely relieved that I decided to take a weapon on a date with his sister.

"Are you okay, Leo?" I ask.

Leo nods. "Yeah. I just…" He takes a moment, looking away. "Just make sure Lyra is safe, okay?"

I smile the most convincing smile I can muster. "Of course, I will, Leo. Lyra will be safe the entire time she is with me."

Leo looks unconvinced until Grendia joins in with an affirmative gesture of confidence. The whimsical skepticism returns to his face, and I am reminded that Leo has had to grow up a lot over the past two days. We're all still figuring out how to make the new arrangements work out, as they develop for us.

"She better be," he says, but I can tell that he has decided to trust us. Well, if not me, then certainly Grendia. Who knew she would be so useful in handling Leo?

"Okay, then," I say. "Now that we're all ready for our evenings, can we go? I don't want to be overly late."

I look at my watch. Well, too late, kinda. But I know dinner is going to be worth Lyra's extra wait.

21

"Oh."

That is it. That is the best response I can muster as Lyra opens the door. To put it another way, Lyra looks so beautiful standing in that doorway that I lose my ability to speak more than single-syllable utterances. Her dark hair is straightened where it is usually tied up and back, and it lightly brushes her shoulders. She is wearing some kind of top that is off one shoulder, a retro vintage look if I remember correctly, and her dark hair against her lighter skin only serves to highlight her curved neckline.

I have never necessarily thought of Lyra as a conservative or modest dresser, just that I have never really seen her dress up much. Maybe once or twice before now, well before I gave any romantic thoughts about her much attention. But now, that's all behind me. These are definitely romantic thoughts going through my head.

"Are you just going to gaze at me all night?" Lyra asks, a hint of teasing in her voice.

I shake my stupor enough to step to the side and let her past me into the hallway. She is wearing wedge heels instead of her usual sneakers and that gives her a little more height than usual. I really like the overall look, especially since she manages to make casual jeans look way more dressed up than I do. Completing everything is her makeup. She didn't go heavy with it or anything like that, but it's more than I've ever seen her wear. A very sultry evening look. I guess I never really have seen Lyra at her best. Until now, perhaps?

"I see you made some effort, too," she says, pausing to

reach out and lift my sport coat just enough to get a glimpse of the entire design on my shirt. She raises an eyebrow and tilts her head before turning to walk down the hallway.

"You coming, Jack?" she says, not turning around as she heads to the elevator.

"Yeah!" I say, much too enthusiastically for my taste. I swear I hear her giggle to herself at my complete lameness.

She's a stunner. There's nothing else to say there.

We are in the elevator before I am able to fully speak again.

"I think you're going to like where I got us a reservation," I say.

"Oh, a *reservation*," Lyra responds. "How fancy. You must want to make a good impression."

I can't tell if she's just messing with me or being serious. She and Leo kind of kid around the same way, but Lyra always throws those eyelashes and bright brown eyes into the mix, and I get all fuzzled about what's being said.

She must see that I am at a loss for what to say next, and she moves close to me. She leans into me a bit. Her touch is electric. I feel every sinew and nerve in my body light up as Lyra lightly bumps me with her hip.

"I know you picked the right place, Jack," she says. "I'm only teasing you a bit because I can, and it's really fun. But that's why I'm here. The hard part is already over, okay? You don't have to be nervous for the rest of the night."

I turn to face her. She is still standing close, looking up at me. Even with her wedges helping her out, I am still over half a foot taller than she is, and seeing her look up at me reassuringly is a memory that I will carry forever.

"I can't promise that," I say. "I've thought about this moment for a really long time, you know."

It is now Lyra's turn to look embarrassed. She blushes

slightly but does not turn away. I take a small step forward and move my hand to her side. Despite all of the right signs, I am hesitant to touch her. What if I am misreading her? Humans are so tough to figure out. Does she want me to kiss her? I have no idea what I'm doing here. Can Prentian's have panic attacks? We don't have a word for it, so maybe not? Wait. But I'm on Earth. Can I have a panic attack on Earth?

Lyra solves the problem for the both of us by grabbing my hand and placing it on her waist, simultaneously going up on her tip-toes, her other arms grabbing my jacket and pulling me down toward her.

Our lips touch, and all I feel is fire. Fire and ice. Fire and ice and the most beautiful sense of touch my lips have ever experienced across all the stars. I hesitate only a moment before returning the kiss, leaning into Lyra and pulling her toward me.

I am so glad we are alone in this elevator. I've never been more glad for anything in my life, and I narrowly avoided being squashed into jelly today!

We hold the kiss for a few seconds longer. She smells like cinnamon and some other earthy fragrance that I can't place. It doesn't matter. It makes me want to kiss her more.

I do not get my wish, as the elevator dings that we have arrived at our floor, and she pulls away. She smiles as her tongue lightly touches her lips before turning toward the opening doors and walking out of the elevator, leaving me standing alone for a moment before I regain my wits and quickly follow her toward the street.

We spend the rest of the way to the restaurant walking. Once out on the street, Lyra grabs my hand and refuses to let go. The sun has just set, and the last vestiges of its glow have not yet given way to night. This is my favorite time of day. All of the troubles of the daytime fade away, and the promise of the night, with its endless opportunities and unrelenting drive toward dawn and the new day, starts to take over and fill the imagination with all the possibilities of what might be.

I know, that's a lot to put on a sunset, but it's how they make me feel. I have always felt that the nighttime is the time that anything happens. Walking and talking with Lyra, I have never felt that way more.

"Here it is," I say, as we come up to a small restaurant a couple of blocks from the hotel.

Lyra's eyes widen when she reads the sign. "You got us a table *here*?"

I nod. "The owner owes me a favor that he couldn't refuse. He's a collector of rare things, and I happen to know how to get most of them."

It's all true. The owner of this place is an alien who has expensive tastes in rare antiquities, and not just from this planet, either. He can be a real pain to work with, but the pay is always *very* good, and very worth it if you ask me, since I'm usually the one doing all the work. But that said, he still owed me for the last few things I was able to get for him. Nothing too dangerous, but enough that he understands that he still owes me. Sometimes life as a shadow vendor is good.

"You really don't have to take me to a place like this just to impress me, Jack," Lyra says. I think she is concerned about this being one of the most expensive places to eat in all of Lexington, but I shake my head and politely hold the door for her.

"That's not the intention, Lyra," I say. "Impressing you would be a bonus, but I know you're the kind of lady who just wants to know that I pay attention. And I think inside you'll see that I have been."

"Have been what?" Lyra asks, walking through the door.

"Paying attention," I say.

At least, I hope I have been. Lyra may say that she doesn't like very fancy things, and for the most part is genuine about that, but over the years she had said things that make me think that just once, if only for one night, she would like to know what it is like to eat her favorite meal like her mother used to make when they were kids. Now, not a lot of people know this, but her mother was a classically trained Italian chef and level-two sommelier. Family dinners during Lyra's childhood were, I am told by Leo, legendary. He only remembers them a bit, but for Lyra they were home for her.

I really hope that I got it right tonight. It probably didn't seem like I had the time to pull this together, but I was able to get most of the details set up before Grendia and I left the booth in Leo's hands earlier in the day. A four-course meal with all the right feels of home. *Some* of the items were not technically on the menu, but I was able to spend a little influence to see that it was all right.

I give them my name at the front, and right away we are led to our table, the best one in the house. The owner, Loman, comes out to greet us shortly after, and I introduce him to Lyra.

"So you are the lovely Lyra that I heard so much about earlier today on the phone," Loman says, bowing his head slightly. The attention causes Lyra to blush.

"I suppose I am," she says, her eyes flickering from Loman to me and catching me staring at her, which of course causes her to blush just a little more.

I know she is not one for attention. She never seeks it. I have never considered her particularly shy, but neither does Lyra try to be the center of attention. That is not my goal tonight, but I do want her to feel as special as she is.

"I hope you enjoy your meal tonight, Miss Lyra," Loman says. "You can do much worse than Jack."

With a little wink, Loman stalks off to attend to something else, and we are momentarily alone. Lyra looks at me, her eyes wide with wonder and not a little bit of trepidation.

"What exactly do you have planned for tonight?" she asks me.

"Just a dinner that I have heard you talk about over the years," I say. "I think you might like it."

And like it she does. The meal is great, as I expected it to be. All four courses. We talk about some things, this and that kind of chatter, as we enjoy the food. I didn't see it before, but I think Lyra started out as nervous as I was and just did a better job of playing it cool than I did.

More than once I catch myself zoning out, thinking about our kiss on the elevator. When I do, I feel a slight pressure on my shin as Lyra touches me with her foot to get me to come back to the conversation. Each time, she gives me a wry smile followed by a nod. I think she is thinking about the kiss, too.

When dessert arrives, Lyra changes the topic of conversation to something that I am not expecting.

"So, about today," she says, leaving the topic hanging in the air.

"What about today?" I ask.

"After we talked," Lyra continues, "you had a really busy day, I am told."

"Yeah…" I try to trail off and leave it at that, but Lyra's expression makes it clear that she wants me to keep talking. "Well, I'm sure you noticed that Leo took over for me at my booth."

"I did," she says. I am back to not being able to tell how she is feeling. I sense that I may be in danger.

"I'm sorry about that," I say. "It was an emergency, and he said that he could handle it. And then one thing just led to another today. It was problem after problem, and nothing turned out right after we talked, and I didn't even think I was going to make it here, and…"

I feel a hand touch mine and look down to see that Lyra has reached across the table to take my hand. The sensation brings back the tingles from earlier, and I feel myself instantly calm down. I was rambling, ranting really. I have no idea why I did that.

"Jack," Lyra says, her voice steady, "it's okay. Leo is a big boy, as much as he doesn't act like it. I knew he could handle it. When I saw that other video, though, I just thought that maybe it was something more serious that had taken you away, and I was relieved to see that it was just another one of those new special effects shows you're apparently doing now. I don't really understand that just yet, but—"

"I have to tell you something," I interrupt her. I have no idea why I just said that. She's being so understanding, and I feel like if she knows any more of the truth that it could cause the whole night, our whole thing that we have now, to erupt into a giant inferno that will make me wish I hadn't lived through the day. But I can't help it.

"Okay," she says, still keeping her hand on mine. "Whatever it is, Jack. Whatever is going on with you, I want to know. You're my friend, and more, now, I hope. I've always wanted to be there for you."

I don't have time to process the realization that I actually haven't been alone this whole time. Nope. Can't dig into that right now at all.

"Well, you see, it's actually about those videos," I start out. I have *absolutely* no idea why I am saying what I am about to say, but I feel an uncontrollable urge inside me to get the truth out. Lyra deserves to know the truth, whatever else comes after.

"Those videos, they are all about something else, something

I haven't told you about yet," I say. My speech is jilted as I try to get the words out, and I see Lyra's eyes narrow slightly as I speak.

"You see, it's really all about…"

"Gia," Lyra says suddenly.

"Yeah…wait, no, that's not what I was going to say," I say.

"No, Jack!" Lyra interrupts my rambling again. "I mean, Gia!"

Lyra pushes her chair back, stands up, and points to the front of the restaurant.

"It's Gia!"

I fly up out of my seat and turn around to see a disheveled and bruised-looking Grendia wading through the tables on her way to us. She collapses to her knees right in front of us and gasps for air.

"It's Leo!" she says, her voice shaky and weak. She has been fighting, and after that running. "He took Leo!"

22

"What are you talking about?" Lyra asks.

I help Grendia to her feet and start walking toward the back of the restaurant. I wave for Lyra to follow us, which she does, her she drags her steps and gives me a wicked side eye.

"Are you going to answer me?" Lyra asks, her tone more forceful. I am trying to get us to a place where this conversation will not attract more attention than it already has. The situation must be very serious for Grendia to have to interrupt us like that.

People are mumbling amongst themselves as I help Grendia through the doors to the kitchen. Lyra follows, despite her continued protests that she be told what is going on. Loman is back there and walks up to offer assistance.

"We need your office, Loman," I say. "It's important."

"Of…of course, Jack," Loman says, getting past his fluster remarkably well. "Anything you need."

Once inside Loman's office, I set Grendia down in a chair and look her over a bit. She's mostly okay, but she took some punches to the face, and probably the ribs, too, if her slightly cracking breathing is any indication.

"*Okay*," Lyra says finally. "*What is THIS about?!*"

Grendia speaks before I can. "He took Leo. We were walking around the convention center, and the next thing I knew we were surrounded and isolated. I tried to fight them, but there were too many."

"Oh! Is this about your stupid cosplay shows?" Lyra interrupts, her voice teetering between annoyance and rage. "You interrupted my date for another viral video? Jack…*SERIOUSLY?!*"

"No," I say and turn to face Lyra. She stops her building tirade when she sees the look on my face.

"This is not about the cosplay shows, Lyra, because there are no cosplay shows," I say.

Lyra looks confused, and who could blame her? She has no idea what's about to hit her.

"Jarokin…" Grendia wheezes, but I cut her off.

"Lyra, Leo was taken because he knows something. Something about me that I have kept hidden for a long time."

Lyra's eyes widen and the color drains from her face as she takes a swift step back. I don't blame her. And I don't know what else I would expect. She has just been told her brother was taken by people who beat up a strange woman she just recently met all while out on a date with a guy who just told her that he's been keeping a secret from her for all the years she has known him.

I am not off to a good start here.

"Jack," Lyra says with a shaky voice, "am I in danger? Please just tell me what's going on."

"Lyra," I say, "I think it would be better to show you."

She furrows her brow as I look to Grendia. She nods, and I take off my sport coat.

"This," I say, pointing to my maccomp, "is a device that alters appearances, in this case my appearance, making me appear to be human."

"Appear…to be…human?" Lyra repeats.

I nod. "Yes. This next part will be difficult to process, but please remember that no matter what happens next, I am still Jack. The same Jack you have known for years, played games with, shared meals with, joked and laughed with, and teased mercilessly because I am slow to catch on to things from time to time."

"Enough with the preamble," Lyra says, regaining her usual composure. "Just hit me with whatever this"—she gestures to me and Grendia with both of her hands—"all is and end the suspense."

"Okay, here goes," I say, and I reach down to my belt, pressing the button to deactivate my maccomp.

The hard light mirage that is my disguise fades away in a flicker, and Lyra sees me for the first time. Sees Jarokin for the first time. Well, kind of. There was earlier, in that video where I should have died, but I'm not counting that since all she saw of that was a phone recording.

Lyra is still for a moment.

And another.

Okay, she's been still for a really long time now. I don't even think she has blinked yet! Okay, is she still breathing?

"Lyra?" I ask, but she holds up her hand to stop me from saying anything else.

She is quiet for almost a minute more, looking at my exposed features. From my gray-tinted skin to the ridge of small spikes that follows my hairline, and onto my hands, which are not terribly different from a human's, just with a great range of movement in the joints, which can be unsettling to watch, I am sure.

Lyra reaches out to touch my hand but stops. She cranes her neck around my shoulder to look at Grendia. Grendia nods, and I offer my open palm to Lyra.

"I'm not going to hurt you, Lyra." My voice is deeper now that the maccomp is not affecting it to sound like a human's voice. Lyra does not show any reaction to my altered voice and tentatively reaches out to me, lightly touching my hand with hers. The electricity is still there, at least for me, and Lyra takes her hand back after a few moments.

"You're...you really aren't human," Lyra says.

I shake my head. "No, but I am me."

"And who, *exactly*, is that?" Lyra asks. "Jack? *Prince Jarokin?* And who is Gia to you? Why is this happening now? And where is Leo? Is he…is he?"

I stop her right there, re-engaging my maccomp to return to my adopted human form and offering to help Lyra to a chair. To my surprise, the usually fiercely independent woman accepts my help. She is still processing.

Wow. Leo really did take this in a lot quicker than other people would.

"Grendia," I say, "who you know as Gia, is from my planet. She originally came here to take me back home, but I didn't see it that way."

"That's one way to put it," Grendia says. "Jarokin has a mind of his own, and I've come to see things his way. My partner, on the other hand, has not."

"Niolan," I say, my voice tightening. "He took Leo."

"Yes," Grendia says. "He had help, too. I was not alerted that he was even conscious let alone healed enough to function nor leave the ship on his own."

"More royal guards?" I ask.

"I don't think so," Grendia says. "They didn't fight like us."

"Whoa! Just…whoa!" Lyra interjects. "You two are moving *way* too fast for the human in the room. You're going to have to slow down and tell me exactly what is going on here. Leo is in trouble, so I'm in for whatever. We'll figure out the rest later, okay?"

She looks up at me, pleading with her eyes for me to accept her terms. We can drop the disaster that had been our amazing first date night for now. She's right.

Grendia takes a moment to explain the situation to Lyra, who listens intently and asks questions when Grendia skips over something important. I interject where appropriate to make sure

Lyra gets the context she needs, and soon Lyra is as caught up as she can be after a five-minute rundown of the situation.

"So, let's set aside the shadow market, the intergalactic community, and the whole prince thing," Lyra says, mentally sifting through the information that we threw at her. "Right now, there's a crazy guy named Niolan who has my brother, who knows about all this, and who is currently bait to lure Jack into being taken home to his psychotic mother and distant father. Did I miss anything?"

"I don't think so," I say. "It's a pretty good summary of the situation as it stands."

"Okay then," Lyra says, standing and throwing back her shoulders. I didn't give her enough credit, I think. She's taking this just as well as Leo. Maybe even better. But she also has a mission. Leo has to be saved.

"So where do we start?"

23

"Why are we back at the con hotel?" Lyra asks.

"Because," I say, hitting the elevator button, "*this* is where the shadow market lives after hours."

"So this shadow market you've been talking about," Lyra says. "How many of you are there?"

The elevator door opens, and I let Lyra and Grendia step into the car first. I follow them and lean over to the button panel, pressing the floor just under the top floor. It's the same floor where my room usually is, where it was before it was compromised, and I know exactly the room we will be visiting.

"There's only about a dozen of us, maybe less, here at this con," I say. The elevator doors close, and we begin the climb up to the twenty-second floor. "But the whole network just in the US is a little over a hundred last I checked. Worldwide it's much more than that. Easier to hide out in some places than others, but the shadow markets tend to exist in both the literal and figurative shadows of real marketplaces. It makes commerce easier all around. Not having to find extra spaces to do business is just more convenient than hiding away. Although, there is this one market in Spain that—"

"You're rambling again, Jack," Lyra says, putting a hand on my arm.

I am rambling. I'm nervous. Not about what we're on our way to do, no, just about the situation. I had a gut feeling that Grendia was right about Niolan being a problem for us. I just thought we had more time. Obviously my mother's crony is way more resourceful than I ever gave him credit for. He *did* find me on

Earth, I suppose, but I was assuming that Grendia did most of that work. I could have been wrong, I guess.

"Being nervous about all of this is *my* job," Lyra says. "And I heard once that there's a rule that only one person in a relationship can freak out at any given time. And since it's my brother who has been kidnapped, the one freaking out is me."

Lyra moves closer to me and rests her other hand on my cheek. "So you have to keep it together for now, okay?"

"Should I leave?" Grendia says from the other side of the car, and Lyra and I separate a bit. I forgot she was here. I think she knows that.

"Uhh, no," I say, and then looking at Lyra quickly add, "and yes, that's a deal."

A…relationship? We're in a relationship now? When did that happen? Was that Lyra's way of telling me that despite the disastrous end to our date and the impending possibly terrible outcome of the rest of the night that she was already thinking of us as…Us?

I shake my head. Now I'm just rambling internally, and Lyra's quizzically raised eyebrow tells me that she knows it, too. I turn toward the door, steadying myself for what I have to do next. Angry Jack is about to make an appearance, and I hope that Lyra is not bothered by what she's about to see.

"Who are we going to see?" Lyra asks.

"A shadow vendor who deals in goods that are out of my wheelhouse," I say. "Many of us tend to shy away from the truly volatile stuff. Weapons, explosives, the really harder drugs that some species have to use in order to get high, or to be properly medicated. But who we're going to see is one such vendor. He deals in all of it."

"Sounds like a really great guy," Lyra says.

"Eh, I don't think you'll think so in a minute," I say. "You know him. And he won't be happy to see us, I can tell you that."

We exit the elevator, and I make a left turn into the hallway. Lyra is following close behind me, with Grendia watching our backs. The floor is quiet, and I know the reason why. Most of the shadow vendors have rooms here, and there are likely many after-hours shadow market deals taking place in the rooms that we pass by. But none of those are of interest to me tonight.

"What room number?" Grendia asks.

"It's 2276," I respond, not looking back. We are only a few rooms away, and I slow my pace as I approach. The door to room 2276 is closed, and I stand in front of it for a few seconds, silent, listening for any noise or voices from inside the room. Hearing none, I nod to Grendia and Lyra. Grendia swaps places with Lyra and has a power blade ready under her jacket. She nods back to me, and we are set.

I sigh quietly and raise my hand, knocking in a pre-described pattern to signal that I am a shadow market customer. Several seconds pass before we hear anything from the inside.

"One moment!" we hear a muffled voice call out from inside the room.

I cross my arms and sigh again. This guy *never* has anything together.

"Ah! I'm coming, don't you worry!" The call-out is accompanied by a crash that sounds like something expensive being shattered followed by muffled curses in several languages, only a few of which I recognize.

Next I hear some heavy footsteps approach the door along with some heavy breathing, and finally the bolt unlocks and the door swings open.

"Hey there, Hal!" I say with a big smile on my face.

"AHHHHHHHHH!!!!!" The high-pitched scream is accompanied by the door being slammed in my face and the sounds of many more locks than should be on a standard hotel door engaging one by one.

"Hal? Really?" Lyra asks, her eyes still wide with shock.

"Yep," I say, stepping to the side. "Grendia, if you would?"

Grendia's face breaks into an unrestrained smile of joy as she steps in front of the door and delivers the swiftest heel kick I've ever seen. The door splinters instantly. Wood, metal, and broken locking mechanisms fly everywhere, and Grendia is already moving inside the room before the last of the debris lands. Soon, another high-pitched squeal accompanies Grendia dragging Hal out of the bathroom. He attempts to struggle and squirm his way free, but Grendia is not having any of it. She smartly cuffs him at the base of his neck with the pommel of her blade, which causes him to go mostly limp and cry out in pain.

We could be attracting some attention at this point, but I'm past the point of caring at the moment. Hal has few actual friends that are likely to come to his aid in a situation like this, and even fewer once they see it's me putting him in that situation.

"Jack," Hal manages to say as Grendia tosses him onto the bed. He attempts to get up, but Grendia's power blade against his neck deters any thoughts he might have once had for that option. I grab a table chair and set it next to the bed, sitting down in it and crossing my arms.

Okay, so I have to admit, this feels pretty cool. If not for the mortal danger that Leo is in because of me gumming up all the works, I would feel pretty much like a badass anti-hero slash criminal do-gooder vigilante type from those old noir and gangster films. But I digress.

"I know they came to see you, Hal," I say.

Hal freezes, likely trying to think of a lie that might possibly get him out of this situation. There isn't one.

"Who is that?" Hal asks, his voice only a decibel below his annoying shrieks of terror.

"The locals he hired," I say. "I know that they came to see you for gear and supplies. He didn't have time to recruit from out of town. And you're the only dealer in town shady enough to deal with anyone you meet."

"I don't know who…" he begins, but Grendia presses her blade against his throat, making the point that it is useless for him to try to lie. I am not entirely sure she's not going to kill him anyway. I don't necessarily want him dead, but I doubt I could stop Grendia if she really wanted to silence Hal for good.

"Okay…Okay!" he spits out, barely able to move or breathe out of fear that Grendia's blade will leave its mark.

I nod to Grendia, and she slightly lets up on the pressure, just enough for him to start to catch his breath.

"I just need to know what you know, Hal," I say. "Where were they going? Who were they going to go see next? I know you know. You always get people to tell you things they don't realize."

Hal frowns. I think he's been under the impression that he's been getting away with his biologically enhanced grifting skills all these years. And for the most part he has, but Prentians happen to be able to see a spectrum of light that Hal's species, the Doogranons, emit from their eyes when they are attempting to lightly hypnotize people. It's not a true hypnosis, but that's about as well I can explain it for now.

"Cannery," he finally says, biting his tongue back the moment he speaks. He really fears them, and I don't blame him, especially if he met Niolan.

"The one downtown by the old track?" I ask.

He nods. "Yeah. They said something about a bunker there. But…but that's it. I swear. That's all they said. Nothing else, Jack, I swear!"

I don't even care what he sold them. Probably some standard-fare guns, power packs, and some light explosives.

Niolan is going to make sure Leo is as hard to get to as possible. He knows Grendia, that's for sure. But I wonder if he really remembers me.

"I told you dealing in this crap would lead to trouble someday, Hal," I say. I nod to Grendia, and she releases him. To his credit, Hal stays in place and just glares at me.

"Well, we can't *all* be princes, I guess, *Jack*," he bites back at me. "Some of us need to do what we have to do to survive."

Lyra, who has until now been quietly observing the interrogation, moves beside and raises a hand at Hal as if to strike him.

"*My* brother is in danger, you asshole!" Lyra says, and she proceeds to reach forward and slap Hal across the face. The alien lets out another brief scream, and I gently help Lyra step away from the situation.

"If they come back," I say, knowing that they probably won't, "you tell 'em I'm coming for them, and they better pray they're ready."

Hal lets out a chuckle of disdain. "Screw you, Jack. I hope they haul your ass back to Prentia."

I have to wave an enraged Grendia off teaching Hal a lesson, giving her a stern look.

"He's not worth the effort, Gren," I say. "Besides, he has to change his sheets now, too."

Grendia snickers as she notices the wet bed sheets, and the three of us exit the room to return to the elevator.

24

"We have to go check out the warehouse," I say, closing the door to the hotel room. We are regrouping here to plan the next move. The cannery is obviously a trap. It is likely that whoever Niolan recruited purposely dropped that information with Hal in case we found him for questioning. Can't take anything for granted at this point. I can't afford to underestimate Niolan, even if that means over-guessing his cunning and capabilities.

"I agree," Grendia says. "Niolan revoked my remote access to our ship. He would have also moved it, but it's possible he overlooked the hunters' ship that is cloaked on the other side of the warehouse. He was, I am hoping, still unconscious when we parked it there earlier."

"So now there are spaceships, too?" Lyra asks. She has not said much since we left Hal's room. I think she is feeling lost, and I don't blame her one bit. I need to give her a focus, I think, something she can be working on to try to get her mind off the danger her brother is in. It probably won't work, but I still have to try.

"How do you think we all got here?" I ask, a goofy smile on my face.

A little too goofy, as Lyra's response is to throw a pad of paper at me. And she's really accurate, too. It hit me in the forehead.

Ah! Another head hit! Seriously?

But I don't blame her. I would have thrown something at me, too.

"Well, yeah, obviously," Lyra says after looking at me to

make sure the paper pad did not actually hurt me. "Of course there would be spaceships. I just hadn't put much thought into those coming into the picture yet. Do you think this Niolan guy will try to take Leo off Earth?"

Grendia and I exchange glances. It is unlikely at this point, since I am his actual target, but anything is possible in this kind of game.

"I don't think so," Grendia says when I am too slow to respond. "Jarokin is Niolan's target, and he would not want to leave without his prize in custody."

Lyra looks simultaneously relieved and disturbed by Grendia's answer, and I sit down in the chair next to Lyra and put my hand on hers. Her hand is cold and shaking slightly. We need to be careful with her. Not that she is delicate. I don't believe that for a second. But her world, her whole universe, is rapidly expanding with almost every new word out of our mouths, and while she is doing a great job keeping everything on track so far, that might not last. I don't know at all what her losing it might look like, or upon whom she may lose it, and I really want to make sure that she has a target other than me or Grendia if that happens. Perhaps that sounds selfish at this point, and it probably is.

"We're going to do everything we can to make sure that space travel is not in the future, for either you or Leo," I say.

Lyra looks somewhat comforted by this. She had no reason, I suppose, to believe me, so it is appreciated.

"The warehouse isn't far," I say. "Grendia and I can be there and back in about half an hour. At least at that point we can assess what assets we have and whether or not we'll have a ready answer for Niolan's space-faring capabilities should it come to that."

Lyra is looking into my eyes as I tell her the next step of the plan. When I stop talking for a moment, she interrupts my next statement.

"Don't leave me here!" she pleads.

I tighten my grip on her hand reassuringly.

"I was going to leave that up to you," I say. "There *is* something you can do to help us while Grendia and I are checking out the warehouse, but I will only ask you to do it if you are comfortable with being left here in the room while we do that."

Lyra considers my offer for a few seconds before responding. "What is it that you need *me* to do, Jack? I'm pretty useless in all of this."

I press my lips together and shake my head slightly. "That couldn't be further from the truth, Lyra. Grendia and I may be able to handle the physical dangers of the situation, but we need help trying to figure out what those dangers actually are. That's where you come in."

Both Lyra and Grendia look skeptical at this. It is not my intention to be cryptic. Lyra has skills we don't, and I have an idea how to use them.

"Leo lives out his whole life on social media," I say.

"Yes," Lyra says.

"So, maybe that public life is about to come to some use," I say, pointing to Lyra's phone that is in her other hand. She has been gripping it as if it will suddenly buzz or ring with vital information, and she is about to be more right than she knows.

"We need you to scour his social media. All the platforms he's on. His posts from this afternoon leading up until he and Grendia were attacked especially," I say.

"What am I looking for?" Lyra asks.

"It's possible that he was being followed for a while before he was taken," I say. "If he was, there might be something in the pictures and videos he took of himself and whatever he was up to that we can use to figure out something, *anything*, about who we're dealing with. It may be a long shot, but it may also give us an edge somehow."

Lyra nods along as I am speaking and opens her phone. Before I am finished with my ask, she is already scrolling through Leo's social media looking for anything that can help us.

"We'll be back in half an hour," I tell her, standing.

Grendia is at the door, waiting for me. I take one more look at Lyra, who has jumped in with all of her attention looking for a way to help her brother. I do not know first-hand the kind of pain she is going through, but she is all the more amazing in this moment for everything that she is. She has a strength that I always knew was there, but until now I had never seen it on display. I do not know if that strength is unique to Lyra or part of her general humanity, but it doesn't matter now. Lyra is strong, and I have a lot to do if I am going to be her match.

I turn to walk out with Grendia, who opens the door and precedes me out into the hallway. It's a subtle gesture, the order of egress, but Grendia has a lot of decades of royal guard and bodyguard training to shake if she's going to stop acting like one. Maybe she never will. Who knows?

"I got it!"

I have almost closed the door when I hear the shout from inside the room. I swiftly throw the door back open and rush into the room. Lyra is already out of her seat and running toward the door. We almost collide, but I am able to avert a disaster by opening my arms and engulfing Lyra in a massive hug. The smell of her hair assaults my nostrils, and I am briefly taken back to the now-dissipated magic that was our date. It gives me a hope that the magic could still be there, after all of this is over, and I gently release her from the embrace.

"Sorry," I say, sheepishly looking away. When I look back, Lyra is staring up at me, the weight of our evening lifted off her face, just looking at me like she did after our kiss in the elevator. But the look is gone as quickly as my feeling, and we are both back in the present.

"It's okay, Jack," Lyra says hurriedly. "More time for that later, but for now, I think I know how we can find Leo for sure."

"How?" Grendia asks. She is still standing near the door and has closed it to allow us to speak more freely.

Lyra holds up her phone. I see a video of Leo walking through what looks like a pizza place.

"And this," Leo says in the video, "is the best pizza place in Lexington." He pans around the dining room, and I recognize the familiar setting of Big Pete's Pie Palace. "Tonight is Gia's first time here, and we're gonna introduce her the correct way with…"

Lyra pauses the video, and I look up from the phone with a quizzical look on my face.

"This guy, right here," Lyra says, pointing to a guy in the background. "He shows up again in later posts when Leo and Gia…Grendia…are walking back, and again right before their attack. He's definitely following them."

"That's great work," I say, "but how…"

"I'm not finished yet," Lyra says, and she flips to another social media app. This one has a profile pulled up for a guy who looks exactly like the man who was following Leo in his posts.

I see it all there. This guy is as addicted to social media as someone Leo's age, and he's definitely one of Niolan's crew. There are secret words, numbers, and symbols scattered in all of his posts that aliens use to identify each other on human social networking sites. And his friends aren't hard to track from there.

"You found all this in…less than a minute?" I ask Lyra.

She smiles. "Wow, Jack, you really are older than you look, aren't you?"

Okay. Ouch.

"I like to think it's because I'm not human," I say, "so that was mean."

Lyra shrugs. "If that's what you need to tell yourself."

Grendia laughs at my expense, and I shoot her a look that causes her to choke a bit. That causes Lyra to burst out in laughter as well.

After their shared moment, I get us back on track. "So what should we do now?"

"Well," Lyra says, "I'm kinda hoping that you have some cool advanced alien tech that we could use to hack into the social app and track where these goons are posting from."

That's…a really *good* idea. I look to Grendia.

"My tablet alone can't do it," she says, "but the communications computer on the hunters' ship can probably do that. Human information security is hundreds of years behind galactic standard."

"Let's go!" Lyra says.

"You're not staying here?" I ask.

"Hell no!" Lyra says. "I already did my part of the splitting up plan, so now I get to go along on the fun part, too!"

"Can't argue with that," I say.

25

We schedule a car and have it drop us off a couple of blocks from the warehouse. Fortunately there are enough places still open even around here that the request does not attract any questions from the driver. They drop us off in front of Keexy's Vapehouse, which appears to be doing a lot of business tonight. One of the locals standing outside tries to get Grendia's attention, and she flashes him a look that lets him know he most definitely does *not* want to have her attention.

"Is it a long walk from here?" Lyra asks.

"Not far," I say. "A couple of blocks, but we're heading into an area with a lot of abandoned buildings that tend to attract a certain crowd. So just be on alert."

"What do I have to be nervous about?" Lyra says, a playful tone in her voice. "I'm more worried about what Grendia would do to anybody who tries to harm us."

I look to Grendia, who is scanning our surroundings like a watchful hawk protecting her clutch of younglings.

"Lyra is correct," Grendia says. "It would be a most dangerous choice for any humans to attempt to hinder us."

"Just don't kill anybody unless you have to," I say, immediately regretting the last part. What Grendia thinks is a "have to" situation might be very different from what I think it is. Another mental note added onto things to keep in mind while adapting Grendia to Earth. Humans are mostly harmless. It's the few making a bad name for the many. Mostly.

Thankfully, the journey to the abandoned warehouse that was Grendia's former safehouse and my new spaceship's garage is without any kind of event that might force me to prevent Grendia from being overzealous in the discharge of her perceived duties. We approach the warehouse from the west, which allows us to enter another abandoned building across the street from it and observe it for a few minutes before we enter.

"Do you see anything?" I ask.

"Nothing," Grendia says.

I am looking into the windows with a set of maxspec binoculars designed to pick up on energy signatures left by alien tech. There's nothing in the building according to the binoculars, which is expected. The hunters' ship's cloaking field should be blocking detection by such devices anyway.

"Is it safe?" Lyra asks.

"It could be," I say. "As far as we can tell, Niolan picked up and shipped out, literally. We just have to get in there to confirm that the other ship is still there."

I pull the ship's control dongle out of my jacket pocket.

"This thing has a limited range," I explain to Lyra. "I won't know if the ship it controls is there until I'm about twenty meters away, which means we have to enter the building to find out."

"No sense dawdling, then," Grendia says. "Let's go."

Lyra nods and takes my hand as we get up to leave.

"Thank you for doing all of this for Leo, Jack," she says.

"Of course," I say. "It's my fault he's in trouble. I'd do this even if it weren't."

"I know," Lyra says, squeezing my hand and then letting go as we walk out of the building to cross the street. "That's why I know you will win."

*   *   *

"It's quiet," Grendia says, and Lyra catches my gaze by shaking her head and giving me a warning glare not to repeat the oft-used response to Grendia's setup. I frown in disappointment and turn toward the middle of the warehouse.

I draw a disintegrator with one hand while the other holds the ship's control dongle. Grendia is right, though. Where a few hours ago this place felt like a regular abandoned warehouse, with ruffling old plastic sheets hanging from windows and mysterious water drips coming from unseen pipes, now it just felt…paused. Waiting for something to happen.

Grendia moves around us in a semi-circle, scanning for threats. After a minute, when none come at us, we both relax a little. I walk over to where the hunters' ship should be parked and activate the control dongle.

Lyra lets out a sharp gasp as the image of the warehouse in front of us shimmers and disappears, revealing a real-life spaceship in front of her. She freezes in place, staring at it. I did say earlier that this is a nice spaceship, but I don't think Lyra's reaction would have been any different if the ship was a piece of junk. Grendia smiles, watching Lyra gaze in wonder at something that to us is the equivalent of a Chevy Equinox.

"So that…" Lyra says, "…goes to space?"

"Yep, it does," I say.

"Can I see inside it?" Lyra asks, her eyes bright with anticipation.

I press a button on the dongle, and the boarding ramp extends, opening up the entrance to the ship. I motion for Lyra to proceed, and she practically runs up the ramp. Inside, she looks at everything, touring all of the rooms and asking what devices she can't recognize might do. Grendia rolls her head at the giddy display of joy as Lyra gleefully forgets the gravity of our night just for a moment and has fun being a human on a spaceship.

"Has Leo seen any of this?" Lyra asks. Mentioning his name does not shake her out of her state of wonderment, and I take that as a small win for now.

"No," I say. "This is one thing Leo hasn't seen yet."

"Ha!" Lyra says, dancing around the ship's main room. "I finally get to know about something *before* he does! Go me!"

Lyra explores a bit more before coming to a locked door. She turns to me,, disappointed, when the door refuses to open.

"Why won't this one open?" she asks.

"I don't know," I say. "I only got this ship a couple of hours ago and haven't been able to give it more than a once over to make sure it's in good shape. It belonged to a group of bounty hunters who thought they could handle me…"

I hear a pronounced grunt from the other side of the room, and Lyra and I both look over to see a conspicuous Grendia doing a terrible impression of someone trying to clear their throat. The message is clear.

"…I mean, thought they could handle Grendia and me." I revise my statement. Grendia adds a curt "mmm-hmm," and Lyra smirks at the royal guard.

Again, I am *not* comfortable with how quickly *my* friends are becoming *Grendia's* friends! It's like they all just want to make my life more difficult. What are friends for, eh?

I turn back to the locked door and enter the new override code that should give me access to the entire ship. Being the new owner should have its perks, after all. I am rewarded with the control panel in front of me switching from red lighting to blue lighting, accompanied by a soft hiss as the door slides into the wall, revealing…

"Whoa," I say.

"Umm…is that…?" Lyra asks.

Unable to handle the anticipation, Grendia walks up behind

us. "So what is it that…oh!"

Beyond the door is a room that looks like one of those grand room-sized closets that the rich and famous install into their yachts and castles and such. But this deluxe closet is *not* full of space shoes. No. The hunters who left behind this ship used it for something else.

"Have you ever seen anything like this?" I ask Grendia.

"Only in the royal vaults," she says.

Sitting here, waiting for the three of us to find it, is the most beautiful armory of intergalactic weapons, gadgets, gear, and accessories that I have ever seen. And I'm saying this as the prince of a very powerful star system!

"So…" Lyra says, "…we're gonna go get Leo back now, right?"

26

We decide to leave the ship where it is. If Niolan knew about it, he would have taken it or destroyed it before we got to it, which means it's just as safe staying where it is as it would be anywhere else. We gear up with new weapons and gadgets, courtesy of the bounty hunters' fully stocked cache, and depart for the cannery location. Lyra synthesized a change of clothes in the ship's fabricator, a device she was *very* loath to leave despite the circumstances. Dressed in much more appropriate-for-the-mission attire, Lyra is adamant that she also gets to have some upgrades from the "fun room." Grendia and I spent a few minutes giving her a crash course in some of the gear she takes, along with her chosen weapon out of the options we judged wouldn't harm a human to use. At least, we hope not.

The cannery is a couple of miles from the warehouse, and we repeat our Uber drop, this time being deposited outside an all-night coffee shop that is hosting an open mic night. I doubt Grendia and I would have stuck out much if we hadn't had active maccomps. From there, we walk past several business buildings that are closed and end up having to pass the cannery on a side street in order to avoid being completely exposed as we approach it.

Grendia was successful in tracking the phones of Niolan's hired goon squad, and they all are pinging from the top floor of the cannery. The floors below them are supposed to be abandoned, but there's no telling what might be there now. It is likely that Niolan has left anything from lookouts and sensors to traps and even explosives on the lower levels in anticipation that one of us is stupid enough to try going that way. Unfortunately for us, this isn't a TV show where we can count on the bad guys to be dumb.

"So going up is likely the hard way," Lyra says.

"Yeah," Grendia says. "But there aren't many better paths. The building next to the cannery is supposed to be empty as well, and we *could* use it to access a higher floor or the roof."

"We don't even really know that Leo is in there, though," I say, "let alone where or how they might be keeping him."

Leo's phone is obviously disabled and has been since right after the attack. That's pretty much Kidnapping 101, so I am not surprised.

"I have a pretty stupid idea," I say.

Grendia rolls her eyes. "Of course you do."

"I'll go in and talk to them," I say in a flat tone. I am dead serious. I have no idea if they will attempt to harm Lyra or Grendia, but I am pretty sure that at the very least they won't kill me.

"You'll WHAT?!" Lyra screams, and she immediately claps a hand over her mouth while using the other hand to hit me in the back of the head.

"You'll *what*?!" she immediately repeats, this time at a lower volume. It is unlikely that anybody heard her. There's nobody nearby, but her alarm is amusing. Not that I can let on that I find it cute and funny.

"It's not the *worst* plan you've ever had," Grendia says, wrinkling her chin and nodding in consideration. "I could sneak into the building while you distract them, and Lyra can position in the fourth floor of…*that* building over there to provide us with some overwatch." Grendia points out the building she means as Lyra and I train our gaze on the building indicated.

"You're serious," Lyra says. "You're going to just hand yourself over to them?"

"Of course not," I say. "Even if Niolan is in there, he will find me just showing up to talk to be highly suspicious. He might even send out some to the goons to try to find Grendia and you."

"That *would* even the odds for you in there if he did do that," Grendia says.

"Yes, but it's not a guarantee," I say.

"So you get in there, talk to Niolan or whoever is in charge, find Leo, and then what? Blast your way out? You *are* aware you're trying to save my brother and not get him killed faster, right?" Lyra says.

She has good points. I can't argue them individually.

"You're right," I say, "but we have to do something. We're currently in a kind of standoff of wits with Niolan, and we have to make the first move. It sucks, but it has to be done. The best we can do is try to do something he might not expect."

"You were going to do something like this the whole time, weren't you?" Lyra asks.

I nod. "Yeah."

"It's not Jarokin's worst plan *ever*," Grendia adds. "And he's right. Someone has to do something to break this situation. Niolan has the power here. He knows that we're coming for Leo, so we have to try to be unpredictable."

"You know this kind of thing only works in movies, right?" Lyra says.

"Well, I hope for tonight, it's not *just* a movie kind of thing," I say.

I raise my hand and knock on the door. I knock one more time for good measure and resolve myself to waiting for whoever is inside and watching on the other end of the camera I am looking up at to realize who I am and what's going on. I imagine right now that the conversation is going something like, "Uhhh…'ey boss? Dat guy you said to look out for is here, and he just knocked on the door."

I give a two-fingered salute to the camera just for good measure and throw in a wink that should give Niolan the proper message. It isn't a minute more before I hear heavy footsteps and rustling from the other side of the door. After a few more seconds, the door opens abruptly, and I am staring down the barrels of no less than six guns. I slowly raise my hands.

"Hey there," I say. "Did someone here order a dozen cookies?"

To my amazement, two of them look at one another with an excited look that says, "Hey! We get cookies, too?" So yeah, not the brightest, these local aliens, but you get what you pay for, I guess.

"Come 'ere, you." One of the others grabs out for my jacket and pulls me through the door.

I am quickly patted down, my weapons removed from my person. But they do have the common sense to leave me my maccomp. My hands are bound with some zip ties, and I am taken upstairs. Three flights of them, actually, to the top floor. After being deposited, roughly, into a broken-down recliner that saw its good ol' days in the '90s, two of the goons are left to keep an eye on me while the rest go into another room.

"So," I say to the goons left to guard me, "you got any odds on the horses for next week?"

"I'm putting everything on Fluffy Buffer Jackalope Jaffy," one says, and the other immediately claps him on the back of the head.

"I told you to keep that quiet, you idiot! It's a secret that he's got the best track times in practice!"

"I'm sorry, Ston," the first guard says. "He asked, and I was just trying ta be polite, is all."

"Polite? He's our prisoner, you idiot! We don't gotta be polite to the likes 'o 'im!"

"I appreciate it, though," I chime in, and both of them look at me with a dumbfounded blankness that can only come from having been already deep into several beers before I showed up.

This might not have been the problem Grendia and I thought it was. Sure wish I knew if Leo was here, though.

"There, ya see? He appreciates us, he do," says the first guard.

Ston shakes his head at this and sits down in a chair across from me. The two continue bickering about Mouthy spilling the beans about their sure-fire horse race for a few more minutes while I patiently wait for them to notice that I have broken out of the zip ties.

"You idiots!" a call comes from the newly opened door across the room.

I look past the goons to see Niolan standing there, fuming. He does *not* look any better than the last time I saw him, and that was when he was unconscious and bleeding out from a gaping chest wound. So maybe he's had a rougher night than I have.

"I wouldn't be *too* hard on them," I say, and the goons turn to look at me for the first in several minutes. I am sitting in the chair with my hands resting lazily on the armrests, clearly unbound.

"Hey, I thought you were tied up!" Ston says.

"I was," I say.

"Get out!" Niolan says, walking toward us.

The goons stand up, and I get up with them, readying to give Niolan the room.

"*Not you,*" Niolan says, raising a blaster in line with my chest. I shrug and sit back down. I guess he's not in the mood for humor tonight.

Ston and Mouthy shuffle out of the room as Niolan repositions one of the chairs to sit right across from me. He takes his time and sits down, blaster still trained on me, and stares at me as if to bore holes in my head with his eyes for several, frankly unnerving, silent seconds before speaking.

"I knew taking the boy from Grendia would bring you to me," he says. "She's always had a soft spot for you, so bringing her with me was the perfect way to get you to drop your guard."

"Oh, you mean Leo?" I ask. "How is he anyway? I'm sure you must be getting along great."

Niolan's left eye twitches when I mention Leo by name. I take that as a sign that the boy is probably still alive and has likely been…well…Leo about this whole thing.

Good. He's got under Niolan's skin. I just hope that hasn't cost him a finger or something.

Niolan ignores my attempt to goad him and cocks his head to the side.

"I'll admit, Jarokin, I didn't see this coming," Niolan says. "Never thought you'd turn yourself in just for a human. I assume you want me to trade him for you, is that right? Playing at being a sacrificial hero for your little humans, eh?"

"Would you be open to a trade?" I ask. Might as well keep him talking if that's what he wants to do. Go ahead big man, gloat all you want. My plan ended at the door, and I'm just winging it from here. As it is, I lost a bet to Grendia when you walked through that door. I thought that there was no way you'd be here. The goof's on me, then, I suppose.

"Why would I trade away a prisoner that you would throw your freedom away just to protect?" Niolan asks. "Instead, I'll just keep you both, and ensure that you won't try anything stupid on our way back to Prentia. Because that's where you're going, *Prince* Jarokin. Back to mommy. She's still raging at me, you know, even after all this time. You broke her heart when you left like you did."

"Ha!" I say, unable to contain myself. "What heart would that have been? Did she find one after I left?"

Not the smartest thing to say, as Niolan leaps from his chair and pistol whips me hard on the cheek. Must have touched a nerve with that one. Dude. Seriously? I'm your prince.

"Okay," I say, using a hand to make sure that my cheek is still there and not across the room in a pile of rat turds waiting to be devoured by the maggots. "Ouch."

Niolan pistol whips my other cheek and leaves me reeling in my chair as he turns and sits back down. If I had to guess based on the look of poisonous glee beaming from his face, he's wanted to do that for a long time, probably since before I left even. This guy is *so* full of himself. He probably thinks my mother will reward him with a dukedom or a like title, with power and money to go along with it. She might. I mean, it has happened before. But then again, she could just as easily have him killed because he knows too much. Time will tell. Part of me wants to be there to see which it is. I might be, I suppose, if this goes badly. But I'd prefer a different path.

"Royal blood mean anything to you?" I ask, massaging my latest series of brutal head woundings.

"It obviously doesn't to *you*," Niolan bites back. "Here, you're not Prince Jarokin. Here, on Earth, you're just a fugitive of the crown, and I'm just the one tasked with bringing you in."

"Yeah, but alive?" I ask.

Niolan shrugs.

I really hope Grendia is making the best of this time. We're in a terrible spot in this room for Lyra to be able to do anything to help me from where she is. It's likely she has seen some of the beating that I've taken, but I'm not sure she has a good angle on Niolan with the *sniper piercer* that Grendia gave her.

"So my mother sent you to find me," I say.

"Yes," Niolan answers.

"Why after all this time?" I ask. "Can you at least tell me that? You *do* at least know that, right?"

Niolan's eye twitches again. Good. Another nerve tweaked. He's not the rock he projects.

"It took us three years," Niolan says. "Three years of being out in this dreadful intergalactic cesspool of filth and biomass waste."

There's the Prentian elitist coming out. Many of my people, especially those in the upper echelons of society and power, view most of the rest of the universe as wretched filth that deserves to be wiped out. It's not like Prentia has the capability to do that, but we are one of the most advanced races, technologically and evolutionarily speaking. Few other societies match us for capability, but that's also a weakness that I saw almost from the start of my education. Prentia is vulnerable, and growing more so with every subsequent generation.

But that may never be my problem to deal with, at least as long as Niolan can be stopped here and I somehow send a strong enough message to my mother that I'm done with her and her planet. However, *that* problem isn't the one in front of me. Niolan is. And I'm running out of time, I think.

"Three years, eh? That's all it took? I'm disappointed in myself. Or impressed by you. I'm not sure which," I say.

This gets a snicker out of Niolan.

"You weren't easy to track down. I'll give you that. Hiding out on this total dump was the best move. I didn't see that as a move you'd make. Thought for sure we'd find you on one of those elite resort planets where royals go to hide from their people for a few generations before coming back with an iron fist."

"Glad I didn't disappoint, I guess," I say. "So what *is* the plan from here?"

"We're leaving soon," Niolan says. "Just waiting for a delivery that should be here soon."

"Going away pizza?" I ask.

"No." Niolan cuts me off. "Stop interrupting me if you want to keep your teeth. You don't need those either, according to the queen."

"What about Grendia?" I ask.

Niolan snickers. "What *about* Grendia? She can rot here for all I care. I'll tell them she betrayed me and ran off on her own. She'll be branded a traitor, killed on sight on a thousand different worlds that she could possibly flee to from this trash heap."

The door opens behind Niolan. Without looking, he calls back, "Is it here?"

"I don't know what *it* is," Grendia says from the doorway. "But these guys aren't exactly in the shape to tell you."

27

Niolan looks over his shoulder at Grendia, and that is all the opening I need. I leap from the chair and slap the blaster out of his hand. But that is all the surprise I get to enjoy. Before I hear the sound of the blaster clattering across the room, I feel the impact of Niolan's other fist sucker-punching me in the gut. I double over for a moment, the rest of my brilliantly planned out assault upon his person stalled by the unexpected counter-attack.

Niolan is on his feet before I recover, but he does not have time to hit me again. Grendia has somehow covered the distance between us and uses her momentum to kick high at Niolan's head. The larger man ducks under the kick and uses his open palms to shove Grendia back. She does not fall down and only stumbles back a few steps as Niolan's action counters her momentum.

I am able to act again, and I swing a hasty haymaker at the distracted royal guard, but I am once again met with disappointment as Niolan's fist rises to block my own. Grendia rejoins the fray, and the next several moments are full of punches, kicks, counter-attacks, and glancing blows on all sides as Niolan not only manages to hold his own against both of us but even pushes us back. Now in the center of the room and breathing heavily, the three of us pause together to assess the situation.

"I am more than your match," Niolan says. "Both of you."

"Probably," I say between heavy breaths, "but that doesn't mean we're going to go easily."

Niolan smiles a large, toothy grin. It is unnerving. It's the kind of smile that you see in the Batman comics where the Joker has done something truly heinous. If this wasn't real life, I would swear I was looking at a comic book character right now.

"I was hoping for exactly that," Niolan says through his grin.

He's a little insane. Maybe more than a little. But I have no time to ponder that thought, as Grendia makes a feint to Niolan's side, which he is quick to counter. I take advantage of the twist in his position and leap behind him, grabbing his arms and pulling them behind him. Grendia takes full advantage of this to land the first real blows of this fight onto Niolan's face. He takes the blows like a champ, though, like they barely register.

Is he on drugs?

Niolan pitches forward, and I decide to let go of his arms instead of letting him take me over with him. Releasing my grip causes him to stumble forward due to overcompensating for my weight, which is no longer holding him back, and Grendia meets his face with her fist one more time as he crashes to the ground.

"Had enough yet?" I ask, knowing it is unlikely.

Niolan only laughs in response, rolling over and jumping to his feet in one fluid motion that I don't quite follow all the way through. He's so fast. Too fast.

As if confirming my assessment, Niolan leaps back toward me, evading a kick from Grendia, and lands a fist to my face before I can react. This brawl is getting painful all around, and I'm not sure if we'll be able to subdue him without causing him grievous harm.

As if Grendia, too, can now read my mind, she responds to Niolan's new offensive by drawing her power blades, the warm hum of their activation accompanying a grunt from Niolan as he recognizes the sound of them coming to life.

"And here I thought we were having just a good old-fashioned brawl amongst old friends," he says, drawing a blade of his own and activating the power button. It sizzles to life with a blaze of plasma cascading around the magnasteel blade.

I am the only one without a weapon, and Niolan seeks to take advantage of that before Grendia can act. I dodge his first few slashes and yell out as a white-hot pain slashes through my left forearm. Niolan's blade is a double hurt. The blade itself would be bad enough, but the plasma sheathe lances into nerve endings, more than doubling the report that the pain receptors send to the brain. It's as much a weapon of demoralization as it is one that causes actual damage.

Fortunately, Grendia takes his attention from me after this, and their blades clash and whirl in a rapid cycle that I can't fully follow through the pain. Grendia is doing well for now, but she will lose the fight if I don't find a way to help her soon. She is fast, but Niolan is somehow faster, pushing her parries and counter-attacks just a split second farther every time. Eventually, she will reach her limit.

Movement by the doorway draws my attention, and I look over to see Leo standing there, his mouth agape at the action scene unfolding in front of him. I move to the side of the room, away from where Grendia and Niolan are playing out their duel.

"Jack!" Leo yells out.

Niolan spares the boy a glance and smiles. Leo will complicate the fight if Niolan can manage to put him in danger and distract either Grendia or myself in any way.

"Leo! Get out of here!" I yell out, but Leo shakes his head.

"No! I don't want to leave you alone!" he protests.

"I'm not alone, Leo. Grendia and I can handle this," I say.

I am not sure that's at all true. And I'm growing more sure by the second that it likely isn't.

"Run out and across the street! Lyra will find you!" I yell out. I have to look back to the duel as Grendia screams. Niolan has managed to disarm her of one of her blades, and there is a bleeding wound near her shoulder. Her arm is not moving well.

"Lyra's here?!" Leo bellows in surprise.

"Yes! And we don't have time for questions. Now go!" I say.

"No, wait!" Leo says.

"Now!" I bite back.

"No, I mean, not before you get these!" Leo holds up my disintegrators and tosses them across the room to me.

I catch them and nod my thanks as he runs by me to the exit.

"Be careful. Come back alive," he says before darting out of the room toward the stairs.

That's a bit of a relief. Leo being safe will definitely make things easier. Now Niolan's leverage is all but depleted.

"No!" Niolan yells, his rage at losing Leo clear. He raises his blade high, ready to strike Grendia on her weak side. I don't think she will be able to block it.

Niolan's blade flies down and is stopped dead as it impacts against my combined disintegrator shield. The force of the blow still drives me to a knee, but I smile up at Niolan through the transparent energy field, and push up against him, throwing him back temporarily. I look at Grendia, who nods at me and changes her stance to fit having her partner back in the fight. Her power blade and my shield versus Niolan's plasma blade.

"Time for round two," I say and run forward, Grendia keeping step with me to attack Niolan as I tie up his blade with my shield.

To his unfortunate credit, Niolan appears to be no more taxed fighting the both of us than he was fighting just Grendia. Every slash, stab, kick, and punch is countered on both sides, with my addition to the fight only serving to even the odds. This is a stalemate, and Niolan appears to be none too bothered by the prospect.

He's waiting for one or both of us to tire out, relying on his conditioning, and whatever combat drugs he took before the fight, to outlast us and wear us down. I take a kick to my knee and wince as it buckles under me, causing me to land hard on my side. Grendia presses an attack in exchange and manages to slash Niolan across his forehead with her power blade before being kicked in her midsection and sent flying back several feet into a chair.

"This has been a real treat, you know," Niolan says, wiping some blood from his face. "It's not often that I get a workout this…unrestrained."

What an asshole. And a liar, too. I can tell that we've done very little harm to him. Fighting him is just stupid at this point, but I wonder if Grendia knows it. She is slow to get up, and I am afraid she might be just about done for now.

"You know," I say, "you really are an asshole, Niolan."

"I know," he says, holding out his hands and smirking. "But I gotta have a little fun to make you pay for all the trouble, right?"

I hear a crash of something coming in through the window and hitting the floor behind Niolan. It rolls past him and into the center of the room, almost perfectly between the three of us. All of us focus our attention on the small, round object. It is beeping. Fast.

Comprehension hits all of us at once, and we look up at each other before trying in vain to jump away.

The grenade explodes, followed by a cacophony of light, sound, shrapnel, and a thousand different pains all making themselves known at once.

28

"Hello in there!"

The voice is far away, and my eyes are not working yet. The ringing in my ears is being replaced by the sound of blood rushing inside my head. I don't think that's an upgrade in condition. But that's not the blood that bothers me. There's also a lot on the outside. Of course, it's not red like human blood. Prentian blood has a yellow tint to it, and it kinda looks a bit more like human stomach bile. Fortunately, it doesn't smell like it.

"I *said*, hello in there!"

I push some rubble off me and try to sit up. That's a mistake. But I'm committed, and it has to be done. I groan as I fight gravity's pull on my bloody and sore body. Looking around the room, I see Grendia lying limp against the wall opposite me. I can't tell if she's breathing or not. I do not see Niolan, though, there is a huge hole in the floor where he was standing just a moment ago, so he could be anywhere now.

I groan the rest of the way to my feet and shuffle over to the window. I see a group of about half a dozen people down on the street. Two of them are restraining two others, and…

No!

Lyra and Leo are struggling against their captors, but they appear otherwise unharmed. Leo takes a slap to the face as he says something to his captor that I can't make out due to him being three floors below me and my head still singing at the top of its lungs a single note that may cause me to vomit soon.

"Well, there he is!" a hazy figure calls up to me. "And here I was beginning to think our little party favor had gone and done you in before we had a chance to talk!"

I recognize that voice. At least I think I do. The person the voice is coming from is still incredibly hazy, but it takes a couple of steps forward as I squint hard to see if I can get them to come into focus.

"Bossy," I say through gritted teeth.

"Ah, so you *do* remember me!" Bossy says, a pleased look altering her usual sour demeanor.

"You're dead," I say casually, shaking my head in disbelief. I am not doing well.

"And feelin' great, no thanks to your little bodyguard chick," Bossy says. "I guess they don't call my species 'the Roaches of Hastorr Cluster' for nothing."

Eh, close enough translation into English, I suppose. Roaches are kind of an Earth thing, but there are other insects out there that are just as tough to kill. I'm not convinced of that myself. I've never met anything as tough to kill as an Earth roach. Well, until now.

"Is that what they call you guys?" I ask. My speech comes slowly and with not a little effort.

"Jack," Bossy says, redirecting the conversation. "You owe me some things."

"Like dinner and a movie?" I ask.

"Like my damn ship, for starters!" Bossy yells back.

"Oh yeah. I *do* have that," I say.

"And your head!" she adds.

"I'll get back to you on that once I locate it," I say, and I start looking around on the floor beside me. "I know it's around here somewhere."

"You and your girlfriend have exactly one minute to come down, or I'll kill the humans!" Bossy yells up at me. Well she's in a mood tonight. Geez.

"But my girlfriend is down there!" I say and point to Lyra. *Oops.*

I am not all here right now. I should not have done that.

Bossy looks at Lyra, who scowls back at the alien bounty hunter. The other aliens chuckle and leer menacingly at Lyra, who understandably cowers slightly before looking up at me.

"Well," Bossy says, "then I guess that means you have less than a minute now! I mean it! I'll kill them!"

I know she will. And while I'm not at all ready for this, I know there's only one way to keep Lyra and Leo alive right now. I do wish I knew where Niolan had gotten off to. He'd be a useful weapon to point at Bossy right about now. Not that I think I could manage that feat in my present state.

"Okay, okay," I say as I begin to stumble away from the window. "Keep your pants on. Geez."

I walk over to where Grendia is still lying on the floor. I kneel down and clear the rubble off her. I have no idea where her weapons are, or mine I guess, too. Doesn't matter right now anyway. Is she breathing? Yes, looks like she is. That's a good sign.

"Hey," I say, nudging Grendia's shoulder. "Grendia, we gotta get up and go surrender to Bossy now."

Grendia groans in that wake-me-up-in-another-fifteen-minutes kind of way, as if she's just taking an afternoon nap, and I nudge her again.

"Grendia," I say louder, "we gotta go. Bossy is still alive, and she has Lyra and Leo. And she wants *our* ship back. Can you believe the nerve of that lady?"

Grendia slowly opens her eyes as I drivel on. She looks as tired as I feel, but I think she managed to come out a little better on the whole grenade encounter thing that I did. That said, she had taken the brunt of Niolan's attacks. So, we look to be in about the same shape.

"Niolan…" she coughs, as blood sputters from between her lips.

I shake my head. "No idea. But there's a new problem. Bossy is alive. And she's on the street."

"I heard that part," Grendia says.

I help her sit up, and we help each other get to our feet. Looking around the room, there's no time to try to recover our weapons.

"So what's the plan now?" Grendia says.

I sigh and start walking toward the door. "We go and surrender for now. They want to be taken to their ship, so that could buy us some time."

Grendia's only response is to also sigh and begin hobbling after me to the stairs.

"Well now," Bossy says as Grendia and I emerge onto the sidewalk, "that's cutting it close. You might be over the minute, but I don't know for sure. Earth time isn't something I'd set my clock to anyway."

"Jack!" Lyra calls out when she sees the shape we're in. "You're hurt!"

"I know," I say. "And thanks for noticing."

Lyra frowns but gives me a slight wink. The gesture is subtle, so I am sure the aliens all missed it. Our little exchange is enough to communicate that we're both okay. I think. I mean, I know I'm not okay. But if I can fake it for now, maybe Lyra won't worry as much as she should.

"So…" Bossy says. "Where is it?"

"Warehouse," I say. "Couple miles back toward downtown."

"Take us there."

*   *   *

"This is it?" Bossy asks.

We are standing outside the warehouse. To be honest, I really don't know much about how we got here. I think Grendia is working at a higher cognitive level than I am right now. I need some help, and soon. I don't think that's very high on Bossy's priority list, though.

"Yep," I say, taking the ship's control dongle out of my pocket.

"Hey, gimme that!" Bossy says, and she swipes the dongle from my hand.

"I was gonna," I say. "Don't gotta be rude about it."

Lyra and Leo are still with us. My attempts to get Bossy to let them go were met with further threats of violence against all of us. I think Bossy means to take us all with her. That's not good. Humans aren't supposed to be taken off Earth. Bounty hunters should know that.

"Come on," one of the aliens says as he pushes me to follow Bossy. She is walking into the warehouse and pressing the dongle button to find where her ship is.

"I'm goin', Dingus," I say. Dingus furrows his brow and scowls at me. I don't think he likes his name.

"Do we have a plan?" Lyra whispers to me as we all walk through the warehouse in search of Bossy's ship.

"No," I say, and I put my finger to my lips as if it's a secret.

No, really. I'm in trouble here. I need some drugs. Some drugs, and a lot more drugs. Probably some blood, too.

Lyra looks at me with concern, and I give her a lopsided grin in return. At least, I think it's a lopsided grin. It totally could be a full-on ear-to-ear Cheshire-Cat-style creepy face. I have no real idea.

"But that hasn't stopped us yet," I say, hoping these are words of comfort. "Just stay close to Grendia and Leo. I'll do the talking."

Lyra looks less convinced than before, and she has a terrible poker face to begin with. So I think I just made that worse. That's okay, though. Because…

"Found it!" Bossy says as the ship's cloaking device shimmers and the ship comes into view.

A few moments later, we are all on board, and Bossy is checking things out to see how the ship is. We have been sat in chairs in the main room, one guard left to watch us as the rest prepare the ship for space.

"Are they going to take us into space?" Lyra asks.

"That appears to be their purpose, yes," Grendia answers. She is watching them work, and I think she is much closer to having a plan worked out than I am. So far I've got Step Five: Victory.

"You know," Grendia says to the guard, "Jack here really could use some medical attention."

"Shut up," the guard replies. "Don't say another word."

"Or what? You'll hurt Jack some more?" Grendia says, taunting the guard. "He's pretty messed up already. Just look at him. Can barely keep his eyes open. Look at that dopey grin on his face. He's probably fading faster than a Crennilian Sunset. You want your bounty to die on you?"

The guard steps forward. He looks like he is about to hit Grendia for her refusal to be quiet.

"Yeah," I say, and the guard stops to look at me, "and there's also the bunny on your head. He's in pretty bad shape, too."

Might as well sell it while I can. I droop my head and stare at a point just over the guard's line of sight.

"I've seen this before," Grendia says. "They call it Prentian Brain Syndrome. Too much concussive force to the head, and the blood turns toxic. Some cases are even known to cause spontaneous combustion in people."

To punctuate this, I make the exploding gesture with my hands and say, "Bshhhhh!"

The guard looks suitably confused about what to do.

"So what am I supposed to do about it?" Confused asks.

"Plug him into the ship's auto-med computer, of course," Grendia says. "Duh."

"Yeah, duh," Leo adds, as if even a human would know that's what needs to be done here.

Confused looks at each of us. We all nod in expectation. He looks around for someone else to help him, but nobody else is in this part of the ship. Maybe we could have taken him at this point. But I wasn't gonna do it, and I think I knew what Grendia was up to anyway. Our time with the ship may have been brief, but we made the most of it. And besides, I *really* wanted that auto-med unit, too.

"Don't move," Confused says to the rest of them. They all hold up their hands as he grabs me by the jacket collar and drags me stumbling over to the medbay door. He presses the button, but the door doesn't open.

"Oh, hey, allow me," I say, and I press my finger against the button. The door opens.

Confused looks up at me. "Uhh, thanks."

Inside the room, he tosses me down on a chair and clamps the auto-med arm collar onto me. I give him the thumbs-up sign and lean back in the chair.

"Thanks, dude," I say, and then everything goes blank.

29

I wake up to the room bucking and shaking violently, then my stomach is sent into my ankles as the ship's inertial compensator struggles to follow whatever is happening out there. My head swims for a second as the maneuver completes and the world levels out again. But that is the extent of my altered perception. I'm back. Well, at least as back as I'm going to be for now. It looks like the auto-med unit did its job.

I unclamp the collar on my arm and stand up. The ship is in motion, obvious from that maneuver that woke me, but where and under what circumstances were the conditions that interested me most. Before I can reach the medbay door, the ship is jolted by what sounds like a blaster bolt. Are we under attack?

I open the door, and my eyes widen at the rampaging action unfolding in front of me. Leo is closest to me, hiding behind an overturned table and ducking down in between firing off blaster shots at some aliens across the room. Grendia catches my attention next as she rushes and drives a blade into the chest of one of the aliens firing at Leo. The other alien next to her repositions to try to shoot her, but Leo's next shot causes him to duck behind a chair instead.

Lyra is last to catch my attention, and she is engaged in what looks like a kitchen utensil battle with a rather small alien who is jumping all over the place like a rabbit on serious speed-enhancing drugs. She manages to swat him out of the air more than once, but the little bugger always lands on his feet and jumps right back in. I am stunned as I watch all of this unfold, unable to figure out where I should be helping first.

"Oh, hey, Jack!" Leo says between shots. "How ya feeling?"

"Better, thanks," I say as the ship banks hard to the side and sends us all stumbling to compensate for the unexpected turn. "What did I miss?"

"Too much to explain!" Grendia yells, now grappling with yet another alien.

Where do they keep coming from?

"Get to the cockpit!" Grendia yells.

I nod, happy to have a task. I run across the room toward the hallway that leads to the cockpit.

"What should I do when I get there?" I ask as I run by Grendia.

"You'll just have to figure that one out," she manages to grunt out as she breaks the alien's arm in a binding hold and kicks him in the sensitive parts.

I wave at Lyra as I run by. She waves back and tosses a lock of hair behind her ear before swinging her rolling pin at Rabbit Guy. On any other day, this whole scene would be the strangest thing I could ever think of happening. But today, it all just fits.

I burst into the cockpit to see Bossy in the pilot's seat, her hands darting out in all different kinds of directions as she attempts to pilot the ship.

"What the hell are *you* doing in here?" she snaps.

"I could ask the same thing," I say. "What's going on?"

"What's going on," Bossy says, "is that we've got a maniac in a spaceship chasing us, trying to blow us out of the sky!"

To punctuate her statement, another blaster bolt slams into the ship, and a bank of previously blue lights change to bright red. Bossy lets out a string of curses in response and flips more switches.

"Are you gonna fight me here, or will you help me get us outta this?" she asks.

"Hmm," I say, folding my arms and leaning on the gunner's seat. "I dunno about that one. It's kinda not in my interest to help you here."

"It is if the ship you're on is gonna get blown out of the sky with you on it!" Bossy yells.

"Fair point," I say, sitting down at the gunner's station and putting on the target goggles.

My viewpoint shifts from sitting in a gunnery seat to the gun camera of the ship's main turret cannon. I swivel it to face aft. There, right behind us in perfect kill position, is a Prentian Royal Guard ship.

Niolan.

"Oh, I know this guy!" I say gleefully.

"Great! Now shoot him!" Bossy says.

I unfortunately can't think of a reason not to. As much as I *do not* want to help Bossy in any way, she pales in comparison to the threat presented by Niolan. I had held out a little bit of hope that the grenade had unalived him for us, but no such luck. Not tonight.

I track Niolan's movements for a few seconds longer before opening up with the dorsal laser turret. The first few shots land, splashing against Niolan's ample energy shielding. But that's where my success stops. Niolan is also apparently an excellent pilot, and he becomes infinitely more difficult to track. Even after getting the ventral cannons into the action, I can't nail him down with their overlapping fields of fire.

"I don't see him disappearing from my scope yet," Bossy says.

"Shut up!" I say, and I re-track the cannons' attack patterns to try to get Niolan to slip up.

Another strong series of blasts against our aft confirm that he's not backing down.

"We're almost clear of the atmosphere," Bossy says.

My heart drops into my stomach. No! Once we're clear of the atmosphere, Bossy can make the jump into hyperspace. That is something we definitely do *not* want to happen. For a lot of reasons. So many reasons.

I have to think quickly. Niolan's avoidance and counter-attack pattern appears to be just ahead of my fields of fire no matter which way I go. Scanning with the gun cameras, I highlight a spot on the ship that is only weakly covered by our remaining energy shields.

That's it! Right there.

If I can modify the attack patterns of the two cannons to get Niolan to open up on that spot on the ship, the jump drives might be damaged enough to prevent a jump. My fingers fly across the controls, and I trace out the altered attack pattern with my eyes, the goggles following my gaze precisely. I engage the new pattern, and the cannons shift their firing fields. Just like I knew he would, Niolan in turn shifts his maneuvers to stay ahead of the shots.

Is there no skill this guy doesn't possess?

Niolan presses his attack, and his shots pierce the ship's shields this time, slamming into the structure. Warning klaxons sound, and I really hope that I didn't just doom us all or cause one of the others in another part of the ship to be injured. I have to push past that now and be ready. I check the ship's systems and mutter a curse to myself. The jump drives still show as operational. My gambit failed.

"We're clear!" Bossy says, and the ship lurches as the jump drives engage.

I lean back in defeat as the familiar sound of jump drives spooling up for a jump echoes throughout the ship. Seconds later, the ship lurches forward into the hyperlane—

—and slams into something *really* hard.

I am thrown out of my chair despite the seatbelt I thought I had engaged when I sat down. I look up and out the forward viewport at a bright, white-hot crater-marked surface.

Earth's moon. We're at the moon. But…

Gravity.

The jump drives *did* fail after all, just not like I wanted them to. They were still operational enough to make a jump entry, but the moon's gravity pulled us right back out. The drives must have been damaged after all.

Bossy is out cold, her face bloody where she slammed into the control panel in front of her. I am relatively unharmed, for once. Just the injuries of the day making themselves felt again. The door to the cockpit opens behind me.

"Oh my!" Lyra says. "Is that the moon?"

"Uhhh…yeah," I say, getting up from the floor of the cockpit. "That's the moon."

30

"So, we're in…" Lyra says, sitting down in a chair.

"Space. Yes," I say.

We're back in the ship's main room. Bossy and the two still-living members of her Goon Squad 2.0 are restrained in the medbay. We aren't monsters, but we also aren't going to leave them in there without tying them up. Leo and Grendia join us, looking not much worse for wear, considering all that happened while I was out. I am incredibly impressed by all of them, especially Lyra and Leo. Grendia I am not surprised about, but I thought she was injured much more severely than she let on. Maybe it was part of the act. Maybe she's just ignoring it.

"Are we safe? Are we going to die out here? I can't die in space with nobody on social knowing what happened to me!" Leo waits for the rest of us to roll our eyes. He threw that last part in to mess with us. We all laugh. The situation is dire. Maybe I shouldn't tell them that just yet.

"Well, we're not dead yet," I say. "The ship still has power, and the only systems that are non-operational are the main and jump drive engines. Grendia and I will take a look in a few minutes to see if they can be fixed."

I see Lyra and Leo both relax slightly. That's not the whole story, though.

"But that doesn't mean the danger is over," I say. "It won't take Niolan long to figure out where we are. The moon is not all that far away from Earth, cosmically speaking. He is probably on his way now. I'd give it about forty-five mins or so."

Leo lets out a low whistle. "Wow. Alien ships are fast."

"Niolan will not give up," Grendia says. "And now that we're not on Earth, any small advantage we had is gone."

"Please," Lyra says, gripping her chair to steady herself, "don't remind me that we're not on Earth anymore. Space is *very* new to me."

"Oh, come on, Ly," Leo says, using his nickname for his sister that he only breaks out when he's actually trying to be supportive of her, "it's not that bad. We're the first humans to reach the moon so quickly after leaving Earth's atmosphere! That's pretty cool, eh?"

Lyra relaxes the muscles in her shoulders slightly as Leo speaks to her. He is very good at getting her to see the bright side of just about anything. I don't know for certain that he's right about being the first humans to reach the moon so quickly, though. There was a rumor several years ago that a human had found out about aliens and managed to stow away on a craft leaving the solar system. Word is they didn't discover his body until they were over nine hundred light years away and were cleaning the ship's atmosphere scrubbers with highly concentrated aerosolized ammonium nitrate. Probably shouldn't mention all that to Lyra, though.

"So he's definitely going to come looking for us," Lyra says. "What can we do?"

"We can be ready for him," Grendia says. "It's our only option."

I stare grimly at the floor. I am still hurt fairly badly. The auto-med treatments were good, but I'm not at a hundred percent—far from it. Grendia's left arm is weak and slow. I can see that much. Leo looks okay for the most part, and Lyra appears to be fine as well. That's a win at this point. Humans are fragile compared to most species, at least where physical harm is concerned.

"He beat the crap out of both of you together, and pretty good," Leo says. "How can we fight him now?"

"First of all, ouch," I say to Leo. "Second, that fight wasn't a foregone conclusion. I was interrupted. And this time, we can be prepared."

Leo raises his eyebrows in a skeptical expression, and Lyra remains quiet on the subject.

"Jarokin is right," Grendia says. "We had a lot of fight left in us. We still do."

"Uh huh," Lyra says, jumping in on her brother's side.

"Well, what do you expect us to do, then?" I ask. "Niolan is coming, we're beat up. You guys aren't trained fighters, despite what whoever is left of Bossy's crew might think."

I gesture around to the state of the ship in general. A few bodies are still lying around. We need to exit those out of an airlock before they start to stink up the place.

"Her name is Proponi," Grendia says.

"Wait, really?" I ask. "Huh. The one that got credit for those bounties in the Goreemi Nebula a few years back?"

Grendia nods. "The same."

"Oh, wow," I say. "I would have expected more out of such a reputation."

"Uhh, guys?" Leo says.

"Well, she's not an issue anymore," I say. "Hopefully she's the last of the bounty hunters to have successfully tracked me. I'll need to be more careful in the future. Between you and Niolan, Bossy, and the Uglies, I've had enough of people tracking me down."

"People," Leo says.

"We can't know for sure that nobody else has," Grendia says. "We may need to…"

"Hey, aliens!" Leo shouts.

We all turn toward Leo. He is standing by the open door to the cockpit. There is a beeping sound coming from inside the cockpit, and Leo is staring into the open doorway.

I get up and walk over to see what he's staring at. When I see what is now beyond the viewport, I freeze.

"Uhh, Grendia?" I ask.

"Well, what is it?" Grendia asks impatiently.

After I do not respond, she gets up and walked over to join Leo and me. When she sees what we are looking at, she freezes in place, too. Lyra sighs and gets up to join us in our celestial viewport sightseeing moment.

"What's got you all in a…oh!" Lyra says as she catches sight of it, too.

A starship is cresting over the horizon of the moon. It's bigger than our ship. Much bigger. It is coming around from the dark side of the moon where it must have been hiding, waiting.

"You think it's friendly?" Leo asks hopefully.

"I do not," Grendia says.

I am the first to move, and I walk forward into the cockpit, pressing the beeping button at the comm station.

"Receiving you," I say.

"This is the free trader frigate *Heptanomist*," a voice on the other end of the channel answers. "I am Captain Liktanto Jorr, and I claim this ship and all of its passengers as my rightful bounty and salvage."

31

"Well, well, well!" Captain Jorr says, walking into the docking bay on the *Heptanomist* where Bossy's ship is now parked.

They used a tractor beam to capture the ship and reel it in, and despite both Lyra and Leo protesting that we should do something, Grendia and I knew that attempting to fight back at this stage was pointless. Jorr's crew is probably nearly a hundred strong, and without knowing exactly who and what we're dealing with, blindly fighting against him would have been suicide.

"What a strange lot we have reeled in this time," the captain continues. "And just who is the captain of your little ship?"

I open my mouth to speak, but Bossy beats me to it.

"*I* am," she says quickly. "These two are what is left of my crew. And *these*"—she indicates the rest of us—"are our bounty prisoners."

Captain Jorr's eyes widen at Bossy's assertion. "Oh, so *they* are the prisoners here, and you three are the bounty hunters?"

"That's right," Bossy says.

"When my crew entered your ship, they said that these four here were sitting in chairs with drinks in their hands, and you lot"—he indicates Bossy and her two goons—"we're tied up in the medical bay."

Captain Jorr holds up a hand to forestall Bossy's answer before she can speak a syllable. He turns and walks down the line until he is standing in front of the four of us. He leans in, carefully appraising each of us for a long moment before leaning back.

"Is this true?" he asks us. "Are *you* the prisoners here?"

"Yep," I say. "She's right. We *are* her prisoners. She

kidnapped us off Earth all by herself. Well, along with her goon squad. You can see what's left of them."

Captain Jorr is silent for a moment, taking in my answer. It is obvious that he is weighing what to do here. I have just admitted to being in the possession of a bounty hunter, but this guy might not care about that. He's a "free trader" according to his crew. But even in space that phrase is pretty much just a nicer way of saying "pirate." Though what he's doing in Earth's orbit, I can only guess. It's possible he did have legit business with a shadow market contact, but I've never heard of him or his ship.

Jorr lets out a long and hearty belly laugh, and Bossy and her goons take this as a good gesture. Why, I have no idea.

"So they…" he says between laughs, pointing at Bossy, "…and then they…" he manages to get out again before laughing some more, pointing at us, "…and then we…"

I am slightly amused by all of this myself. The situation to an outsider like Jorr has got to look all kinds of bizarre. Despite this, none of the four of us laugh. I think Lyra and Leo are a bit too scared, but Grendia knows the trouble we're in, just as I do. Captain Jorr appears to be a good-natured fellow, but I am not convinced. He did claim us as his rightful salvage, after all. That's not a good sign.

Almost a minute passes while Captain Jorr has his laugh over the whole thing. Bossy and her man start to question whether he's laughing at them or with them, but Jorr's crew is definitely in on the joke, chuckling amongst themselves and pointing at us all, mostly at Bossy and her goons. Captain Jorr composes himself and stands up straight, his demeanor returning to that of a space captain.

"No, but really this has got to get cleaned up now," he says, his tone serious. "These two are humans, and that's not allowed. They won't even sell well at market. But the law says if we find them off Earth and not on a craft manufactured by humans, they have to die."

He makes a *tssk* sound with his teeth. "Nothing personal, ya see. But them's the rules, and some rules not even *I* am too keen on breaking."

"Yeah, that's not going to be happening," I say. I take a step forward, and no less than twenty blasters are raised to point at my chest.

Captain Jorr does not react to my movement and stays still, feet firmly planted where they were. We stare at one another for several seconds, neither one of us blinking. We're probably all going to die here, but I'm going down with at least some kind of final, epic showdown that I hope will be worthy of all the fandom stuff I've consumed since coming to Earth. Not that I've got an ego about it. No way. I just don't want to let Lyra and Leo be killed without at least making them go through me, first.

The tension in the room is broken by a member of Jorr's crew running in and whispering a message to Jorr that I can't make out. The captain snaps his head to the messenger, who nods and steps back, a look on his face that says "I have no idea what to do next."

Jorr turns to his crew, most of whom still have their weapons trained on me. "Put them in cells. I'll have to deal with them later, and…"

He stops and walks up to me, returning my challenging gaze with one equally immovable in its surety of state.

"You," he says, "there's something about you."

And with that, Jorr turns on his heel and walks out of the bay. His crew gives us instructions to follow them, and we march out of the bay through a different door. They take us deeper into the ship and into a conveyor. From there we are taken down several levels and told to disembark into a grimly lit hallway that is lined with doors. They pair us off, with Leo and me getting put into one cell and Lyra and Grendia put into another. I assume they do the same with Bossy, who insists on protesting that she is *not* a prisoner. Though I have no particular love for her, I still wince when I hear them use a stun blast on her to get her into her cell.

Stun blasts aren't really like they are in Earth sci-fi. While most shows and books make the stun setting on a weapon appear to be more humanitarian and kind, it really isn't in reality. To get that kind of result, you have to massively overload the central nervous system. The closest thing humans have to that kind of weapon is a taser, but those are incredibly inefficient and ineffective compared to stun settings on blasters and other energy weapons. I'd rather get shot by a bolt for all the pain that stun blasts cause.

"So, they're going to kill us?" Leo says. He looks frightened, and I don't blame him.

"Not if I can help it," I say.

Leo sighs and leans against the cell wall. "I'm sorry, Jack, but that's not exactly a comforting thing at this point. You haven't really come through on any of your promises to keep any of us out of harm. Actually, it seems like you're just really good at getting us into more trouble than we're already in."

"Leo!" Lyra chides her brother from the cell across from ours.

We can't see each other, but there are open slats in the doors that allow for sound to travel in and out.

"What, Lyra? Tell me where the lie is!" Leo bites back.

I can't blame him, really. Ever since he walked into my room the first night and saw me with my maccomp turned off, things have just got progressively worse for him. Granted, *he* hasn't been shot, beaten, burned, and exploded, but I get where he's coming from. And he's kinda right. I haven't really done anything much to protect either Lyra or him. I was relying on things to continue as normal, even when events shouted at me that they were not going to. It's my fault we're in this mess, and that means it's up to me to figure a way out for all of us.

"It's okay," I say. "Leo is right. I've bungled nearly everything, especially tonight."

"Jarokin," Grendia says.

"No," I say. "If Leo wants to blame me, I can't fault him for it. I got us into this, and I have to get us out."

"That's not how this works now, Jack," Lyra says.

"Not how what works?" I ask.

"You're not alone in this, not anymore. The truth is that you haven't been for a while, even if you've been too stupid to recognize it. Even before tonight, before our date, and everything that went with it, I would have jumped into this mess with you without a second thought. Sure, I'm scared, and some of the punches have been kinda tough to roll with, but I'd still choose to be here no matter what. And *no matter what* Leo says over there, he would be, too."

Lyra's words hit my chest like a grenade going off. And I know what that's like now. I haven't been alone? This whole time, I thought I was just fitting in, being a human. It hadn't until now been a possibility to me that anybody liked me for the real me, the one under the maccomp disguise. Sure, they knew the personality under it all, but I am still an alien to them.

"It doesn't matter that I'm an alien? That I have been the whole time?" I ask.

"Of course it matters," Lyra says, "but that doesn't change that I like you, the guy who is always there no matter what. You've been there the whole time I was struggling to raise Leo, to make it through my parents being gone, to be a friend when no one else would be, to play games with us, to show Leo how to be himself *and* be responsible at the same time. You've done all of that not because you're an alien or you were just trying to blend in. You did it because you are you."

I turn to Leo, who is nodding along with what his sister is saying. He shrugs and smiles.

"I did?" I say, loud enough for only Leo to hear me.

"Lyra's usually right about this kind of thing," Leo says. "You know it, too. I may be mad at you for the moment because of where we are, but that doesn't mean I hate you. And Lyra *clearly* isn't holding any of this against you. She's too good for you, dude."

I nod. I can't disagree.

"But that doesn't change the fact that we are all still here, in a cell, on a pirate ship orbiting the moon," I say.

"No, it doesn't," Lyra says. "But it *does* mean that you're going to have to find that alien part of you again, the one that you've been keeping hidden for all these years, and get us out of here."

"Yeah, bro," Leo says. "I believe in you."

"And I as well, Jarokin," Grendia says. She has been silent this whole time, and I am curious to know what she thinks about all of this. I am not the same person I was when I left Prentia, and I wonder how it makes Grendia feel to hear how different I have been among the humans.

A slow clap starts from somewhere down the hall. It continues for a few seconds before being followed by a cynical laugh.

"Touching as all this campfire talk is," Bossy says, "we're all still stuck in these cells."

"Oh, you're still alive," I say.

"And if I ever get out of here, you probably won't be," Bossy retorts.

The door to the cell block opens, and several of Jorr's crew walk by our cells, stopping at Bossy's cell. They open the door and order Bossy and the goons to follow them.

"Ah, good," Bossy says. "Looks like Captain Jorr has come to his senses and wishes to have a word with the *true* victims of Prince Jarokin and his Band of Outlaws."

"Oh that's rich," I say as they pass by. "Don't forget to add in extra drama about Grendia jumping you in an alleyway and kicking the crap out of you out of sheer spite!"

"Oh, I'll make sure Captain Jorr knows all about your little bodyguard chicky's special skills," Bossy says.

With that, the guards take them away, and the door to the cell block slams shut.

32

Almost an hour passes before we hear anything else. Leo and I spend the time looking around for weaknesses in the cell. There are none. Lyra and Grendia are mostly quiet. Grendia is likely taking advantage of the time to rest. She didn't get the benefits of a bunch of meds earlier like I did, but I also feel those beginning to wear off. I don't think I'll sink back down to the cognitive level I was at, but things might start hurting a bit more soon.

Leo yawns. "What time is it, anyway?"

"Probably around six a.m. in Lexington," I say.

"Whoa, so we've been up all night just running around with aliens and flying into outer space," Leo says.

I don't have a response. Leo has it right. We've been up all night. We should be at least trying to get some rest like Lyra and Grendia have been. At least, I assume that's what they've been doing. Neither of them have said anything for a while now.

"Why don't you sit down and try to get some rest, Leo?" I say. "There's no telling how long we'll be in here before something else happens."

Leo sighs and gives up his inspection of a seam in the wall paneling. I don't blame him. Anything we find could be the advantage we need to get out of here.

"Okay, Jack, but you, too," he says.

I have no argument against this. I nod and move to sit down next to the door. I want to be between Leo and whoever comes through that door, at the very least. Leo sits down next to the wall across from me and almost immediately nods off. For all of his youth and energy, he's exhausted. I am, too.

I close my eyes, telling myself that I won't sleep but for just a few minutes.

The door to the cell block opens, and I open my eyes. I am not sure how long I have been out, but it could not have been too long. Leo is still asleep as I get to my feet and attempt to look out the door slats to see who is out there.

"So," Captain Jorr says, "it's *Prince* Jarokin of Prentia, is it?"

"Yeah," I say. "That's me."

"You're a long way from home, Prince, and word is that you've been gone a really long time, too. Who'd have thought that all this time you were hiding out on a backwater like Earth?"

"So Bossy told you who I am," I say.

"She did her share of talking, yeah," Jorr says. "Offered to cut me in on the bounty if I helped fix up her ship and escorted them to deliver you back to Prentia. It was a tempting offer."

"Did you have another offer on the table?" I ask.

"As a matter of fact," Jorr says as the lock to the cell door is released, "I do."

Leo wakes up at the sound of the cell door opening and quickly stands. I look across the hallway, past Jorr, to the other cell. A member of Jorr's crew is opening it as well, and soon we are all walking along a different corridor than the one we came in through. Jorr says nothing else on the walk, and I manage to exchange a look with Grendia that confirms that they, too, have no plan at this point. We will have to wait for an opportunity.

Eventually we reach a large cargo bay that looks like it has been converted into a workout space for the crew. There is a large empty space in the center, almost like a sparring mat or fighting circle. Grendia gasps, as she sees him before I do.

"I was beginning to wonder what was taking so long," Niolan says.

He is standing on the far side of the room, leaning against a cargo container. Annoyingly, he looks like he did not have a grenade explode right in front of him a couple of hours ago. His smile is the worst part about him, I decide. That smug grin that says he is always winning, always on top of whatever the situation happens to be. I have to drum up memories of him from a couple of nights ago just to remember that he's not invincible. He *can* be hurt. And I have a feeling that I'm going to have to figure out how to do that very soon.

"Niolan here has been telling me about how difficult you have been to capture," Jorr says, moving to and taking a seat in a raised, very comfortable-looking chair.

"Well, he hasn't managed to yet," I say. The dig hits Niolan right where I want it to hit—in his pride. Nolan's grin fades to a scowl, and the royal guard pushes off from the cargo container he's leaning against and walks into the center of the room.

"Okay, Jorr," Niolan says, "now that Jarokin is here, what is it that you want? I've already offered to pay you for him, so what's the big deal?"

"The big deal is that I am bored. And agitated. The bounty hunter was a pain to talk to, and letting her go outside for some air, though amusing for a moment, was not at all the entertainment I thought it would be."

I wince. Not out of a particular pity for Bossy or her goons. Jorr obviously didn't like what she had to say. I would wager it was her attitude that led to her impromptu space walk. I'm not gonna cry over it, but it's still a pretty brutal way to go. Wait, can roaches survive in space?

Regardless, I don't like where Jorr is going with this. A feeling in the pit of my stomach is forming, turning it sour.

"So," the captain continues, "I am in a mood to provide just such entertainment for myself and my crew."

"And what entertainment is that?" Niolan asks.

"Why, I make you and Jarokin fight to the death, of course," Jorr says. "If you win, you at least get to complete your mission by taking the prince's corpse home to his oh-so-grieving mommy. You've already said this is one of the options she gave you, albeit the least desirable of them, and I'm sure the princey here will jump at any chance to not go back."

"And what do I get if I win?" I ask.

Both Niolan and Jorr look at me. Everybody does, actually. Grendia looks like she's about to pop, and Lyra's eyes are tearing up. Leo is…Leo. I nod at them and smile, mouthing the phrase *I got this* and getting a very mixed reply of facial expressions in return.

Jorr laughs. "What do *you* get? I suppose that's fair, all things considered. What would a prince who has everything want from a humble space captain?"

"Well, for starters, you'd let my friends and me go, taking us safely back to Earth. Then, you put this solar system in your rear camera view and you don't come back for a very, *very* long time."

The voice I am speaking with sounds more like Prince Jarokin than Jack. The authority I put behind every word is, I hope, a message that I will not be bullied no matter the circumstance. I may hate it, but I am a royal of a very powerful planet. That may not mean much on Earth, but maybe it does to the likes of Jorr.

Jorr laughs again. "I think the princeling thinks we're standing in the royal palace of Prentia and not in the belly of *my* ship, where I am captain."

Okay, then again, maybe not.

"*If* you win, princeling," Jorr says, stopping to look between Niolan and myself, "and that's a very big *IF*, I'll let your friends go back to Earth, the humans anyway. But you and the other

Prentian, the traitor royal guard, stay with me. You're too valuable to lose on just one measly fight."

"Done," I say.

"No!" Lyra protests, and I look at her. The tears are rolling down her cheeks now. I'm sorry, Lyra, but it has to be this way. The galaxy is a lot harsher place than humans know, and it could use more people like you. I know this, but they don't. So if this is what it takes to make sure you stay in your world, then I will do it without a second thought.

Grendia throws her arms around Lyra, who has nothing else to say. There's nothing else she can say.

"Kick his ass, Jack!" Leo yells out.

"Very well," Jorr says. "A fight we shall have. You have ten minutes to prepare."

I walk over to Grendia and Lyra and wrap them both in the biggest hug I can muster.

"It's going to be okay, Lyra," I say.

"You don't know that," she manages in between sobs.

"But I do," I say, bending down to meet her gaze. "I know it will because you told me exactly what I needed to hear in that cell. All this time I thought I was alone, and I wasn't. I just didn't know it. Now it's my turn to repay the favor of kindness that you've shown me. I can do this."

"But, even if you beat Niolan, you still have to stay here, and I have to leave you!" Lyra sobs.

"We'll see about that," I say. "We'll see about that."

33

I have to give Captain Jorr credit for his selection of dueling weaponry. From basic power blades to energy mauls and even a one-shot dueling pistol, the variety of violent implements of destruction is commendable. Jorr informs us of the rules. They are unsurprisingly simple. We may each select one item per hand. No armor is available outside of a few shields. The order of picking is determined randomly, and wouldn't you know it, Niolan gets to pick first.

He saunters over to the weapons table and looks at the options. After only a few moments, he picks up a large power maul and an energy whip that buzzes with barely contained galvanic energy. Getting hit by that thing will hurt.

My turn now. I select an energy shield that reminds me of my lost disintegrator shield. Old habits and whatnot. So I like a shield. That gives me one more pick. My eyes gaze from item to item while I take my time.

"Oh come on, Jarokin," Niolan taunts. "It's not like your decision will matter. Just pick something, and let's get this over with!"

I ignore the taunt and study what I have available to pick from. Most of these weapons are unwieldy and slow. Niolan's speed will make using such a weapon a bad choice. Maybe Niolan is right. Maybe it doesn't matter what I pick. I promised Lyra that I would get her back home, and I'm not at all sure how to do that. It means I have to kill Niolan. I suppose that was unavoidable after all. I didn't want to kill him, even after he took Leo. Killing him would likely just lead to more problems with my mother. I had been thinking that if I sent him back to Prentia with the clear message to leave me alone, she might listen. It was a fool's hope to think that would work. Niolan has made the decision for me.

"Two minutes, Princey," Jorr says.

I frown. Nothing is leaping out at me as a good option. I can't meet Niolan for power or speed. He has those in abundance thanks to his decades of warrior training. I, on the other hand, have decades of video games and dice rolling under my belt at this point. Relying on my old royal court training days has only gotten me so far, probably as far as they will get me.

Then I see it. A clutch of six vibro daggers weighted for throwing. It's literally the least imposing weaponry on the table. Even a second shield would be more imposing as a weapon, but something about the daggers makes me smile on the inside. A strategy for the fight begins to form in my head as I reach out and select the clutch. Niolan snickers as I pick them up and fit the chest strap over my head, fitting the pouch to sit on my chest and allow for easy pulls of the daggers.

I look over to Grendia who is giving me a "what the hell, man?" kind of look. Lyra and Leo also look suitably confused. I give them all an enthusiastic thumbs up, which is not returned by any of them. Lyra rolls her eyes, I assume to prevent them tearing up again, and Leo just shakes his head. It's clear he thinks I've lost it. And maybe I have.

I turn to Niolan. But then again…

"Okay," I say. "Let's get this over with. I have better things to do tonight."

"Oh, I'm gonna enjoy crushing your bones, Jarokin," Niolan says. "Your mother might not be pleased that it had to be this way, but at this point I'll take my chances with presenting her your corpse."

"Heh," I say, drawing one of my throwing daggers and

walking into the center of the room. "You sure do talk a lot for a guy who still might lose."

Niolan cocks his head to the side as I take my position across from him. We wait only for Jorr to tell us to begin. I have no idea how this is going to go, but I do know one thing. I am not going to fight this duel in any manner that Niolan will see coming.

"Okay, gentlemen," Jorr says. "First, a few rules. This is to the death, and I mean it. You'd better give a good show, too, or I might just kill whoever wins if I'm not entertained."

This elicits a cheer from the gathered crew members, more of whom appear as Jorr begins his monologue. Now that I am studying the battlefield more closely, I note that the circle is not a true circle in the middle of the room and more of an oblong semi-circle with one of the short ends extending to a wall. Crew members are standing in front of the wall at present, but I make mental note of the feature as Jorr continues his self-aggrandized pedantry.

"Other than that," he continues, "the boundaries of this fight shall be this cargo bay. Either of the combatants are free to move anywhere, except to within striking distance of my person. Upon doing so, you will be shot. Also, there is to be no aid from any of the spectators. Any aid rendered to either combatant will result in the person providing aid being shot, probably by me."

Captain Jorr pauses for a laugh that he shares only with himself. I'm glad somebody is enjoying his speech. I'd rather get to the task at hand. Niolan looks like he is losing patience as well.

"That's about it," Jorr says, "except that whatever else I say during the fight goes. And…yeah, I think that's it, then. Fight on!"

The crew cheers at Jorr's declaration, and I suspect it is just as much because Jorr has finally stopped talking as it is that the fight is commencing.

Niolan gives me little time to think as he leaps into action, slashing out with his energy whip as he closes the distance between us. I anticipate the whip and side-step his attack. Unfortunately, I realize too late that I moved exactly where he wanted me to as his power maul swings from the side, using his momentum to add a terrible strength to the swing. I manage to raise my shield to block it, but the force of the blow knocks me back. I stumble several steps backward, trying not to fight the force of the attack any more than I have to in order to keep my feet.

Niolan gives me little time to think about my next move as he lashes out again with the whip. This time it catches me just above the ankle, and I scream in pain as an energy shock travels up my leg. I spin with the force of the whip hit, going down on my knee, but I now have my back to Niolan. Knowing what is coming next, I raise my shield over my head, behind me, and I feel the concussive force of the maul meet the shield, the two energy weapons clashing in a brilliant flash.

The force of the block drives my knee further into the floor, and I feel it bruise as I strain to keep upright. Slashing out behind me with the vibro dagger, I am rewarded with the feeling of the blade hitting something followed by Niolan yelping in pain. But my victory cannot be enjoyed as I feel a kick to my back that sends me sprawling forward.

I roll out of the forward pitch and come up quickly, spinning around and flinging my dagger blindly in what I hope is Niolan's direction. Niolan parries the flying blade with his maul, and I hear someone in the crowd yell, "AHHHH, my knee!" as it finds another, unintended, target.

Laughing, cheering, and jibing of the wounded spectator follows the next several moments as Niolan attempts to maneuver me with his whip once more, trying to get an angle with his maul. I draw another dagger and look for my own opportunity.

Five.

My breathing is already fairly heavy, but Niolan does not look taxed beyond a slight limp on his now-injured leg. I may be able to use that to my advantage later, but for now I am more concerned with maneuvering him where *I* want and not the other way around.

"I didn't see you lasting this long, even," Niolan says between whip cracks.

"Surprised?" I ask.

"Heh, perhaps a little amused," Niolan says. "I didn't know you had this much grit in you, Jarokin. But it won't last."

"Probably not," I say, making a hard dodge away from his whip. My leap is in the wrong direction, technically, if I want to keep avoiding giving him an attack angle with his maul, but I have my own strategy here.

"Enough talk!" Niolan yells, and he leaps forward for another close attack.

I throw my dagger at him. He is slow to parry it, but he manages to deflect it. I raise my shield with both of my arms to meet his raging maul swing. When we connect, I do my best not to give any ground and instead swivel on heel and toe to divert the maul to one side instead of attempting to stop it cold.

Four.

The gambit works, and my arms are not broken in the exchange. My back is now to the wall at the end of the fighting circle. I risk a glance back at it. It is a dozen feet away. Niolan smiles with a feral fire in his eyes. He is about to have me cornered against the wall. I draw another dagger and fling it at him in one fluid motion. This one manages to clip him in the shoulder, and he almost drops the energy whip.

Three.

"Gah! Those things are like little gnats!" he bellows. "They'll never kill me, Jarokin, just piss me off more!"

Good. That's exactly what I want. I think. I hope so, anyway. If my crazy idea is going to work, then there's only one way it will. He has to be raging mad when we reach the wall, and I'm running out of daggers.

I start to slowly give ground. He has not attempted to close the distance with me just yet, preferring to keep me moving with the whip again. I draw and throw another dagger in the space between another whip crack. This one he deflects with the whip itself, and I see crew members across the room ducking to avoid the deflected missile attack.

Two.

I look back to see the wall getting closer. I am almost where Niolan wants me. At least, that's what he thinks. If I can do this right, I can hopefully even this fight up. I draw one of my two remaining daggers, but I hold on to it. This one isn't for throwing. My timing has to be spot on here, and I prepare myself for the pain that my sacrifice move is about to bring me.

Just like I expect, Niolan steps forward one more time, and I take a step back, the last step I have between me and the wall. I'm now close enough to reach back with my hand and place my fingers on the wall, which I do to make sure I am where I mean to be. I watch Niolan's feet to see what his next move will be. He shifts to the right, indicating that he will attack with the whip again.

Good boy.

As the ship cracks out, I step to the wrong side of the arc and let the whip catch me on the side. I cry out in pain as the whip rakes down my ribs and across my abdomen. I hear someone, Lyra I think, cry out as I take the hit. My eyes become unfocused, but I don't need to see all that well for what comes next. Just as I predicted, Niolan moves in for the kill shot, taking advantage of my lowered shield arm that is attempting to clutch my newest injury.

I hear more than see the attack coming in, and I don't have to look up to know the look of savage ferocity, of pure satisfaction, that is on his face. But I am afraid that I have to disappoint him again. He's fast, but predictable.

I duck under the maul's swing and feel it lightly scrape the top of my head. Okay, so he's *a lot* faster than I thought, but still. I hear the maul slam into the wall paneling behind me with a satisfying crunch. The force of the blow carries the head and part of the haft of the weapon into the paneling, and I hear stuff behind the paneling break and shatter at the force visited upon it.

In the same motion, I pivot around, reversing my grip on the dagger and slamming it into Niolan's hand, pinning it to the wall, even as it still grips the maul. I take a step back and shake my head as it is Niolan's turn to scream out in pain.

One.

I take a few moments to breathe as Niolan cries about his injury. Oh please. Get over yourself. It's just a knife wound. Like I haven't had worse tonight. The din of the crowd rises as some of the lucky bastards who bet on me realize their longshot might have just paid off. I wish I could have gotten in on that action, if only to see the look on the bookies' faces when I come to collect.

Niolan is still trying to pull the dagger out with his other hand, having dropped the whip to try to free himself from the wall. I draw my last dagger and walk forward, pressing the point of it to the back of his neck. He freezes.

"Do it," he says, defiance and haughty superiority still in his voice.

And I intend to, until…

What's that?

The force of Niolan's strike against the wall dislodged another panel that is now bent outward and hanging to the side.

Behind it, a glowing tube of concentrated plasma energy pulses, quietly doing its job to power the ship. I look to the left and the right before making my decision. This is it. This is my way out of this.

I pull back with my knife, and Niolan bows his head, ready for the killing blow. But he is not the target of my final blade thrust.

I yell out a battle cry because I know this is going to hurt. It's a theme I've been embracing lately, causing self-harm, and why stop now?

I thrust the dagger forward, and it flies past Niolan's head, plunging into the plasma conduit behind the wall panel. The reaction is instantaneous, as the vibro energy of the blade ignites the concentrated plasma in the conduit, causing a massive explosion that encompasses everything, and everyone, in the cargo bay in its blast.

34

My energy shield, and Niolan's face, take most of the blast for me, but the force of the shockwave still hurls me across the room. I see cargo containers flying, people getting ripped off their feet, and even a few heads becoming instantaneous party poppers. I don't have time to be concerned about how Lyra, Leo, and Grendia fare in the blast before I hit the wall on the other side of the cargo bay. I feel something crunch in my shoulder. Pretty sure that just popped out of its socket. Yay.

Warning sirens are blaring as I try to get to my feet. I look around the cargo bay. It's perfect. Utter chaos no matter which way I look. Nobody is paying any attention to me. Crew members, the ones still alive, are getting up, running around, and screaming bloody murder to try to get things back under control. I do not see Captain Jorr, but I am not concerned with finding him. The muffled sounds of explosions elsewhere in the ship tell me that I have done some good damage. I just hope not too good. We need time to get out of here.

I grit my teeth and groan as I use an overturned cargo container to pull myself upright. I can't see Lyra, Leo, or Grendia anywhere. Making my way through the debris near me, I shove past a crew member who attempts to stop me. I bash him in the face with my shield, which thankfully is still strapped to my arm, and move on.

"Lyra!" I yell out. "Grendia! Leo!"

The din in the cargo bay drowns out my voice. The plasma conduit has ruptured in multiple places now, and the venting fire is louder than any other noise save the sirens that will not stop blaring. I move my way to the center of the bay, toward where I last saw the people I am looking for. Thankfully, I run into no bodies of said people, but neither do I find them.

Looking around, I see signs that someone was dragged toward one of the doors. It could have been them. The way to said door is mostly clear, and I start making my way to it. A few pitfalls and a couple of ignored crew member bodies later, I reach the door. Hoping that I am following them instead of leaving them in there under a pile of cargo containers, I manually open the door and exit into the corridor.

Things look only marginally better out here than in the cargo bay. Crew members rush past me, none of them paying me any mind. They have jobs to do, after all, and even if I'm the cause of their current trouble, I am sure that they consider their present task of keeping the ship from exploding as more important than restraining me. No argument here. I follow the corridor down to a junction that splits off four ways from where I entered it, and I stop for a moment to catch my breath and perhaps figure out where Grendia might have taken Lyra and Leo.

My arm throbs in protest, perhaps thinking I have forgotten that it is currently not where it is supposed to be, internally speaking. I walk over to a corner and take a few quick, deep breaths, preparing myself for the pain. Without pausing to psyche myself up for it, I slam my shoulder into the corner and yell loud enough to drown out the sirens, just for a moment. I feel the joint pop back into place with a splooshy ligament-scraping sound that echoes in my ears for a few seconds. My vision goes blurry again, and I have to reach out to steady myself.

"Is pain just my way of life now?" I say out loud to myself after I am able to breathe again. The pain is subsiding enough for me to remember that I need to figure out where Grendia and the humans have gone.

I look around on the floor. I don't want to find something like a bloody trail, considering that one of the three people I'm trying to find would need to be bleeding in order to leave one for me, but it would be helpful. I can't decide if I am disappointed or relieved to not find any blood indicating which way they went. That means whoever was being dragged out of the cargo bay might have woken up and been able to walk on their own.

I try my best to guess which way they might have gone. It's been a bit since I've seen anybody else, but the sirens are still going off. The muffled explosions are less common, but they haven't stopped entirely. I really did something bad to this ship. But I'm not leaving without the people I came here with.

I decide to make an educated guess and choose a corridor that leads to what I think is toward the aft of the ship, closer to where the docking bay should be. This ship is a maze with no indicators on the walls or floors to tell me where I might be. I just have to keep guessing each time I am presented with a choice. It has been some time since I ran into anybody, and that worries me. Am I headed to a dangerous part of the ship? Am I alone now, as I thought I was before? I have no idea where everyone else could be, or even if they are still alive.

Maybe jamming my dagger into the plasma conduit wasn't such a good idea after all. It hasn't really gotten me anywhere. Maybe Leo was right to be mad at me. My decisions have not helped at all. I just keep making things worse.

I round a corner and find myself face to face with two crew members who are just as surprised to see me as I am to see them.

"Hey!" one of them yells over the siren noises. We aren't very close to one of the klaxons, so the siren is slightly quieter in this corridor.

"Hey yourself!" I yell back.

"You're not supposed to be here!" he says.

"Well then where am I supposed to be?" I ask.

The two of them exchange confused looks. I think they have no idea who I am. Judging by their uniforms and the tools they are carrying, they appear to be below-deck mechanics. Very little chance they know about me or who I am. I hope.

"If you don't know, then I'm gonna continue this way," I say.

"Where are you trying to get to?" the other one asks.

"My station at the docking bay," I say. "I've never been in this part of the ship before, and I'm a bit lost."

"Oh! In that case, take the corridor behind you to the left and take your third right after that. Should get you back to the right place eventually."

"Much obliged," I say, and I nod to them and turn around.

"Wait a second!" the first one says, and I turn back around to face them as he takes a step toward me. "Why do you have an energy shield?"

"I work security for the captain," I say, holding up the shield and showing them.

They exchange another confused look and shrug.

"Okay, well, good luck finding your way out of here!" the second one says.

"I appreciate it," I say, and I turn again to leave. This time they don't say anything as I make my turn and head down to where they told me to go. The way is clear, and I pick up the pace a bit, hoping to get to the docking bay in time.

After a couple of minutes, I begin to hear a rumbling sound at the end of the corridor. There is a door at the end that looks like it is jammed open with a metal pipe, and I rush to the end of the corridor to see where I have come out. I use the pipe to force the door open, my shoulder protesting with each pull.

On the other side of the door is an antechamber with a

large, wall-sized window that looks out into the docking bay where I see Bossy's ship. The rumbling I heard is the ship's start-up sequence, and moments later the engines blaze to life. Someone must have done some kind of work on the ship while we were in the ship's brig.

My eyes go wide when I realize that it is possible that the people on that ship might be Lyra, Leo, and Grendia. No! Did they think I was dead or something? Why didn't they try to find me? I was right there! They can't be *that* mad at me for blowing up the ship. Is the ship still blowing up?

I am not idle while all of these questions and more race through my head. I run over to the door on the bay side of the room and open it, quickly darting into the bay, waving my arms and shouting at the top of my lungs.

"Wait for me! I'm not dead! Grendia! Lyra! Leo! Don't leave without me!" I am quickly out of breath as I run and shout at the same time.

As I reach the center of the bay, the engines whine with power as they are fed power, and a blast of air whirls around me as they screech to full life, sending the ship hurling out into space. I watch as the ship careens away from the moon, making top speed out into space.

"No," I say, gulping in air and trying to come to terms with being left behind. "I'm still here. I'm still here."

"Oh, I see you," a voice behind me says, and I turn to see a much worse-for-wear Captain Jorr standing in the open door that we were marched out of just a while ago. "And I'm glad for it, Princey. Cause you've cost me a ship, and now I'm going to take it out on your hide."

35

"Oh you are, huh?" I ask, turning to face Jorr. "You look about as bad as I feel, and that's saying a lot, believe me."

It's not hyperbole at all. Captain Jorr looks *rough*. Part of his face is covered in burns. I think he's missing what passes for an ear for his species, and he is bleeding from a dozen other cuts. I think I even see a compound fracture on his forearm poking out. He'll want to set that sooner rather than later.

"You," Captain Jorr says as he raises a pistol at me with his unbroken other arm. "Your kind are all alike. Think you can run amuck across the cosmos, using the rest of us as pawns in your schemes and games."

"My kind?" I say, ignoring the pistol for now. I think he's in a talky mood at the moment, more so than a shooty one.

"Yeah, the upper echelon, the privileged, you snakes who take from whoever you want and then squash anybody who gets in your way," Captain Jorr says, becoming more animated as he speaks.

The warning sounds of the ship are background now, the explosions less frequent, but I have a sense of impending doom that tells me that Jorr knows his ship does not have long. And he has decided to use the time left to him to berate me for my highborn birth. Well, if that's what floats his boat, I suppose. I am apparently not going anywhere at this point.

"Sounds like you have some issues to work out," I say.

Captain Jorr pulls the trigger on his pistol, and the bolt flies past me, dissipating on the environmental force field that keeps the bay pressurized and full of breathable atmosphere. Guess I touched a nerve there.

"Issues?!" he barks out. "You lot *always* think you can take what you want without consequence, and you, your little royal brat spat with your parents, has now doomed so many innocent people to die. There are good people on this ship, *Prince* Jarokin. Good people that will now die because you had to take out your problems on the rest of us."

"Ya got a pretty weird way of saying that you pirated yourself into disaster," I say.

I raise my shield as another bolt flies by me. He really needs somebody to listen, I suppose. Too bad for him that I'm a terrible listener.

"It wasn't me who killed all the people on this ship," I say. "It was you. You made it my only option in order to have a chance to live."

"Oh please," Jorr bites back. "You know how the universe works. You would have been ransomed back to your parents eventually, and anyone whose hands you passed through along the way would have gotten rich because of it. *You* are the reason for all of this, and I'm done with wanting to get rich off your sorry hide."

Captain Jorr shoots again, this time with much better aim. I am able to block the shot with my energy shield, but the shield is damaged while absorbing the shot. It fizzles out, sparking with one last burst of life before deactivating with a low-pitched whine. I look up at Jorr. He is smiling a toothy grin and adjusts his aim.

"I might still get off this heap before it goes," he says. "But not you. No. You will die here, alone, abandoned. Your friends took off, and it looks like they aren't coming back. Oh well, it seems this was how it was meant to be anyway. One less privileged spoiled brat in the universe isn't a bad thing anyway, and I'll tell your—"

I jump, startled as the sound of blaster fire fills my ears. I wait for the pain to come. Good move, Jorr, shoot me when I expect you to keep talking. Wish I'd have thought of that more than once before now myself. Well, this is it I suppose. I really expected more pain from a shot like that. Wait a minute. Why am I not in pain?

I look back over to Captain Jorr, who is staring blankly into space. His gun hand drops slowly, and he topples over, landing hard on the bay floor. Behind him is a figure. No, three figures. One of them is holding a pistol of her own, a look of grim satisfaction on her face.

"He talked *way* too much for his own good," Grendia says.

Lyra runs over to me and wraps me in the biggest hug I've ever received. I cry out in pain, and she lets go for a moment. But I tighten my grip despite the discomfort.

"I thought…" I say, through breaths of relief, "I thought you left without me."

Lyra steps back a half step and stares up into my eyes. "Why the hell would you think we left you?"

"Bossy's ship," I say. "You…You weren't in it, then?"

"Obviously not," Grendia says.

"How did you survive the blast?" I ask.

They all look a little roughed up, and Grendia has a cloth tied around her head. It must have been her who was knocked out, and Lyra and Leo found a way to drag her to safety.

"It's a long story," Leo says. "The short version is that Grendia pulled a really large alien dude in front of all of us, and he got turned into swiss alien cheese by the explosion. Then when we couldn't find you, Lyra and I dragged Grendia out of the cargo bay until she woke up, and we started looking for you. Grendia was right. You'd go for Bossy's ship. Looks like someone beat us to it, though."

"Yeah," I say. "So what do we do now?"

"I don't know," Grendia says. "Finding you was the only plan I really had."

"What about Niolan?" Leo asks.

"What *about* Niolan?" I ask. "I'm pretty sure he's dead. He was between me and the initial plasma blast. Probably toasted remains in a cargo container soup at this point."

"No!" Leo says, suddenly excited. "I mean, how did Niolan get here? On his ship, right?"

Grendia and I exchange excited looks. Of course! The Prentian Royal Guard ship has to be here somewhere! Only Grendia is keyed into biometric access functions of the ship, which means nobody could have taken it!

"Leo, that's brilliant!" I say. I hug Lyra again quickly before we all head to the far side of the docking bay.

There is a lift there that provides access to the other docking bays, and it appears to still be functional. I press the button, and we all get into the car when it arrives.

"Any idea how long until the ship explodes?" Leo asks.

"Could be soon," I say.

"What did you stab into anyway?" Grendia asks.

"The main power drive plasma conduit, I think," I say.

Grendia's eyes widen in horror as she realizes what that means.

"How? What were you…? Why didn't we all…?" Grendia goes through several more partial questions before landing on, "That shouldn't have worked, Jarokin."

"Again, I know," I say. "That happens a lot around me lately."

"Yes…" Grendia agrees.

The lift reaches its destination, and the door opens. Grendia and I are the first out into the bay. Grendia's ship is here, just sitting and waiting. It doesn't look like it has been harmed. The only one of us with a weapon is Grendia, so I let her take the lead on clearing the rest of the bay. We are alone for now, but that could soon change.

"Okay," I say, "let's get on board."

Grendia nods and walks over to the exterior control panel. After placing a thumb on the control pad, the panel beeps a negative tone and turns red. I'm pretty sure that's not a good thing.

"Uhh, Jarokin," Grendia says.

I already know the problem. Niolan thought to de-authorize Grendia from the ship before leaving it. That clever bastard is still managing to be a thorn in our side.

"Can you override his lockout?" I ask.

"I can, with some time," Grendia says. "But I'm not sure we have any of that left."

"No other option," I say.

The double doors on the side of the bay open, and a dozen crew members, most of them armed with pistols, storm into the bay. One of them shouts orders to shoot us, and those that are armed start taking aim.

"Trouble!" Leo yells out as he and Lyra take cover behind a container.

Grendia tosses me her pistol. "You deal with that. I'll get us on the ship."

I catch the blaster and snap off a shot, catching one of the crew in the chest. He drops his blaster, which is quickly recovered and picked up by another alien.

"Please," I say to Grendia before running into the thick of yet another fight I have no business trying to win. "Hurry."

36

When did I get into the habit of just running into fights? This was never my life before setting foot on the floor of QUASITASTICON 9, but now it's like I can't get enough of them. I mean, yeah, I can totally get enough of them. But I haven't exactly gone looking for the fights, either. They've pretty much all found me. Do I have a tracker on me that fights use to hunt me down?

As risky fights go, this one ranks up there. I haven't been able to get my shield to turn back on, so it's just me, a blaster pistol, and my good ol' Jack-can-do attitude. I yell out what I hope is an intimidating shout that is actually half battle cry and half my arm freaking hurting because it was dislocated less than twenty minutes ago.

My first shot must have been pure luck, as now three of my fingers are numb, and I can barely figure out where I am aiming. But that does not stop me from pulling the trigger, and often, as I run toward the ten or so crew members who are attempting to simultaneously shoot me, shoot Grendia, and move around to get an angle to shoot Lyra and Leo. Lots of attempted shootings going on in this cargo bay at the moment.

All of this should deter me from running straight at them, but it does not. Three of the crew, upon seeing my unwillingness to listen to reason, decide that I am too much for them and turn around to run away back through the double doors. I guess they don't understand the advantage that superior numbers give them and would rather take their chances with the still-exploding ship. I'm not going to argue with them, especially since one of them was kind enough to drop his pistol as he stumbled away.

"Free pistol!" I shout out as I bend down to pick it up. Several blaster bolts zoom over me, right where my torso was a moment before, and I stand up with one arm each extended to the left and right. I start pulling the triggers and rotating around, spinning just enough to vary my position but not enough to further agitate my multiple concussions.

I get lucky and unlucky as it goes. Two more crew members get winged to varying degrees. I think at least one is down for the count, but I also get grazed on my good shoulder and my thigh.

"Let us help!" Leo yells out from a dozen feet away. He and Lyra have worked their way over to me, and I am glad to see that they are not just sitting there and being helpless. I really like these two humans. Not a peep of self-pity out of them when the chips are down.

"Come on, Jack!" Lyra shouts as she jolts me out of my internal monologue. I really need to concentrate right now.

Looking around, I see a couple more pistols on the floor next to bodies, so I toss both of the pistols I am holding at Lyra and Leo. Without stopping to see what they do next with their new space weapons, I bolt for the nearest unattended pistol. I feel a hot poker jab into my leg and know that I have taken another hit.

Adrenaline don't fail me now!

It kinda doesn't. The next step onto that leg causes it to collapse, and there's the pain. But it does pitch me forward and into a couple of bodies who were thankfully both armed when they died. I grab the pistols and start shooting at anything not human and not Grendia. I hope so, anyway. They're all kinda just blurs right now. That hot pain in my leg is fierce.

"Jack! Can you move?" Lyra shouts out as she pops out from behind a container and nails a dude between the eyes with her blaster.

Wow. Just wow. I mean, who knew that Lyra was also part

warrior woman? Freakin' hot, if you ask me.

"What was that?" I have completely forgotten the question.

"Can you move?" Lyra shouts again.

"Maybe, why?" I say between shots.

There are not only a handful of crew left, but they are the smart ones who have, like us, taken cover. Now I am reminded of that really ridiculous cop movie where two guys are like three feet away from each other and popping up and down while they exchange gunfire. That's really what our situation would look like to an observer.

"Cause we have to get out of here!" Lyra says.

"Grendia hasn't got the ship open yet!" I yell back.

"Yes, I have!" Grendia calls out, jumping in between us and blazing away with a rapid-fire blaster carbine.

"Hey, where'd you get that?" I ask. I am still on the floor, leaning on the two dead bodies whose pistols I have been shooting for the past couple of minutes. My leg is bleeding, and I am sure that from Grendia's point of view I look absolutely ridiculous.

"Where do you think I got it from?" Grendia says, and she nods toward her ship. The boarding ramp is down, ready for us to run up and into the ship.

I guess it's time to see if I can move.

"Okay," I say. "Get them to the ship, and I'll cover you."

"Like hell you will!" Lyra yells past Grendia to me. "Get up, spaceman!"

I yell out as I use my good leg to prop me up onto my knees. In response to our need to leave immediately, the double doors open again and let in almost a dozen more armed crew members. I guess those guys that ran away earlier found some friends.

Grendia turns and lays down a barrage of suppressive fire, causing the newcomers to the fight to scatter as she screams at us to get on the ship. I don't have to be told a third time, and I hobble up to my feet. I almost collapse with my first few steps, but Leo is there to catch me on his shoulder, and we make progress toward the ship. Lyra takes one of my blasters and joins Grendia in providing cover fire for our retreat.

A few moments later, Leo has deposited me in the nearest chair, and Grendia and Lyra are running up the now-closing loading ramp. There is still fire hitting the ship's hull, but I know the armor plating on this ship will never even feel a scratch from such small arms.

"Make sure he's not going to bleed out," Grendia barks at Leo as Lyra follows her toward the cockpit. The ship is already going through its automated start-up sequence, and my experience with such vessels earlier in life tells me that it will be ready to blast out of the docking bay very shortly. Military-grade hardware versus even the black-market stuff is usually no contest, at least where the Prentian military is concerned.

"Over there." I point Leo toward a medical pack on the wall. "Grab that and bring it over here."

Leo sets it down on the table next to me and opens it up.

"What now?" he asks.

"Those two paddles," I say.

"The ones that look like a defibrillator?" he asks.

"Yeah," I say. My breath is ragged. I think I am losing a lot of blood. "They aren't defibrillators. Slap one directly over my wound, and the other one on my chest."

I open my shirt and indicate where he should place it. He follows my instructions.

"Now," I say, trying my best to stay conscious. "Push that green button, and then strap yourself into the seat next to me."

Leo follows my instructions, and moments later I feel a soothing painkiller entering my bloodstream, and the bleeding from the leg stops. Just as I breathe a sigh of relief from the latest round of drugs to flood into my system, the ship's engines roar to life, and we blast out of the *Heptanomist*'s bay to the sounds of explosions and a shockwave behind us.

Moments later, Lyra comes running back from the cockpit. I smile, but she only gives me a look of concern in return. I am touched that she is so affected by the state of my well-being, but she does not come over to see how I am doing. Instead, she grips the side of the doorway as the ship is rocked by an impact.

"We're not out of this yet," she says. "Grendia needs you up front, Jack."

37

"What is it?" I ask Grendia as I walk into the cockpit.

Comparing this ship to Bossy's, there is just no way to properly describe it. While Bossy's ship is a perfect example of what the best money and most dangerous connections can help one afford, the Prentian Royal Guard ship is an expression of wealth in its truest form. Not to the point that function is compromised—no, the truest high-end art accomplishes both aesthetic masterpiece and the peak of functional operation. I never hated that part about being Prentian. The rest of it, though. Well, no time for that now.

"There's a damned ship out here shooting missiles at us!" Grendia says, banking the ship hard right and heading closer to the surface of the moon.

I hobble over the secondary pilot seat next to Grendia and happily take the pressure off my leg by sitting down. A rapid review of the display station in front of me summarizes the situation. Yep. Those are missiles. And they're closing in on us fast.

"Deploying countermeasures," I say, and I press a series of buttons that activate everything from a laser infrared jammer to a screen of micro-particles that are all intended to help confuse incoming projectiles.

The two blips on the sensor screen disappear a few seconds later. To whatever did the job, I am thankful. But there is still a larger contact on the screen a little further back that is closing on us. I make sure our energy shields are operational and toggle the controls in front of me over from copilot controls to gunnery.

"Who are they?" I ask Grendia.

She is making for the moon, and I agree with her decision. Getting as low to the surface as possible is our best chance to lose our pursuers.

"No idea," she says. "Could have taken off from one of the other bays on Jorr's ship and decided that this ship was the cause of their problems."

That theory seems sound. So it's likely that Jorr's crew is after us.

"Not a lot of places to hide down there," I say.

"More than up here," Grendia replies.

"What do you need us to do?" Lyra asks.

I had no idea she and Leo had followed me into the cockpit.

"There's not a lot at this point," I say. "Strap into those seats, though. This is going to get bumpy."

In response to my prediction, the ship behind us opens up with its blasters and scores several hits on our rear shields. Lyra and Leo do not have to be told twice at that point, and they both quickly take a seat and fasten their crash webbing harnesses.

"Are you going to shoot back?" Grendia asks.

She is zigging and zagging, rolling and diving to avoid taking many more hits, but the ship that's chasing us must have a seasoned pilot and gunner. They are not letting up.

"Yeah, yeah," I say, and I zone in on my tactical display screen.

As soon as they give me an inch, I unleash a stream of fire from our ship's rear cannons. The scarlet bolts fly out into space. Some even hit their mark, and I give a little whoop in celebration when I see that I managed to actually land a hit on them.

"A little early for celebrating, don't ya think?" Grendia says.

"I'm learning to take the little wins," I respond, not looking away from my screen. This pilot is annoying me now.

Grendia hauls back on the control yoke, and the ship levels off from the nose-down dive that she put it into. Moondust flies up behind us as Grendia skims the surface of Earth's biggest satellite, granting us a temporary cloud of cover from the ship behind us. I continue firing into the cloud, hoping to score some lucky hits, but I imagine that I am as off the mark as they are when they return fire.

"What's the plan?" I ask, still blazing away with the aft cannons.

"Scanning for one," Grendia says. "One of these craters has to be near an outcropping of rocks of some kind."

"The moon is pretty well pummeled into oblivion at this point," Leo says. "Maybe on the dark side?"

Grendia nods her agreement as we fly past the horizon line separating the sunlit side of the moon from the dark.

"Oh wow!" Lyra says, and Leo echoes her sentiment of wonder.

"Look at those stars, Lyra!" Leo says, straining in his seat restraints to lean over and get a better look out the viewport.

"I know," Lyra says. "They don't look anything like that from Earth."

I wish I had time to stop and admire space the way the humans are. I had not thought about how they would have never seen space like this before. The stars are so dim on Earth compared to out here. They say that's actually affected human development over the years, with light pollution dimming the night skies more progressively over time. But I'm glad they are getting to see it, even if we're in the middle of mortal danger. Maybe we'll stop to look around here in a moment, but not yet.

"They're closing on us!" I yell to Grendia.

"I know," she says. "That's intentional."

"What?" Lyra asks. "But why?"

"No time, just trust me," Grendia says as she banks the ship into a deep dive over a crater wall and punches the throttle forward, using what little gravity the moon has to help pick up more speed.

I think I know what she's doing, but she has to get the other pilot going a lot faster than they are now. Fast enough to mitigate their reflexes. Her play works, though, and the other ship crests the crater ridge and matches Grendia's maneuver, picking up a ton of speed and gaining on us again. Grendia gooses the throttle a bit more again to goad the other pilot into closing even closer.

The return of scarlet laser blasts flying past the viewport and the report of splash damage across our aft shields confirms that they have once more closed. Which means…

I pull the trigger on my controls, and the aft cannons open up again, this time scoring many more hits than before. The pilot of the other craft is concentrating on gaining on us more so than attempting to avoid our fire. They must be confident that their energy shields can handle whatever we throw at them. Well, for a while anyway. No shields last forever.

In response to this thought, our aft shields begin showing a power drain, and I check the systems report. They shouldn't be that low, unless…

"Hey, did you…?" I ask Grendia.

"Divert power from the aft shields to the maneuvering thrusters, yeah," Grendia says. It's the only way this is going to work.

A red warning light accompanied by a rapid beeping flares up on the command console.

"They're going for another missile lock!" I yell.

At this range and speed, avoiding a missile may not be an option. Grendia banks and climbs up out of the other side of the crater and levels off, once more skimming the surface as close as she dares. The lock warning does not break, though, as the other ship is close enough to maintain us on their sensors. As soon as they level off, they launch two more missiles at us.

My eyes widen as I rapidly press all the buttons.

"Incoming!" I yell. "Brace for impact!"

Sometimes energy shields can stop missiles, but since Grendia transferred a bunch of our shield power to the maneuvering thrusters, I am pretty sure a hit will mean bad things for us. Along with the countermeasures, I add the aft cannons, creating a field of overlapping fire that I hope will catch one, preferably both, of the missiles while they are still at range.

The small red dots on the tactical display keep heading toward us despite my efforts, and I tighten all my aching muscles in preparation for the impact. Just before they impact, one of the bolts from the cannons hits a missile, and it explodes only a couple dozen meters from our hull. While sound doesn't travel very well, or at all really, in space, the force of the explosion is still felt as an impact on the ship. No damage, though. But it was only one missile that I managed to hit.

I do not unclench, as I expect the other one to hit soon after, but the impact doesn't come. I look around to see if we're just dead, and maybe I missed it. Nope. The humans are looking like they're both about to chuck up whatever might still be in their stomachs, and I don't blame them. This is not the fun part of space travel.

"Get ready!" Grendia yells.

"For what?" I ask, looking at the tactical display once again, afraid that they had fired more missiles.

Instead, I hear several metallic bangs from back in the ship as their renewed blaster cannons have broken through our depleted shields. The ship's damage-reporting computer does *not* like any of this, and it starts yelling at me.

"Get the forward cannons ready!" Grendia yells.

"What?" I ask again.

"Just do it!" Grendia yells, and she flashes me a look that sends a chill of pure fear down my spine.

"Okay," I say quickly and switch my gunnery controls to the front heavy-blaster cannons.

As soon as I look through the gun cameras, I smile. I get it now. She has us perfectly positioned, and it'll be up to me to make sure her immaculate setup is not ruined. I don't need to wait long for the payoff of Grendia's masterful tactics.

We are swiftly coming up on another crater ridge, and like last time, Grendia pours on more speed right before reaching the ridge. But unlike last time, as soon as our ship crests over the ridge, Grendia pulls back on the throttle and shoves all of the power into the reverse and downward thrusters.

The result is that we are all thrown forward in our restraints, and my vision turns slightly red at the g-forces Grendia's maneuver puts on all of us. But, the other ship flies right over us, perfectly into my sights. I do not hesitate, despite the disorienting effects of Grendia's move, and I pull all the triggers.

All four of the forward-facing heavy blaster cannons blaze to life, their fire zeroing in on a pinpoint area of impact right above the other ship's engines. Their energy shields never had a chance to stop such a barrage, and the ship virtually disintegrates from the aft to the bow, the cannons making short work of our former pursuers.

"WOOHOO!" Leo yells from behind me, and Lyra and Grendia join in on the celebration as Grendia re-engages the engines and we sail past the remains of the pirate ship that are slowly falling to the moon's surface.

I am breathing heavily in all the excitement, my chest heaving as I take in fresh air.

"That was amazing!" I say, turning to Grendia.

She has a huge smile on her face, and she reaches over to punch my shoulder.

"And you thought I was crazy to divert that power from our aft shields," she says.

"Wait, we didn't have shields?" Leo asks.

"Eh," I say. "We didn't need them after all."

Leo does not look convinced. Lyra unfastens her crash webbing and leaps forward to hug me from behind, kissing my cheek and nuzzling my neck with her face.

"Lyra," I say. "Really? In front of everybody?"

"Oh please, Jarokin," Grendia says. "Let the lady be glad that we're all somehow still alive."

"Thank you," Lyra says, still holding on to me and nodding to the other alien in the cockpit. "Jack, you really need to get used to it, anyway."

I shrug. "Yeah, you're right."

"And get used to it," Lyra says.

"Well," Grendia says as she steers the ship up and away from the surface of the moon, gaining some altitude. "What should we do now?"

"Home?" Leo asks.

Grendia nods. "Earth, you mean."

"Well, yeah," Leo says.

"Yes," Lyra echoes, "home."

I shrug when Grendia looks at me. "I guess the humans want to go home. The whole galaxy in front of them, and Earth is where they want to be. Go figure."

It is Lyra's turn to punch me in the arm, but this is harder than Grendia's hit, surprisingly.

"It's your home, too, you jerk," Lyra says. She sits back down in her chair, doing her best to act insulted.

Leo laughs at this exchange. I think he is enjoying someone else being the target of his sister's attitude for a change.

"Well, then," I say. "I guess that means home it is."

Grendia nods once more and smiles. "Yeah. Home."

And that is when the second missile hits.

38

Explosions. Explosions everywhere. Over there. In the back of the ship. Under my feet. That thing isn't supposed to explode. Neither is that.

I wait for the inevitable loss of atmospheric pressure, for the ship's main systems to be compromised. Holding my breath isn't going to cut it. Losing atmosphere is game over. Those pirates won. Damn pirates. What did I ever do to them?

Lyra and Leo are freaking out. Screaming and crying, clinging to one another as the ship crackles, fizzles, thunks, and screeches around them. It's a terrible sight to behold. Grendia is keeping her calm, at least comparatively. She is flipping switches and pressing buttons on consoles at such a rapid pace that I suspect she's reached the point of "Press all the buttons!" just to try to activate the right ones that will somehow save us from this.

But me? Well, I'm tired. I know it's over. I'm sure I look like a mess, too, just maybe one that has accepted his fate and is really tired of the night that never ends. It really has been a long night. If this is the end, well, such is life, I guess.

I wait.

But the end doesn't come.

"Are you just going to sit there, or are you going to help me?" Grendia yells and breaks me out of my death vigil.

We're not dead, yet. Why didn't that missile kill us?

"How are we not dead yet?" I ask.

"Oh, you actually *wanted* to be dead?" Grendia fires back.

"Well, no, but…" I attempt to say.

"That missile," Grendia says, "it wasn't a conventional

warhead."

Oh! That explains the not dead part!

"EMP?" I ask.

"Or something like it," Grendia says. "The systems are all fried. Those explosions must have been some of the power cells overloading."

Before continuing, Grendia shuts down most of the alarms. That doesn't mean that alarms aren't trying to vehemently go off and let them know about the problems they represent, just that Grendia doesn't want to hear what they have to say at the moment.

"So, are we going to die?" Leo asks.

"Remains to be seen," I say. "But that missile wasn't a conventional warhead. They wanted to disable us, not kill us. Not sure why."

"Could we have been wrong about who they were with?" Lyra asks.

"Huh?" I ask back.

"We assumed that they were on Jorr's ship, but what if they were *other* bounty hunters, maybe more of Bossy's people even?" Lyra asks.

I open my mouth to refute the idea and immediately close my jaw. No, that's not a bad theory. At least, it's no worse than anything else the rest of us could come up with.

"Jarokin," Grendia says, "you need to get back into engineering and stabilize the drive coils."

I nod to Grendia. "Leo, you're with me. Lyra, take my seat and see if you can help Grendia get the rest of the systems back online remotely."

"How do I start knowing how to do that?" Lyra asks as Leo and I jump up to run to the back of the ship.

"Grendia will tell you what buttons to push," I say. I give

her a brief hug. "We'll be right back. We're still here, and that's a win. Just gotta keep moving on. What was it that American astronaut said? 'Solve enough problems, you get to go home.'"

"That was a character in a book," Lyra says.

"Doesn't mean he's wrong," I say as I leave the cockpit.

I can hear Lyra shaking her head at me as Leo and I walk aftward.

"Where are the drive coils?" Leo asks.

"Down on the engineering sub-deck," I say, crossing over to the access hatch on the floor and pushing the button.

The seal hisses slightly, and I am afraid that there might have been a malfunction in the safety sensors and that the engineering deck may be unpressurized. But a moment later we are not being sucked into the open hatch, and I breathe a very relieved sigh. Leo gives me a strange look, as if he realizes that we just dodged death again. I mean, maybe. I'm not going to tell him that, though.

The engineering deck is, surprisingly, a bit of a mess. I think it did lose atmosphere for a bit, which would explain at least one of the wrenching explosions that I heard right after the missile hit us. I look around after Leo and I climb down and locate a pair of breather masks for us and hand one to Leo.

"Will we need these?" Leo asks.

"It's a mess down here," I say. "The deck obviously lost pressure at least for a bit. We'll need to see what the problem is before we can assess anything else."

Leo nods and puts on the mask. Our priority just became finding the hull breach and figuring out if it needs further attention. I press the button on the vox box mounted to the wall beside us.

"Grendia," I say.

"Jarokin," she says back.

"We're down here, and it's obvious it lost pressure at some point. We have to find the breach and make sure it's secure before we can assess the drive coils," I say.

"Copy that, but hurry," Grendia answers. "The drive coils are fluctuating, and if they don't get stabilized soon we're not making it back to Earth."

"Copy that," I say and switch the vox off.

"Well, that's grim," Leo says.

"Nah," I say, doing my best to make a confident face from behind the breather mask. "This is gonna be cake."

This is *not* cake. It's nothing like cake.

I tilt my head to the side, hoping that the altered angle of what I am looking at will help me assess the problem and figure out a solution. The missile head is poking into the hull of the ship. It's like it was made of something harder than diamond. Probably is. The missile's nose looks like a drill bit. Must have had a rotational spin on its axis when it hit. Very nasty stuff. Not sure even the energy shields at full power could have stopped it.

"Is that gonna explode?" Leo is hiding behind me, using my body as a shield between himself and the missile.

"No," I say. "It's already done its damage. See all the exposed wiring halfway down the body of the missile?"

Leo pokes out from behind me and takes a quick look at the warhead.

"Yeah," he says, ducking back.

There's no way he saw it.

"Well," I say, walking toward the missile, "it's plugging its own hole in the hull right now. So, I guess that's good. But that won't hold forever. We'll need to fastweld around the missile to make sure it doesn't retreat out of the hole it made and leave us back in a worse spot."

I inspect the area around the break and realize what happened. The drilling motion of the missile's nose not only pierced the armor, but it also super-heated it to the point that some of it became molten as the missile passed through. It cooled quickly, but not too quickly that it didn't fuse to the missile's body, temporarily sealing the breach. But that will not last forever.

"Leo," I say.

"Yeah, Jack?" he answers.

"In that toolbox there, a device that looks a bit like a nail gun. Grab it for me and bring it over."

Leo opens the toolbox and roots around in it for a moment before coming up with a triumphant look on his face, holding the tool aloft in victory.

"This?" he asks.

"Yep." I nod, and he swiftly brings it over, stepping back again once it successfully changes hands.

A few minutes later I am staring at the weld line I fused between the ship's hull and the body of the missile. I made sure to cut into the missile and weld solid joints internally as well, ensuring that the missile won't spring a leak and turn into a straw through which Leo and I would get sucked out into space after being compressed into blood-and-bone milkshakes. I shudder a bit at the thought and turn back to Leo.

"Okay, well, we won't be sucked out into space while we're fixing the drive coils," I say.

"I'm not comfortable with how casual you are about that," Leo says.

"Oh come on," I say, clapping him on the shoulder. "No reason to be like that. You're currently in the least amount of danger you've been in all night."

"Am I?" he asks.

"Y—yeah," I say.

"You hesitated there," Leo says as I walk past him toward the aft, where I will find the drive coils.

"I did?" I ask. "Hmm…doesn't seem like something I'd do."

"Not funny, Jack!" Leo protests as he follows me down the narrow corridor.

*　　*　　*

"Are those supposed to be so…technicolor?" Leo asks.

The drive coils, all four of them, are rapidly pulsing in multiple colors and at random intervals. No. They are *not* supposed to be doing that. This should be fun.

"Well," I say, "no."

"I don't suppose welding them back together will be the answer again, huh?" Leo asks, holding up the welding gun.

I shake my head as I look around for the diagnostic panel. Spotting it, I walk over to it and press a button. Nothing happens. I hit the panel. Still nothing. It was worth a try. I may have spent too long on Earth. Hitting sensitive equipment to make it work properly again isn't a real thing. But I'm not going to be the one who dispels the human notion that it is possible.

"Probably not," I say.

Now this one is going to be interesting. Plasma drive conduits, not too unlike the one that I jabbed with my dagger on Jorr's ship, can be fickle things. From what I can see, it just looks like the EMP blast that rocked the ship de-synced the coil sequence when it fried the other systems. There's probably a better way to do what I'm thinking I am going to do, but I'm not an engineer. So, bad idea it is.

I walk over to the vox box in this room and press the button. "Uhh, hey."

"I don't like the sound of that at all," Lyra responds.

"What's wrong, Jarokin?" Grendia asks, her voice strained.

"Well, the digital diagnostic and control panel for the drive coils is fried," I say. "Not sure how long, or even *if* it can be repaired without some serious downtime. But, we don't have that kind of luxury right now."

"We do not," Grendia says, and I become suspicious that there is something she is not telling me.

"What aren't you telling me," I ask.

Pause.

"Nothing," Lyra says.

"Grendia…" I say.

"Well…we're…" she stammers before she pauses again.

"Grendia…" I say again.

"We're coming up on Earth *really, really* fast because the pulsing of the drive coils has us in a super-sublight speed. I'm not sure we're going to be able to slow down enough to make a safe atmosphere entry, meaning we might just skip off the atmosphere and…"

"Become some pretty sky lights for someone in Asia, mostly likely," I finish the thought for her.

"Yeah…" Grendia says.

"Well," I say, "best I can do then is try a manual reset of the drive coils. They might come back online, or they might not. Either way, our speed will be fixed, and our only hope is for the drive coils to come back online in time for you to hit the breaks and control our entry."

"That's how it is, yeah," Grendia says.

Lyra cuts into the conversation. "Okay, now that you two have figured all that out, do it."

"Do you still need Leo down there?"

"I don't," I say. "Not for what I have to do."

"Good. Leo, get your butt back up here and strap back into your seat, now," Lyra orders.

Leo and I exchange nods of understanding. Even if he wanted to stay with me, there's no way he's going to risk us surviving this and then having to face disobeying his sister. I don't blame him, and I watch him walk away toward the hatch to the main deck.

"He's on his way," I report.

"Okay," Grendia says. "Run the reset cycle quickly, and get back up here. We don't have much time."

"Roger that," I say and switch off the vox.

The manual controls for the plasma drive reset are not hard to find. Grendia and I know the risks, and I could hear it in her voice when she spoke: this kind of thing doesn't always work. Manually resetting something this sophisticated, roughly the alien equivalent of a human unplugging a sensitive data server while it's still running, is a twitchy thing. Still, it's the only shot we have. I prefer maybe dead to definitely dead.

I open the panel for the manual controls and pause my hands at the toggle switches. This is still pretty risky, no matter the situation. I grab the handle for the main power drive, take two breaths, and pull it down in one swift motion. Main power for the entire ship shuts down, with battery backups kicking in less than a second later to keep some low-level lights and the air processors running. I float off the floor as the gravity gyro spins down. Sneakers aren't exactly made for space travel and thus do not have magnets in the soles for gripping the decking.

Now that I think about it, I really hope I left Leo enough time to get to his seat before I shut off the gravity. Oops.

One. Two. Three. Four…

It's kinda like resetting a modem, really. You have to let the system purge its memory and default to previous programming.

That's the theory, anyway. Interesting how human technology picked up on that little nuance of pretty much all technology in the galaxy. Must be one of those laws of technology that binds the universe, or whatever science people would call it.

Ten.

I flip the main power switch back into the engaged position, and nothing happens.

"Oh, right!" I say. I reach over and press the breaker button to re-engage the connection, and I am rewarded with the sound of the drive beginning its start-up cycle. The gravity gyro engages a few seconds later, and the moment my feet hit the floor, I am running for the access hatch to get to the cockpit before we hit Earth.

39

"You could have warned me about the gravity thing," Leo says as I run into the cockpit and start strapping myself into a seat.

"Yeah, sorry, um, is it the time for this?" I ask, rapidly locking my webbing into place.

"Oh, I'm sorry," Leo says. "Are you busy?"

"Shut up, both of you!" Grendia says. She slaps a red button with enough force that I think I hear it crack and the atmospheric entry retro boosters engage, throwing us all into our crash webbing with a massive amount of g-force that I don't want to think about.

All of my collected war wounds and injuries scream out at once, reminding me that I've been fairly thoroughly beaten and battered for pretty much the last twenty-four hours.

"Oof," I grunt as the pain hits me in a solid wave.

Earth looks really beautiful, and I think that it is odd that my mind has the spare processors to take notice of that fact. The planet is filling the viewport, and I feel a sense of pride and possessiveness about the blue marble in front of me that I haven't felt in a long time, not since I left Prentia decades ago. Lyra is right. In the time that I've spent here, Earth has become my real home, not just the place that I chose to hide out from the galaxy.

The retro boosters scream in protest, and all of the screens go red.

"That's not good, right?" Lyra says, her face now tinted bright red by the plethora of red screens and lights all around us.

None of us have the time to answer her as the ship hits Earth's atmosphere and we are rocked hard by the resistance it attempts to bring against the foreign object attempting to breach its perimeter. The ship bucks violently, but we do not explode. Grendia is somehow still managing to flip switches and keep a hand on the control yoke as we dive down toward Earth's surface.

As the ship bucks one last time, something explodes. I would guess it is one of the main engines. At least it's not the drive core. At least, please, don't be the drive core.

"We've lost engine two!" Grendia screams out.

Oh good, just an engine. We can survive that.

Another explosion.

"And engine one!" Grendia adds.

Okay, that makes landing safely a bit more complicated. Engines tend to help with the whole planetary gravity issue.

The ship stops vibrating, which means we are successfully in the atmosphere. One more problem solved. On to the next one.

I turn to the controls at my station. I am in the navigator's seat, and within moments I have global positioning and flight data up on my screen.

"Hey," I say, "you're *not* gonna believe where we are."

"Try me," Grendia says.

"We're on target for eastern Kentucky," I say.

There is a moment of silence from everyone else in the cockpit.

"So we're going to land basically back where we took off from?" Leo asks.

"Kinda," I say.

Grendia looks at the navigational data and turns her head to give me an incredulous look.

"No," she says, "not just *kinda*."

"What do you mean?" Lyra asks.

Grendia turns back forward and sets her jaw. "We're going to crash into the convention center."

"Oh…" Lyra says.

"The good news is that we're going to make it in around the time the vendor hall opens," I say.

Everyone slowly turns to look at me.

"What?" I ask.

I turn to the control panel, my eyes sifting through the data rapidly flashing from a dozen different readouts. There's no way that hitting the convention center dead on would play out like in a movie. People are going to get hurt, and I can't accept that. There has to be a way to avoid human casualties. Something has to be here, and…

"There!" I yell, pointing to a screen near Grendia.

"What?" Grendia yells back, her eyes following my pointing finger to the display screen.

"Push that button!" I scream.

Grendia slams a fist into the button without asking for an explanation, and we are all rocked sideways as a port thruster, the only one still operational according to the control panel, roars to life. The ship's fall is not slowed, but that was not my intent. The change in thrust has turned us from our collision course with the convention center, and we are now, according to the flight computer, headed straight for a used car lot about a block away from the convention center.

"Prepare for impact!" Grendia says.

"The retro boosters have one more burst stored in them," Lyra reports. She has learned a lot very quickly.

"We'll hold until the last possible moment to mitigate our crash as much as possible," Grendia says.

There is very little I can do at this point but wait the remaining moments before we hit. Something else in the back makes a shrieking, tearing sound, and I guess that part of the hull plating has just been ripped off by the wind that is whipping around the ship. Less hull means less weight on impact, but that does mean that pieces of a Prentian Royal starship are now being scattered over the Kentucky countryside. I'm sure that won't come back to haunt me.

I get an idea and start searching through the ship's inventory logs, hoping for a last-minute miracle that could keep us in the clear. My eyes grow wide when I read one line on the manifest, and I turn to Grendia.

"Hey, it looks like we have a—" but I do not get to finish my sentence as the ship takes out a row of light poles and plows into the used car lot, sending cars, trucks, and pieces of alien spaceship flying in every direction.

I see Lyra and Leo pass out due to the force of the impact, and Grendia makes a painful scream as I see blood spurt out from somewhere on the front of her torso. The ship buckles and bends as it merges with cars and asphalt of the car lot. Several of my own injuries open back up or re-break as the ship continues its wrecking ball landing.

A few seconds later, the crash is over. Well, we've stopped moving downward, at any rate. The viewport is completely blocked by fenders, headlights, and chunks of parking lot, and I have no real sense of where we have actually ended up.

I unfasten my crash webbing and move across the cockpit to check on Lyra. I sigh when I see her breathe. She probably has a broken rib or two, but who doesn't at this point? Leo groans as he regains consciousness. He opens his eyes and looks at me with concern as I stand over Lyra. I give him a smile and a thumbs up to let him know Lyra appears to be okay, and I turn around to see how Grendia fared.

She is unconscious, and bleeding from a short piece of rebar that somehow pierced the hull and jabbed her in the side, but she is breathing. I am not worried just yet. Breathing is always a good sign. After a few tries to wake her, she jumps to consciousness and lets out a painful roar as I attempt to limit her from moving.

"You have something in your side," I say.

"Always knew you were a genius," she says, coughing. Fortunately, she does not cough up any blood, but a cough could mean her lung on that side is damaged.

"Can you move?" I ask.

"If you get this webbing off me, yeah, maybe," she says.

Lyra is awake now, and Leo helps her out of her webbing as I help Grendia. The four of us walk out of the cockpit and into the main deck area. We walk across to the hatch, and I press a button to open the door and let down the boarding ramp. They do not appear to be blocked, which brings me some relief. I pause at a storage locker, reading the number on the door, and I open it, grabbing what is inside it and putting it in my pocket. Grendia spares me a puzzled expression, and I just shake my head as I help her to the top of the ramp. There is light at the bottom, and we take our first steps down.

At the bottom, we are met with thunderous applause as the ramp deposits us onto a sidewalk where I see a very confused-looking MC standing at a raised podium and a gathered crowd of humans in cosplay outfits. Grendia and I both give a wary wave toward the mob of at least a thousand people, maybe more, staring at us in disbelief and shouting at the top of their lungs.

Of course. The Downtown Cosplay Parade. QUASITASTICON always does that on Sunday morning. And we have arrived just in time.

"And look!" the man at the podium says. "It's the mystery hotel lobby fight crew, back for another special demonstration of what they can do!"

The crowd goes wild, another round of cheers going out when Leo and Lyra reach the bottom of the ramp.

"Noooo!" a voice from behind a pile of mangled cars calls out. Grendia and I only have time to exchange looks of confirmation before the pile of cars is torn in the middle by an energy blast. Niolan emerges from the chaos as I try to shout above the din for the crowd to get back, but they only cheer louder, believing this to also be part of the show.

Niolan looks like he's been shot, stabbed, blown up, and burned by a blowtorch, but I would still recognize the crazy look in his gaze no matter what planet we crashed into. He is holding a plasma blade in his hand, and I can see in his one remaining eye what he plans to do with it.

"I'll kill you if it's the last thing I do, Jarokin!"

As he rushes forward, Grendia plants her feet and pushes me out of the way. I stumble back and land hard on my back. Fearing that Grendia has just sacrificed herself to protect me, I roll to my side and get up just in time to see Grendia produce a blaster from under her jacket. Before I can do anything more, she aims and fires, hitting Niolan in the forehead. Niolan's body flies back from the impact of the bolt and disintegrates in mid-air before it has a chance to hit the cars behind him.

The street is absolutely silent for several seconds before someone in the crowd lets out with a huge, "YEEEEEAAAAAAHHHHHHH!" and the crowd goes wild, unable to contain itself any longer.

40

"Jarokin," Grendia says to me under the din of the crowd. "What do we do?"

She looks freaked out. We just crashed a ship into a used car lot right next to a street parade of a thousand humans. I really hope we didn't kill anybody. Doesn't seem like it, based on the lack of humans running around asking for help because a space ship just fell on their loved ones. So, there's a win.

"Just follow my lead," I say. "I have an idea."

I walk over to Leo and Lyra and make sure they are okay. "How are you guys doing?"

"What kind of question *is* that?" Lyra asks. "This is way more attention than I'd ever want. Ever. And all of your secrets are exposed now. Isn't…isn't that really bad?"

Leo looks just as freaked out as Lyra, and I don't blame them. The situation *is* really bad. They're not wrong. We all turn and wave at the crowd, and the MC standing at the podium waves at us to come over to him. Something needs to be said, for sure. But what?

"How do we get out of this, Jarokin?" Grendia asks as I walk past her to the podium.

"I have one more ace up my sleeve, courtesy of my mother," I say.

Grendia gives me a look of mixed surprise and horror. I have to be quick about this. Can't let there be time for the humans to catch on that this whole thing really is what it appears to be.

"Hello, QUASITASTICON 9!" I say as I get up to the podium. The crowd cheers for a few moments longer before calming down a bit. Somewhere behind the ship, a car explodes, sending a fireball into the air as if on queue. I wince, but the crowd only cheers in response, as if it's all part of the show.

This is a decision point for me. I can feel it. Everything is about to change. The old life I had just a couple of days ago, that's gone now. There's too much at stake to cling to that old life. Not that I'll be leaving all of it behind. No, far from it. Lyra's coming with me if that's what she wants, too. And Leo and Grendia, too. But no more Jack the Shadow Market Vendor.

No. I have to do this. I lean forward, toward the microphone, and then I change everything.

"My name is Jack Grant, and I'm sure a least a few of you have seen some of the pretty cool special effects shows we've been putting on this week, right?"

The crowd goes bananas again for a moment, and I wait for them to calm down. While I wait, I pull out the item in my pocket. It's a much more advanced version than the one I used earlier. A standard issue device in all Prentian ships sent out into the galaxy. The irony is that it was my mother's idea to make them a standard-issue piece of equipment. Not out of a want to help anyone, mind you. No, she was thinking only of Prentia and what the rest of the galaxy might think if a Prentian delegation or soldier, or her son, violated intergalactic law. Or even worse, made Prentia look bad. Can't have that.

I set the Fix-It-All device on the podium as I wait and press the button. Just like the smaller, less sophisticated one that I used in the hotel lobby, this one begins its pretty light show, sending out millions of nano repair bots to seek out and deliver their services to the destroyed materials nearby. I press a couple more buttons on the device to give them some direction, and the clean-up commences. The crowd is stunned into silence, and Grendia, Lyra, and Leo step up next to me as the little bots start their work.

"Yes," I say, getting the attention of the crowd back on me, at least mostly, "this is some amazing special-effects technology, but I can assure you that at no time was any single one of you in any real danger. It may have seemed like it, yes, but that's the magic of this new technology. We chose to debut to the world our new technology here at QUASITASTICON 9 because we knew you all were a crowd who would appreciate what it could do. Beginning with the LARP shows at the hotel and later during the cosplay contest, and culminating in this grand finale here today. I can confidently, I believe, say that the technology is a success, right?"

The crowd roars once more. The whole time I have been talking, the nanobots have been hard at work, cleaning up the mess. I instructed them to use Grendia's ship as extra building materials in the repair process, so the used cars at Lance's Auto Bonanza and Insurance Depot are about to get a Prentian tech upgrade that includes space flight worth materials and, perhaps in some cases depending on exactly how the bots do the work, a slight technology boost that I'm sure won't cause any problems.

"What is your company called?" someone in the crowd shouts out.

"I can't say at this time," I respond. And I can't. I have not thought that far ahead with this just yet, but I should do so in the near future, I think.

"We are preparing a more formal press release that will be forthcoming in the next few weeks. For now, suffice it to say that there is something big coming to the entertainment and fandom industry, and you, the fans, are going to be the first ones to hear, see, and use the new technology this time around!"

This draws a last, huge surge of supportive cheering from the crowd, and I stand there for a few moments, waving. I motion for the MC to join me back at the podium, and we shake hands as I turn the podium back over to them. We gather ourselves together and start walking along the sidewalk back toward the hotel. I pause and shake a few hands in the crowd and hang back just a moment longer than the others, telling them to go on ahead. I need to stay just a few minutes longer to see the nanobots finish their job. When the last of the light show fades away, the crowd is in awe, and I take my leave. A little magic is good for a crowd, but there's still a lot to be done now that I've set the ball rolling.

"You've changed everything now," Grendia says when I rejoin them.

Lyra moves in front of me and stops me from walking, wrapping me in a big, tight hug. I don't care what hurts as she hugs me. It's worth it.

"Are we safe now?" she asks.

"The danger of last night is over," I say. "Yes, we are safe."

"What are we going to do now?" she asks, refusing to let go of me. "Will you…will you have to go now? Will you leave?"

She is crying, and I look over to Leo who also appears to be getting emotional about the prospect that Grendia and I are going to have to leave.

"No," I say. "We're not going to leave. But things *are* going to change a bit."

"Wh…what things?" Lyra asks. She still seems unsure if she should be emotional right now, and it's causing a lump to form in my throat as well.

"We have plenty of time to discuss it later," I say. "But for now, I think we can still make it to the vendor hall."

"Work?" Lyra asks. "You just want us to go back to work? I look terrible. I haven't showered. I've been to space! I saw the moon! Like…THE MOON! And now I'm just supposed to sit in my booth surrounded by rocks for the rest of the day?"

"Well," I say, looking to Grendia and Leo for support. I find none. "Yeah, for now. It's the best we can do."

Lyra looks at me skeptically. "You're up to something new now, aren't you?"

"Maybe." I shrug. "But you're gonna have to wait for our second date to find out what."

Lyra punches my arm and hugs me again. "Wow. This was our *first* date. How are you going to top this one, Jarokin?"

My ears buzz and butterflies come to life in my stomach as I hear Lyra use my real name for the first time. It is a euphoria that I didn't know could exist. I'm myself with her now. Wow.

"I'm sure I'll think of something," I say.

*   *   *

We decide to head back to our respective hotel rooms to at least change clothes before we all head to the vendor hall. It makes us a little bit late, which puts the QUASITASTICON 9 vendor coordinator into a bit of a tizzy, but all seems to be okay otherwise.

The floor is abuzz with the excitement of the day, and business is better than it ever is on the last day of a con. At least, it is for my booth and for Lyra's. Everyone wants to talk to the four of us, to try to find out what has been going on all weekend. It's not like the "shows" aren't all over social media at this point, but people want access to the people involved, and part of me can't blame them. I mean, the way that I presented it is that this was exactly our intention.

I start to notice that some of the shadow vendors are avoiding my presence or my eye contact. They are skittish, and understandably so. I've pretty much brought us all dangerously close to being out in the open. The two exceptions to the shadow vendors who are willing to talk to acknowledge me are Kinno, to whom I owe not only a drink but also an incredible apology, and

Hal. Kinno tells me that he expects the drink conversation to be worth it, and I doubt I will disappoint him. Like me, he's been on Earth for a really long time. So the excitement of my weekend is going to thrill him like a streaming service action movie.

Hal, on the other hand, is just plain weird. He waves at me to get my attention, and I sigh as I walk over to see what he wants. I know I should just ignore him, but his stupidity might brighten my day somehow.

"Hey, Jack!" he says as if we're good old friends who are about to continue the same conversation we've been having for years.

"Hal," I say.

"So, uhh, no hard feelings about all that other business, right?" Hal asks, his eyes glancing over my shoulder, I would guess to see if Grendia is nearby.

"Oh, Hal," I say, smiling and taking his hand to shake it. I pull him close in a similar manner to how we spoke before the show. "Of course there's hard feelings, you little maggot. You nearly got Leo and Lyra killed, not to mention me captured. We all almost blew up, and in case you missed it we crashed a whole damn ship into a used car lot in downtown Lexington not an hour ago. So yeah, there's some hard feelings. So guess what I'm not gonna see from you anymore?"

I step back just enough to look him straight in the eyes, but I keep my hold on his hand, tightening my grip to make sure he gets the point I am making. His whole body tenses, his palm growing damp with sweat as he glances around nervously. Nobody is paying any attention to us at the moment, as we are hidden fairly well by the mess of Hal's booth.

"Jack," he squeaks out, "of course. Anything you say. I'm gonna pay my taxes and get right with the humans, so there's no danger whatsoever to the shadow market ever again."

"And I don't want to see you at any con I'm at ever again," I say.

He looks up at me in shock. The hurt on his face may be real. I don't care.

"O…okay, Jack," he stammers. "Just, please. Please don't ever send *her* after me again."

"Hal, if you stray again, give help to the wrong people, and I hear about it, I promise you that Grendia will be the last person you ever see."

I think he just wet himself. I tap him lightly on the cheek with my other hand before letting him out of the handshake.

"Good talk," I say, and I walk out of his booth.

When I get back to the booth, Grendia is animatedly talking to a small group of fans about the special effects shows that we have been putting on, promising that there will be more information coming soon. The group, all teenage girls from what I can see, all want to take selfies with Grendia, telling her again and again how absolutely badass she was for pushing me out of the way and shooting "that creepy alien guy" who ran at her with the huge knife.

I turn away from the Grendia Fan Club to see who else is in the booth. A woman in a flowing purple robe has just walked in and is looking at some of my most expensive collectibles. I walk up to greet her.

"Hello," I say, "is there something I can help you with?"

"Tell me, Jarokin," she says, "is this *really* what makes you happy? Was running away from home really worth all of…this?"

I open my mouth to try to form an answer before my brain properly comprehends what has just been said. I stare at her in disbelief. She just called me Jarokin. And she's…no. Can't be. The likelihood of that is. Well, I mean, considering the last twenty-four hours, not that unlikely, really. Still.

"Are you going to just stare at me, Jarokin, or are you going to say something?" she asks.

My knees get weak, and my mouth is suddenly dry. She can't actually be here. This isn't possible.

"Mother?" I say.

41

"What are you doing here?" I ask my mother when we are in my hotel room and the door is shut.

"Well, I'm here for you, obviously," she says, as if the past two decades of separation had vexed her no more than if I had stepped out to get some milk at the corner store.

"What do you mean, here for me?" I ask. My tone is not respectful. The one person I left Prentia to get away from, the one who drove my whole odyssey across the stars that eventually brought me to Earth, is standing in my hotel room, and I am terrified of what all that means.

"Well, originally I came to bring you home," she says.

"But Niolan and Grendia—" I start, but she interrupts me.

"Oh, that fool of a girl never knew I was following them, and Niolan followed my orders perfectly as instructed; too perfectly from the look of you," she says, looking me over and spotting the telltale signs of many of my injuries.

"And what does *that* mean?" I ask. I am losing my patience. She hasn't changed. This is all a game to her. It's just that in games my mother plays nobody is allowed to have fun except for her.

"Well," she says, pausing to look around at the room. I have never known her to have trouble finding the right words. More likely she's appalled at the "peasant"-level accommodations I am living in presently. "I had to know for sure that you were still worthy of the Prentian throne, Jarokin."

"By having Niolan try to kill me!" I have instant rage. She's exactly the same. This is the new worst possible day ever, which happens to be following the previous worst possible day ever.

Where does this insanity end?

"I didn't tell him to kill you," she says, shaking her head in disappointment. "You must have driven him to that point all by yourself. And I have to admit I'm not surprised you were able to do that. You do have that effect on people."

"I take that as a compliment," I say through gritted teeth. "So where does that leave us, then? You know I'm here. You know how I have been surviving all this time. I'm beginning to think that you've known for a while and just didn't tell Grendia. And what about the bounty hunters, huh? You sent them, too?"

"Well," she says, casually taking a seat in a chair after passing on the prospect of lowering herself onto the couch, "I had to make it look convincing, didn't I?"

"Mother! You're impossible!" I scream.

"And you're a derelict prince who ran away when his responsibilities became too much for his sensitive nature to handle!"

"That's *not* why I left!" I yell. "*You* are literally the worst person. IN. THE. UNIVERSE. And I know, because now I've seen most of it, and there's nobody out there worse than you. You manipulate. You lie. You put me in ridiculous amounts of danger. You don't care if anybody that I care about gets in the way or dies because of your insane games. So I'm done! I have been done. For twenty years, Mother! Didn't you get the hint when I left? I'm done being Prince Jarokin because I can't stand another moment being your son!"

She is silent throughout my rant, and I know that nothing I have said will have hurt her. She has no feelings. Never has. My father is only still alive because he's the royal blood. I'm only still alive for the same reason. Well, kinda, I guess, seeing as how she didn't exactly care if I died because of her whole Everybody-try-to-kill-Jarokin game.

"You've not grown up at all," she says. "Still the same selfish boy that you ever were."

"Mother," I say, my voice calmer. "Did you not hear anything I said just now? I'm...DONE. WITH. YOU."

She guffaws at my insistence that I am done with her and waves her hand. "Well, that may or may not be true, Jarokin, but there are other people who are not done with you. And you would be wise to accept my help in dealing with them."

"What *other people*?" I ask. "You're the only one who has been sending people after me. If you would just call them off, then I won't have to deal with anybody else. See how that works? It all comes back to your insanity."

"Well, maybe and maybe not," she says, her voice pitchy in a sing-songy kind of tone that is a clear drop she is hiding some key piece of information from me.

"Mother," I say. "What are you not telling me?"

"Nothing," she says quickly. She's a good liar, but I'm her son. I may not like that I inherited part of her, but I did.

"Mother," I say again.

"What?" she asks.

"*Mother*," I say, putting the tone of authority behind my voice that I know brings her pride for me to use, but I am done playing this part of the game.

"Oh, it's nothing," she says. "Our activities here on Earth, especially your 'Grand Finale' entrance back to the planet today, have attracted the attention of authorities that even our crown may not fully protect you from."

So, she heard about my speech to the crowd. But that's for later. Intergalactic level authorities *do* exist for the purpose of intervening and regulating commerce, travel, and, when necessary, conflict between star systems and larger governmental bodies when those issues threaten the balance of galactic stability and security. That's not to say wars don't happen. There are probably several dozen raging across the stars right now, but the Authority, as it is most often referred to, is there for when the galaxy gets more unruly than it is civilized. To have their attention, things have to be bad.

"I was fine here, Mother," I say. "You were the one who sent everybody after me and made it so that Earth has been exposed. This is on you."

"It's on *us*," she retorts.

"No," I say.

"Well, *they* disagree," she says.

So *that's* why she's really here. Her games have finally got her in trouble with the Authority. Pushing things too far as a way of life has finally become a problem for her as well as for me.

"Oh, no," she continues, "the problem is not *mine*. In fact, they have no idea I am involved in any of this, and I doubt they would believe it or care if they were told so. No, they have a problem with *you*, Jarokin. And I'm here as a courtesy to tell you that the Prentian crown will not be extending its protection to you in this matter. Earth has been your problem since the moment you sat foot on it. And now, thanks to *your* actions, there are Authority agents on their way here now to collect you and take you to your trial on *Unbeknownst*. I only wanted to lay eyes on you one last time, my son, before you are carted off, never to be seen again."

As she is speaking, my heart begins to race. The Authority *has* to know they're being manipulated. She's done this. But why?

"Why?" I ask.

"It's for your own good, Jarokin," she says. My mother rises from the chair and walks across the room, wrapping me in a light hug that is a perfect metaphor for all of the love and affection I received as a child. Cold and done only for show.

"Heh," I chuckle as I step away from her. "My own good.

Not that you would ever know anything that was for my own good."

There is a knock at the door. So soon? Is that the Authority? Grendia? Oh no! Please don't be Lyra or Leo! Meeting my mother and putting them on her radar would be the absolute worst thing in the galaxy. We might as well have all blown up during one of our many opportunities last night than endure my mother learning of my affection for Lyra.

"I would answer that," my mother says.

My eyes narrow, and I reflexively drop my hand to a spot inside my jacket that is now empty. Didn't have time to get new weapons before starting our day. Didn't think I'd need any. I'm a fool. I walk over and open the door.

"Jack Grant," a lady says. She is holding a Lexington Police Department badge in her hand and is accompanied by a large fellow, both in suits.

"Yes?" I say.

"I'm Detective Josephs," she says. "You need to come with us."

42

"Of course," I say. "I can come right now if that works for you."

Detective Josephs and her partner appear to be pleased with my willingness to go with them. I exit my room, closing the door behind me. No need to give them the chance to ask any questions about who might be in the room with me. My mother can look after herself anyway, and I'm not concerned with how she does so. We were done talking anyway. At least I was.

"That works for us, Mr. Grant," Josephs says. "This is Detective Yates. Please follow him to the elevators, and we will walk you to our car."

"Your car?" I ask. "Going downtown, are we?"

"We would prefer to talk to you at the station, yes," Josephs says. "Unless you object to that?"

"I'm guessing you're not going to tell me what this is about until we're somewhere more secure, are you?" I ask, following Yates down the hallway.

"No," Josephs responds.

"Am I under arrest?" I ask.

"Not at this time." Her voice is clipped.

I send a text message to Grendia that I am about to be questioned by the Lexington PD. She replies, asking if I need assistance, and I tell her that I do not. I'm not exactly sure what this is about, but if I had to hazard a guess, it's likely something about crashing a ship into a used car lot. Or, at least making it *look* like I crashed a spaceship into a used car lot.

I would be naive if I didn't expect something like this to

happen eventually. I've spent a whole weekend causing a terrible ruckus, and there's basically no evidence to show that any of what's in the viral internet videos was real, fake, or part of some kind of crime or not. I don't blame the police for having no idea what to make of all of it. But there is one good thing that the arrival of Detectives Josephs and Yates has brought me. Time. It is unlikely that any agents of the Authority will attempt to bother me while I am in the custody of Earth law enforcement. That would not be a good move on their part. So I have some time to think about how to handle that situation. The problem is, I have no idea what they will say I have done wrong.

*　　*　　*

They make me wait in an interrogation room for over an hour. I'm missing all the fun of the last day of the con, and that's making me a little grumpy. After all the effort I put into surviving the past three days, you would think the universe might let me at least enjoy one last day of the event. But nope. This is the con from hell, and the Lexington Police Department is making sure I know it, too.

The door finally opens and in walks Josephs and Yates. They have removed their jackets, no doubt to make it seem like questioning me is a more casual affair. I've seen this kind of thing on TV, but I didn't know that real detectives actually do things like this. I wonder which one will be the bad cop?

"Comfortable, Mr. Grant?" Yates asks.

I shrug. "Just lonely. But you're here now, so I'm getting better."

Yates has a good poker face, but not a perfect one. He wasn't expecting that kind of answer. Maybe he's new at this? I would have thought criminals are way more clever than I am at split-second one-liners.

"I'll cut to the chase, Mr. Grant, so I don't waste anybody's time," Josephs says, ignoring my exchange with Yates. "You feature in quite a few viral internet videos that have been posted this weekend. Videos that show a hyper-realistic amount of violence, destruction, and death. Yet you claim that all of these videos are just a 'show' that apparently are put on with the help of some new kind of special effects technology that you announced today after, seemingly, crashing some kind of spaceship into a used car lot in downtown Lexington, not two blocks from convention center."

I listen with a passive face as Josephs gives her summary of the weekend. They haven't missed much, except for all of the important stuff.

"We even have security cam video of one of your little 'shows' in the alleyway behind the convention center," Josephs says.

Oh wow! There was a security cam that caught that?

Josephs turns her tablet toward me and shows the security cam video of Bossy's men dragging me into the alley, Grendia's grand entrance, and the fight that ensued. In the video it looks like I fare much better than I actually did, and I am at least happy that me getting my ass thoroughly kicked looked somewhat as cinematic as I imagined it at the time.

"Yeah," I say. "That's one of the shows all right."

"But there was no audience," Yates says. He's standing off to the right, leaning on the wall instead of in a chair across from me at the table. I'm not sure yet if he's waiting for an opportunity to be the bad one.

"Looks like there was," I say, pointing to the tablet. "I doubt you're the only ones who have seen this camera footage."

Josephs' eyebrows sink down a notch at my answer. She's

not stupid, but my answer gives her nothing to go on. They're sniffing up all the right trees, but they aren't going to shake anything loose at the rate they're going.

"This fight looks pretty convincing to me," Josephs says, not letting up on the subject. "And I don't see much of the fancy pyrotechnics and special effects that are present in the other videos. Why is this one different?"

I shrug again. "It didn't need a lot of effects. Shortly after this we did another show in the Cosplay Contest Hall."

"Yes, that," Josephs says, turning the tablet back to her and selecting another video. "Convention staff says this was not planned and interrupted a scheduled event. In fact, nobody connected with the QUASITASTICON 9 event, the convention center, or the hotel had any idea that anything like your little cosplay shows would be taking place this weekend."

"Detective," I say, stopping her before she says something else, "I don't mean to be rude here, but are you leading up to a point? Have I broken any laws? Is there a reason the police have an interest in questioning me about any of this?"

Josephs frowns and leans back in her chair. Yates steps forward and puts his hands on the table, using his size to loom over me. I'm still not convinced he's gonna be the bad one, but the move is definitely in that direction.

"A detective went missing yesterday," Yates says.

"I'm sorry to hear that," I say.

"I bet you are. According to his last check-in, he was on his way to see you, Mr. Grant," Yates says, letting his statement hang for a moment.

Oh crap! Detective Sergeant Collins was *yesterday*? That was a really long day. Yeah, I guess he *is* missing. Well, not much I can do about that. Bossy's crew double-crossed him, and he was pretty much dead no matter what. Just a hard luck case there. But now I get why they are talking to me. I'm the last person that Collins is known to have spoken to.

"To see me?" I ask. I'm betting they don't know he actually did make contact with me, considering the circumstances he was in. "You guys are the first detectives I've spoken to."

"You sure about that, Mr. Grant?" Josephs asks.

I mean, it is a lie, sure, but I'm fairly certain that Collins would have covered his tracks pretty well while working for the bounty hunters. I decide to trust in Collins and lean into the lie.

"Yeah," I say. "It's news to me that another detective came to see me."

"We found his car parked in the convention center parking lot this morning," Josephs says. "Are you sure you never saw this man?"

She turns the tablet around again, and I see a picture of Detective Collins. I look down at the picture for a moment before looking back up, right into Josephs' eyes.

"I've never seen him before," I say. "Whatever he was doing at the convention center, he didn't come to see me."

"Mr. Grant, you're being far less helpful than we were hoping you would be," Josephs says, and Yates pounds a hand on the table and stands up.

"It sounds to me like you're not telling us everything you know, Mr. Grant," Yates says. "I think you did meet with Collins, and you may even know what happened to him. Hell, I'm willing to bet you're involved in his disappearance."

I do not let Yates' tirade affect me. He's looking for a response out of me, but I take a few breaths before I respond. What I say next may be the difference in my ability to get out of here any time soon or in needing to make myself comfortable for a while.

"I really wish I had something for you," I say, looking up at Yates and then looking to Josephs. "Nothing in those videos is anything but what I've told you—just a bunch of performance cosplayers showing off some new technology and having some fun at a convention. As far as your missing detective, well, the convention can be a pretty busy place, and I can't even hazard a guess as to where he might be."

I pause for a moment. They are letting me talk, to let me talk myself into a corner, no doubt, waiting for me to say something stupid. Well, that's not going to happen.

"Again, and for the last time, I *really* wish I could be of more help, but I just don't know anything," I say. "Am I free to go?"

Yates turns around to hide his face of anger and disappointment. Sorry, dude. I'm not going to give you what you want. Even if I could, the real explanation of what happened to Collins is *way* above your paygrade. Josephs closes her tablet and sighs.

"You're free to go, Mr. Grant," she says.

"Thank you, Detective," I say. "Any chance I can get a ride back to the convention center?"

"No," Josephs says, and Yates snickers as I get up to leave.

"Thank you for the hospitality," I say.

43

"No, they left me to get back on my own," I say. Grendia is on the phone. I am standing outside the front of the police station, waiting for my ride to get here.

"Rude," Grendia says. "Do you need me to come get you?"

"No, I can manage. I've already ordered a car to come pick me up and take me back to the convention center," I say.

"What about the other problem?" Grendia asks.

"Oh, my mother?" I ask.

"Yeah," she says. "I'm so sorry, Jarokin. By the time I realized who you were talking to, you were already on your way out of the booth. I had no idea she was on Earth. What happened with that? And then when you texted me about the police, I was incredibly worried."

"I didn't mean to cause you any concern," I say. "I handled my mother, at least as well as she will be handled for now. We have other problems on the horizon, but I don't think she'll be a problem for the moment."

"Really?" I can hear the disbelief in Grendia's voice. I don't blame her. My mother has been at the center of all of our recent troubles, and for her to suddenly not be an issue is a bit of a turn.

"I know, it's a tough one to believe, but she actually dropped an even bigger problem on me before the police knocked on my door. I'll have to tell you about it when I get back," I say.

My car pulls up to the curb in front of me, and I step forward to open the door. I get in the back and sit down, greeting the driver and confirming the details of my destination.

"I'm in the car now," I tell Grendia. "I'll see you soon."

When I get back to the convention center, I stop by my hotel room first. Mother is gone. I am not surprised. I access my lockbox and grab a new pistol. Nothing as exotic as a disintegrator this time, just a regular hold-out style laser pistol that will do in a pinch but is useless in a protracted fight. It's all I have left. I never had much of an arsenal anyway. I could count on three fingers the number of potentially lethal fights I've been in since arriving on Earth, before this weekend. The quiet was nice.

I head back down the vendor hall, and I see a relieved-looking Grendia when I walk back into the booth. I smile, and we both go back to helping customers. The crowds die down the closer to the end of the day we get, and eventually there is no one left. The five-minute warning is announced, and a few more people scramble to get some items they have been thinking about. But after that, things are quiet, and the breakdown begins.

*   *   *

"So you survived, too, eh?" Leo asks.

We are all standing around, waiting for the transport companies to finish collecting our pallets, so we can sign off on the shipments and get out of here. I'm hungry, as I haven't eaten anything all day, not since dinner last night, and I can feel myself beginning to get grumpy the longer we wait.

"Yeah," I say, "via a little visit from my mother and the Lexington PD."

Lyra's and Leo's eyes widen. I have not had a chance to update them on anything about the situation. Grendia only knows a little bit more than they do, and we all need to sit down and have a talk.

"So, it's not *really* over, is it?" Lyra asks.

I shake my head. "Not like I hoped it was this morning. We're not in any physical danger at the moment. The danger has moved into more of an existential plane of existence at this point."

"That's not better, Jack," Lyra says.

We let the subject drop until we finish up in the vendor hall, and we all walk out to head to the hotel restaurant. Once seated, I explain everything that has happened since this morning. Lyra and Leo go from faces of surprise, to shock, to concern, to confusion, and finally landing on staring out into space in a pale-faced stupor. Grendia might be keeping it together a bit better.

"So what do we do now?" Lyra asks.

"Well, my mother said that the Authority is coming for me," I say.

"Just for you?" Leo asks.

"I think so," I say, "but I'm not a hundred percent sure."

"Who *is* the Authority, really?" Lyra asks.

"It's a council of the most powerful individuals in the galaxy. Not personally powerful, but they are placed in their positions by the most powerful governments in the cosmos," Grendia says.

"Is your planet a member of the Authority?" Lyra asks.

"Yes and no," I say. "The Prentian government controls only a single star system. We're technologically advanced beyond most places, but only just enough to make it so that we're not as reliant on the intergalactic trade markets as most other systems. This puts Prentia in a weird place. The Authority can't put an economic squeeze on Prentia, but neither can Prentia present enough of a presence to demand an equal voice in the Authority. Prentia isn't the only system like this, and the Authority generally does not like dealing with such star systems. Tends to be a pain for everybody involved."

"But you're not under the protection of the Prentian crown

anymore," Leo says. "What does that mean?"

"Essentially, it means that my father and my mother are not willing to stick out their necks to save me politically. I don't know what might have changed in my absence. Grendia would know better than I, but this also does not surprise me. Father never used to let us get kicked around by the Authority, but something might have changed. More likely, as I'm talking about it out loud, is that my mother convinced him to withdraw his support of me in order to gain more standing with the Authority. She's always after more power and more standing in the intergalactic community. That's her way."

"I agree with Jarokin," Grendia says. "It is very likely that leaving him out in the cold is the queen's doing, though the king would have to agree to make it legally binding. I am sorry, Jarokin. I had no idea about any of this."

I shake my head. "It's not your fault, Grendia. They kept you in the dark on purpose in the hopes of using our connection to someday manipulate me should the need arise."

Grendia appears to take comfort in my words. Shortly after, the food arrives, and we move on to talk about other things. The last day of the convention was fun for the rest of them, and I wanted to hear all about their visits with their new fans. We talked a little about what my announcement at the podium would mean, and I laid out an initial plan that I came up with to figure out a way to buy a tech company that is working on some obscure technology and come up with a product that could be sold as a first generation of the "prototype" stuff we used this weekend.

"That's a huge leap," Lyra says after I am done explaining the initial plan. "From convention booth vendor to tech company owner."

"It is," I say, "but I can think of no other way to explain to the humans what has happened here this weekend. We're out of the Fix-It devices. I doubt I could get my hands on one even if Grendia and I somehow managed to get back into space and visit the nearest trading outpost. That's pretty rare technology. Luck was on our side, and there's no two ways about that."

Leo yawns and stretches. "Anybody up for a card game back at the hotel to finish out the night? Seems to me like all of this isn't going to work itself out tonight, and I need to wind down with a game or something before I sleep."

"I could drop right now," Lyra says, and Grendia nods in agreement with her.

I get where Leo is coming from, though. My body is tired and sore, but my mind is working on all of the new problems that have entered my orbit. There's a lot to do, but Leo is right. None of it will get done tonight.

"Yeah, Leo, that sounds like a good idea," I say. "I'll get the check and meet you all in the lobby."

I open the door to my hotel room, and the four of us file in. Leo is talking about the newest card game he picked up at the convention this weekend and how he can't wait to try it out. Lyra and Grendia seem less enthusiastic, but I think they understand that Leo needs the relaxing game time. And I think we do, too. We all need to remember, even just a little bit, what normal is like.

"You certainly took your time at dinner."

I am beat by Grendia at drawing my blaster as both of us step between the humans and the man sitting in the chair in the corner of the room. He has moved one of the lamps to be just behind him, and the effect is dramatic and imposing. Full marks to him for that one. Excellent dramatic entrance material right there.

"Who are you?" I ask. Grendia and I both have our blasters pointed at the man, but he makes no move for a weapon of his own. He casually puts down his cigar. Yeah, thanks for smoking in my non-smoking room, jackass. That's one deposit I won't be getting back.

"I am here on behalf of them," he says. He slowly reaches into his front jacket pocket and pulls out a small item. Leaning forward, he sets the item on the coffee table in front of him and leans back.

"The Authority," Grendia says.

I am looking at a badge of one of the Authority's field officers. So, they are here already. I thought it might take them longer, considering how big the universe is and how small a part Earth plays in the grand scheme. I am disappointed, and it shows on my face. I lower my pistol and nod for Grendia to do the same.

"I need you all to come with me," the man says.

"*All* of us?" Leo asks, poking his head over Grendia's shoulder.

The man nods. "Yes, Leo. You, your sister Lyra, Grendia, and *Prince* Jarokin. You're all coming with me."

44

I'm getting very tired of people needing me to go places with them. The latest in the line of law enforcement, Authority Agent Palle, is at least extending us the courtesy of not putting us in cuffs or bringing along armed goons to make sure we're compliant. Lyra and Leo had their objections at first, but Palle made it clear that the Authority could make a lot of trouble for Earth if they refused his polite request.

"Doesn't sound very polite to me now," Lyra says.

"I think that's as polite as he knows how to be," Leo responds.

"Uhh, guys," Grendia say. "He's right here, in the room."

"We know," Lyra says as she glowers at Palle.

Leo echoes the look, and Palle looks at me, as if expecting me to do something about their attitudes.

"It's not like humans are pets," I say. "They're people, just like you and me. I can't control them."

"We'll see," Palle says as we get on the elevator. Palle presses the button to go up instead of down, and Leo and Lyra look at me with puzzled looks.

"Ah, yeah," I say. "He isn't exactly taking us to the Authority by car."

Lyra sighs. "*Another* freaking spaceship?"

"I'm afraid so," Palle says. "The *Unbeknownst* doesn't make house calls."

"You aliens keep mentioning that place. What is it, exactly?" Leo asks.

"It's a space station, of sorts," I say, "located in a space between galaxies."

"*Between* galaxies?" Leo asks.

"Yeah," I say, "it's a little weird to get your head around if you don't know a few things about intergalactic space travel. There's what Earth scientists might call time travel, and weird science that doesn't make sense, and physics becoming magic and vice versa kinda stuff."

"Oh, magic," Lyra says. "That's all you had to say. Magic space stuff. That works for me."

"What?" I ask. "Seriously? That's all the explanation you need?"

"Well it's not as if we have time to learn the whys and hows in this elevator, do we?" Lyra responds.

I look to Palle, who has remained silent, and he just shrugs. "The human's understanding may be primitive, but I am impressed that she is willing to just accept what is."

"I'm *right here*, ya know," Lyra says.

"I know," Palle says, with a slight upturn in the corner of his mouth.

Leo laughs, and Grendia and Lyra can't help but join him. Palle might not be a bad guy individually, but the organization he represents has me scared. Grendia has an idea, I am sure, about what we are going to face, but the humans have no clue. The Authority could do anything. They could decide that Earth has been too exposed, too early ahead of schedule, and that could result in all kinds of problems. They could kill me for being the problem. Fortunately, the Authority *does* believe in the sanctity of life and civilization, but that also means that they play the survival game at the species level and not a rung below it. If we've somehow disrupted humanity's perceived progress too much, the four of us, and up to and including anybody we may have come into contact with, could be in serious danger of not being alive this time tomorrow.

Well, there *is* the Mind Wiper, I guess. It's just a rumor, but it could be real. They could just wipe our memories back to a certain date and make sure that things play out differently. I've heard about them doing that before. I'm not sure how often they play God like that, but the rumors have to come from somewhere, right?

The elevator doors open, and we exit out onto the roof. It looks pretty darn good for having been our crash pad, literally, about eight hours ago. My eyes meet the third spaceship that I've encountered on this roof in as many days. I'm counting the crash.

"Please, if you would," Palle says as he motions for us to board the ship.

"Back to space it is, I guess," Leo says. "Who would have thought that in just one day I'd be not thrilled with the prospect of going out into space for the second time?"

"It's an odd feeling, yes," Lyra says.

The ride back into space takes almost no time at all. Palle's ship is automated, with robot brains taking care of the functions of the ship. One of the many perks of being part of the Authority. Even Prentian tech looks a bit behind the curve after seeing the inside of this ship. The Authority vessel takes us to the edge of Earth's solar system in a little less than an hour.

"Why didn't we jump to hyperspace or something like that when we got to space?" Leo asks.

"Because that's not how you get to the *Unbeknownst*," Palle answers.

"What does that mean?" Lyra asks.

"There's a different type of technology that is used to get there," Palle says. "I don't suppose there's any harm in telling you about it at this point, at least in the case of you and your brother your exposure is pretty much absolute."

Lyra and Leo exchange nervous looks with me and Grendia. I smile and make a reassuring gesture, trying my best to let them know that it will all be okay. I have no faith that it will, mind you, but I don't need two survival-crazed humans thrown into Fight-or-Flight mode in a spaceship on the edge of the solar system. I have a hunch that it won't go well for Palle, or this ship, as I am sure that Grendia would not hesitate to help them. And then I'd be forced to jump in, and everything would go to…what's the human phrase? Ah, hell in a handbasket. I've always liked that one. Such a cheerful, nihilistic way to express certain doom.

"There's a nexus point not too far ahead of us," Palle says as if just saying that will answer all of Lyra's and Leo's questions.

"Oh, a nexus point, yeah," Leo says. "It *all* makes sense now that I know that."

Palle turns around in his seat and glares at Leo. "If you'd ever shut up for a moment, I *was* about to explain what that means."

"Oh, uhh, sorry," Leo says. I don't blame him for his attitude. I don't like being told to get on spaceships and going to get judged by celestial peoples, either.

"Oh, so *that's* a nexus," Leo says.

The ship is approaching a large structure that looks like a hexagonal gate with a large energy field in the middle. And that's exactly what it is. This is how Palle got here so fast. The Authority can establish one of these in any star system it wants to, as long as the technical officers on the *Unbeknownst* know the celestial coordinates of the gravity-null point, or the point where the system's star or stars ceases to be the strongest pull on objects in the vicinity and wild space takes over as the ruling celestial body, and can recall them to send them elsewhere at any time. It's *a lot* faster than hyper-travel, and a highly restricted and regulated technology that only the Authority has access to.

"Yeah," I say, "it's best to think of them as re-deployable wormholes, at least that's how I initially thought of them."

"That's not far off from the truth," Grendia adds.

The ship takes us into the center of the nexus, and we cross the barrier of the energy field that stands between regular space and nexus space. The other side looks like…

"There's nothing here!" Leo says.

"Now that's mostly true, yes," I say. "Nexus space isn't really a space at all but rather the extra dimensional pocket that exists between two sides of the same nexus field. It's kind of like Einstein's bridge. That guy wasn't wrong about much, really."

Just as quickly as we are in nexus space, we exit it, and the viewport is taken over by the sight of the space station *Unbeknownst*. It is very big, like bigger than the Death Star big, and it takes up the entire vision granted to us by the ship's viewport.

"You were not kidding about the size of this thing," Lyra says. "Have you ever seen it before?"

Grendia and I are as awestruck as the humans. I'd only ever heard tales of this place before today. It is beyond massive. The administration of the known universe resides within this structure, so that part shouldn't surprise me at all. And yet, I was not prepared for its massive and looming nature. Not that it feels evil, per se, just ominous. This is the big leagues of intergalactic relations and government, and we've managed to attract the attention of the people who are in charge of it.

Lucky us.

"Wait here," Palle says and walks through an open door that hisses shut behind him.

We are standing in a receiving antechamber that I assume is not far from where we will be meeting with whoever at the

Authority wants to see us. The walk from the docking bay was mind-boggling, with so many turns, loops, lift rides, and more hallways that all looked the same. Always the same. I couldn't make any reasonable attempt at leaving this place on my own, and I know that's the intent. Palle never seemed lost, and I never saw him reference any kind of screen or wall markings to make sure he was going to the right place.

I haven't seen anybody else but the four of us and Palle since we got off the ship. I'm surprised about that one. It's like they are isolating us to make sure we don't contaminate anybody else on the station. That *could* be accurate, the more I think about it. Lyra and Leo are the first humans ever to visit this place, as far as I know anyway. They could be skittish about Earth contaminants for some reason.

"How long will they make us wait, I wonder?" Grendia asks none of us in particular.

"There's no telling," I answer, just to have something to say. "We really have no idea who we're meeting here. It could be some bureaucrat who oversees some swath of space that includes Earth, or it could be some law enforcement official who will take issue with the fact that two humans were removed from Earth without a proper Authority clearance. We have, unfortunately, inadvertently crossed a few lines over the past few days, despite my efforts to keep things quiet."

"*That* was keeping things quiet?" Lyra asks. "I doubt there's anyone on Earth with a data connection who hasn't at least seen a thumbnail article of some kind that has to do with what went on in Lexington this weekend."

She then shrugs. "No matter how believable any of it may be, I suppose."

"Why do we have to keep all this a secret, anyway?" Leo asks. "Plenty of humans believe in aliens, and many people even think that the government has been keeping all this from us for decades, too."

"The truth is that the Earth governments know nothing concrete, but they have been sniffing around the presence of aliens on Earth for a century now," I say. "It's a mess, really, and all because humanity's observational capabilities have outstripped its technological space travel development."

"So if we'd kept pushing into space like we did in the mid-twentieth century, we might be part of the intergalactic community by now?" Leo asks.

I shrug. "Maybe. There's a lot of species who put political pressure on the Authority to make sure that a species is suppressed from being allowed into the intergalactic community until they reach certain levels of *both* technological *and* societal progress. Humanity has some issues as a whole that go beyond just technology, at least socially speaking."

"So all alien societies are utopias?" Lyra asks.

"You know that's clearly not the case," Grendia says. "But one of the main issues is usually that a planet needs to be united as a single society before it can be accepted. There are exceptions, but they are special cases and usually have to do with when two or more different sentient species coexists on the same planet."

"Oh," Lyra says, her shoulders dropping as her gaze trails off. "So humanity has a *long* way to go."

"I'm sorry," Grendia says. "For what it's worth, the very short time I've been on Earth, I like it very much. Humans are a very interesting species, and I am glad to have met both of you."

Lyra and Leo both smile at Grendia. I am also glad to have met both of them. They are, in fact, my favorite humans of all the ones I have met. Even if I had not ever developed romantic feelings for Lyra, I think that would still be true. They represent some of the best that the species has to offer, and I am glad they are here to represent their planet.

The door Palle walked through a few minutes earlier opens, and a small-statured blue alien walks through it. We all turn and wait to see what will happen next.

"Prince Jarokin, Grendia of Prentia, Lyra, and Leo of Earth," the alien says in a squeaky but forceful voice, "the Authority will see you now."

45

We file into the gallery of a formal meeting chamber. There is a podium for each of us, and we are directed to stand at them. The Authority Council chamber is a lot smaller than I thought it would be. This must be the chamber where they conduct their more private business, the stuff not meant for many onlookers or not of a particularly positive political impact. That's fine with me. I'm not in the mood to entertain any more crowds at the moment, let alone a bunch of self-important alien bureaucrats who only want to cause trouble for people who want to live their lives in peace. But maybe that's another rant.

A rather distinguished-looking alien, with a long neck and an extended mandible that is almost birdlike and anteater-like at the same time, addresses me as we step into the gallery. "Prince Jarokin of Prentia."

"Council," I say, nodding to them as a whole.

"This council meeting has been called to determine the fate of the planet Earth as it hangs in the balance after the events of the past three days, local Earth time, and to determine any personal culpability in the tainting and ruination of a technologically inferior species," the bird-eater lady continues. Her voice is kinda drone-like, and I'm in danger of being lulled to sleep by it.

"Wait, what?" Lyra blurts out. "The fate of the planet Earth? Jack, can they even decide something like that?"

"Quiet in the gallery!" The bird-eater lady forcefully taps a dark, polished rock in the shape of the Authority seal into a stand in front of her.

I make a gesture at Lyra, trying to get her to calm down,

and she flashes me a face that reminds me that humans really don't like being told what to do. Nor are they as a species very comfortable with the idea that their fate may not be in their own hands.

"These are *very serious* allegations, young lady," the council member continues, addressing Lyra directly. "We will not have our proceedings further interrupted by inappropriate outbursts. Decorum rules in this chamber."

"Which one of you is 'Decorum'?" Leo asks, and many of the council members guffaw and begin muttering things, mumbling to one another as they lean over and whisper in each other's ears for a moment.

"Which one of us is…" The bird-eater lady looks flustered. I don't think she's dealt with humans before.

"Yeah, that way I can ask *him* why we're here instead of you, since he's in charge and all," Leo says, continuing as if he didn't just upset the ruling body of pretty much the entire universe with his highly inappropriate and absolutely hilarious question. I know he's not stupid, either. He knew exactly what he asked.

Grendia is doing everything short of physically slapping her forehead with her palm right now. She looks horrified, and not a little scared, for the humans, who have no real idea of the forces they are currently being defiant toward.

The council members glare at him, but Leo does not cower nor apologize for his question. Good job, Leo. You've got guts. But guts aren't gonna get us out of this one.

I may need to step in here.

"Council members," I say, trying to bring their attention back to me. "I believe the next step in the proceedings is to formally state the allegations against the defendants, correct?"

I stare down each one of them, trying to bring out some of my old I'm-the-prince vibes. If I'm going to be treated like one, I might as well use it to my advantage if I can.

"Uhh, yes, Prince Jarokin—"

A very large and scaly-looking council member is talking now. He is incredibly blue. Like, *so* blue. I can't remember the last time I saw a blue like his scale color. I wonder if Earth scientists have it wrong and dinosaurs were more like this guy?

"—the offenses alleged against you and your companions are many, and you *are* entitled to hear each one of them *before* these proceedings continue." Blue Scales motions to a scribe.

The scribe clears his throat before beginning to speak. "In the matter of the Authority Council vs. Prince Jarokin of Prentia, Grendia of Prentia, Lyra of Earth, and Leo of Earth, the following offenses have been alleged. First, that Prince Jarokin and Grendia of Prentia did knowingly and willingly participate in multiple altercations with Authority citizens on an unsanctioned conflict planet, being hereafter designated as Earth, resulting in the deaths or grievous injury of said citizens, that in the commission of the previously stated actions, Prince Jarokin and Grendia of Prentia did knowingly and purposely expose dozens of human beings to advanced technology that is not legally available to the dominant Earth-native species, either through trade or other commerce activity, and that they, in the course of their previous actions, did knowingly and willingly involve human beings in the affairs, action, and knowledge of intergalactic activity that humanity at large is prohibited, by way of international treaty and bound by law, to have both knowledge of and participation in. All this being sworn in a warrant to Authority personnel and granted evidence via discovery of admission of personal testimony and digital corroboration, leads the council to indict the said parties for the high crimes of murder and public disregard.

"In short, the number of statutes and intergalactic embargoes that have been breached on Earth in the past ninety-six hours reaches the dozens, and as the Authority Council's want to do in situations like this, we need to assign blame and punish the guilty parties, then determine what the clean-up procedures will look like," Bird-Eater says.

"*That* was the short version?" Leo asks. "And public disregard is a high crime? Dude, space is terrible. Take me back to Earth."

"Agreed," Lyra says, an edge in her voice. She crosses her arms and stares down Bird-Eater. I am highly entertained when it is Bird-Eater who breaks visual contact first.

"Furthermore," Bird-Eater continues, pretending that Lyra totally didn't just win a stare-down with her, "it is this council's understanding that the Prentian Crown has formally withdrawn its support of Prince Jarokin, meaning that he cannot claim any kind of diplomatic immunity, should the council even be inclined to grant any in a case of a violation of the Primitives Clause of the Authority Charter."

She really does like to talk. I'm not surprised. Anytime someone like this gets a chance to hear the sound of their own voice, they take full advantage of it. As she speaks, attempting to impress on me the legal crapstorm I'm in because I'm no longer considered a "prince" by any legal definition the council cares about, I look at the other members sitting in front of me. They are all up on a raised dais and sitting comfortably behind a long, lavishly decorated and carved table. It's kind of like they're the Intergalactic Supreme Court. That's what a human might think of them as, I suppose, at least one from the United States. They look about as old and out of touch as some of those people, too.

"Yes," I say, and Grendia, Lyra, and Leo all look at me with eyes wide, and mouth open in the case of Leo. "My family has withdrawn their support of me, which means I now address this council as a sovereign without a system, an alien in my own land."

"Then you must know," Blue Scales interjects, "that we can use the full force of the law in our rulings on the allegations against you."

"I do," I say.

"Hey, what about us?" Leo asks. "None of those allegations mentioned anything about Lyra and me doing anything wrong. Why are we even here?"

"In short," Blue Scales says, turning his *so* very blue head toward Leo, "you and your sister know too much. Just the fact that you're here, taking all of this in, and you're not displaying the common signs of traumatic stress that other species demonstrate on being brought into the intergalactic community for the first time, is incredible reason for concern."

"But they're pretty much all like that," I say.

"What?!" Several Council members blurt out the inquiry at once. I am pleased that I have their attention.

"Humans are one of the most amazing species I've ever encountered," I say, "and this body tends to overlook them and others like them simply because they have not met the standard benchmarks of species-level development that you arbitrarily decided was needed for membership in the intergalactic community. But they can surprise you. Hell, these two have done it just by standing in front of you and, despite all of the danger and the power you represent, questioned your very authority and your ability to use it on them. Pretty powerful argument that humanity might not be as unevolved as you believe them to be, isn't it?"

The council doesn't just mumble this time. The eruption of comments, questions, and raucous verbalizations is only this side of complete bedlam. I smile, as I am pleased to see that at least a couple of the council members appear to be on our side on the issue. How far on our side remains to be seen, but the council has yet to reveal its intentions for Lyra and Leo, and I am hoping that we can avoid whatever those intentions may be. I promise that they are not good in any way.

"Thanks, I think," Lyra says to me. "For sticking up for us 'primitives' like that."

I open my mouth to clarify that I don't think that of them, but she winks at me as one corner of her mouth pulls back and up in a lopsided grin. She tilts her head toward the council and laughs. I laugh with her, and I see that Leo, and to a lesser extent Grendia, appear to be enjoying the momentary chaos. I hope we don't end up paying for it.

Though it has been fun to see the council squirm a bit, we're still far from being out of danger.

46

"You still haven't answered my question," Leo says.

The council members look at one another, none of them willing to address the elephant in the room. It's a fair question. Even for an organization as totalitarian in its use of power as the Authority, if it got out that they were just rounding up inconvenient people until they figure out what to do with them, it might cause them some trouble. Not that they don't do that, but if it ever got out, it could be interesting.

"As I said," Blue Scales eventually says, "you and your sister are anomalies."

"So you just kidnap people who don't conform to how you think they should act?" Leo fires back.

"Prince Jarokin," Blue Scales says, ignoring Leo, "you would do well to remind your human friend that this council is the highest body of law and justice in the known universe."

"I think it would be better to tell us why you have really brought us here," I say. "I mean no disrespect to the council in saying this, but even after the reading of the offenses against Grendia and myself, along with the anomaly study of the humans' ability to quickly roll with a rapidly changing universe, you still have yet to clearly state what the purpose of all this is. Do you mean to sentence us? Are we to be incarcerated, exiled?"

I let my statement hang to give the council members a chance to respond. While Leo has been making good points, and his questions *do* deserve answers, I feel like the council has something else going on behind the scenes. From what I know of them, their actions here are…off. I have a suspicion that they have yet to reveal what they are really after.

"This council has yet to vote on the ultimate fate of the four of you," a council member who has not addressed us yet says. This one looks like he is made primarily of some kind of sentient gas that inhabits a seashell-looking series of joints and limbs. I have no idea how he is speaking, but the universal translators at work in this room appear to understand him well enough.

"What we are currently determining," Gassy continues, "is whether or not to hold the humans to the same standards of intergalactic law and infraction punishment as you who are from Prentia. With their exposure level and subsequent actions since arriving on the *Unbeknownst*, it is currently up for debate if these two humans have indeed risen above their species' citizenship level and ascended into the stratosphere of full citizen."

"Has that ever even been considered before on an individual basis?" I ask.

"It has not," Gassy responds, "which is why the debate is taking as long as it is and why the four of you have been called in to testify before the council."

"I don't want to be a citizen," Lyra says. "Not if the price I pay for my knowledge is simply to be raised up in stature only so you can feel better about being on some stupid moral high ground before you squash me. If that's where this is headed, then I've got something to say about your crappy Authority."

"Yeah!" Leo adds in. "And there's also the videos that I scheduled, too!"

All of us. Everyone in the room, Council members, Lyra, Grendia, the bailiff, the reporter, and me, immediately focus all of our attention on Leo. He looks around and shrinks back slightly.

"What?" he asks.

"What videos?" I ask.

"The ones that I took while Niolan kidnapped me. Oh! And

from the night before when I happened to see you and that other guy in your hotel room without your mac-thingy's on." As Leo speaks, Lyra's shocked face turns into a smile, and by the time he is done, she is laughing quietly to herself.

"So, you recorded Niolan's kidnapping of you?" I ask.

"Well, yeah," Leo says, shrugging. "Those guys weren't the brightest. They forgot to check me for a second phone after they snatched the first one out of my hands when they attacked Grendia and me."

"Are you alleging that you have in your possession evidence that your exposure to intergalactic truth is through no fault of your own?" Gassy asks.

Leo nods. "Yep."

"Let us see it, now, human!" Bird-Eater pipes up. I am getting the impression that she might be on the side of the council vote that wants to treat Lyra and Leo as citizens, and that Gassy may, in fact, be one of the closest things to an ally that any of us have in this room

Leo produces his phone and hands it to the bailiff, who takes it up to the council table and sets it on a technology interface pad. Most any technology in the galaxy can be remotely accessed, displayed, and sifted through once it is placed on one of those pads. One of the perks of being Authority. One of the many, many perks.

A holo-screen projector drops down from the ceiling and begins projecting in the middle of the room for all to see. Just as Leo said, there are videos, pictures, and even audio recordings of his time being kidnapped by Niolan and even Bossy. This kid is awesome! He's got all the evidence that we need to show the council that none of what happened was our fault.

"Yeah, so ya see, illustrious Council, or whatever," Leo says, doing his best to sound formal, "there's all this evidence that other people made Jack—er—Prince Jarokin's weekend pretty terrible, and not him. He actually saved all of us, and more than once."

"All this evidence proves," Bird-Eater says, "is that Jarokin's and Grendia's complete lack of discretion in all of these matters led to the continued exposure of the intergalactic community to a non-member world and makes it even more likely that there may have been other witnesses, that even we do not know about."

"Young man," Gassy interrupts Bird-Eater before she can say more, "did you say something about scheduling this evidence to be posted somewhere?"

"Oh…uhh…yeah," Leo says. "I didn't know that I was going to be rescued, so I scheduled all of the Niolan-related stuff, along with some other pictures and videos that I had taken over the weekend, to be posted to pretty much all of my social media accounts on Monday morning, unless I cancel them. At the time it was meant to be how I would let Jack and Lyra know what happened to me, ya know, in case nobody found me in time."

"No one will believe these videos after what Jarokin said in his press conference!" Blue Scales jumps in with actually a pretty good point.

"Maybe not." Leo shrugs. "But a few might believe it. And then a few more after that. And then eventually you'll have a problem on your hands."

"*Leo*," Grendia says quietly, "do you know what you're doing?"

"I do not," Leo says in a hushed tone, as if the aside cannot be heard by anyone else in the room.

"It is clear this human is out of his depth here," Bird-Eater says, "and on that note, I propose that we sanction and punish—"

Bird-Eater is interrupted by the other council members,

who all begin speaking to one another again in rushed and hushed voices, away from their microphones. They appear to be debating how to best incorporate Leo's gambit move into the situation. Their goal at this point has got to be containment. The early exposure of a sentient race to the intergalactic community has resulted in epic, Armageddon-like disaster *every single time* it's happened. And a turnover of power in the Authority has *always* followed afterward. After several minutes, the council members all return to their seats and face us once more.

"Prince Jarokin," Gassy says.

"Council member," I respond.

"While the human known as Leo may not have a grasp of the gravity of his actions, you no doubt do."

"I have some understanding of the—"

"I was not finished," Gassy interrupts. "Because *you* exist as a citizen under Authority dominion, and in light of the evidence that has been presented by the humans that at the *very* least gives weight to your assertion that the events of the past seventy-two hours are not your fault but in fact a construct of outside forces beyond your control, this council is inclined to explore alternative means of resolution for the problems before us today."

Outside forces? He means my mother, of course, but he won't say it. Not even a power member of the Authority Council wants to cross someone like my mother. No doubt she has at least a couple of the members by the short and curlies in some way. My money would be on Bird-Eater, but maybe I just don't like her. At least they appear to have taken death off the table. At least I think that's what Gassy is saying. I better make sure to listen more carefully.

"...decision of this body that you shall be installed as the Regent of Earth, effective immediately, and charged with the preservation of the virtual bubble of secrecy that surrounds the neighboring planetary and solar systems."

Wait, *what?*

I blink several times as I try to catch up with, and fill in the blanks for, what I missed Gassy say as he was droning on.

"Did you not hear him, Jarokin?" Grendia asks, her tone awfully close to berating me. I probably deserve it.

"Pretend I didn't," I say.

"You've managed to be put in charge of Earth, Jack!" Lyra blurts out, clearly distraught that I had zoned out and missed the biggest bomb drop in the history of…well…Earth.

47

"Oh, yeah, I heard that part," I say, doing my best to remain calm.

Crap. Crap. Crap. Crap. Crap. This is so much worse than death. Can I just die instead?

"Do you have anything to say, *Regent*?" Gassy asks, clearly looking for me to do something.

I turn toward the council and take in a slow breath. This is terrible. And I did not see anything like this coming. I walked away from this when I left Prentia. And now I have my own planet, at least in the eyes of the Authority. I feel like I'm not doing a good enough job expressing how big this is. Even to myself. It's a bit esoteric as concepts go, really. Being in charge of an entire planet, even if they know you're the one in charge, is nearly impossible.

Have to think about what's really happening here. I'm being set up to fail. That's clear. The hardliners in the council have been outvoted. That's a good thing, for now. It means we, and Earth, get to live to see another day. But they didn't lose by so much that they can't influence how the alternate solution plays out. And it's me. I'm the alternate solution. It's kinda brilliant, really. I never saw it coming. Putting me in charge is the best move my detractors could have come up with. Was this mother's doing as well? I hate that I can't help but see her hand in all of this. It would be just like her to punish me for leaving Prentia by leashing me to my adopted hiding place.

I open my eyes, my expression taking on the bearing of Prince Jarokin once again. This will not be pleasant.

"Honorable members of the council," I begin, "it is with a humble mind and spirit that I accept your judgment on this matter."

Whatever their personal reasons, most of the council members look pleased. Blue Scales is wearing a toothy grin, but I have no idea if that's just how he smiles when he's happy. He could be pleased, or he could be savoring the impossible position I've just been put in. Refusing this appointment would have doomed us all, and I can't have that, now can I? Earth and humanity don't deserve that. So not to get all noble out of nowhere, but apparently now I'm the planet's protector. I wonder if I'll have a swearing-in ceremony?

"Approach the bench for the swearing-in ceremony," Gassy says.

"Oh," I say, "like right now? We're just doing this right here?"

"Would you prefer a parade?" Gassy asks, his tone bordering between bemused and stern.

"Ahh," I begin.

"Approach," Gassy says.

"Jack, is this for real?" Lyra says to me. "Are you really about to do what I think you're about to do?"

I turn to Lyra and give her a wink and a big smile. "Why, my dear, if you mean to ask if I'm about to selflessly pledge my life and my service to the Authority, placing my body and self between Earth and the rest of the universe until such time that humanity is ready to join the intergalactic community, then yes. That's what I'm about to do."

"That's really hot, Jack," Lyra says. Her expression is…stoic? But her eyes and her words are…not. Humans are *so* complex.

"I don't think so," Leo says, "but not dying right now

sounds pretty cool to me!"

"Jarokin," Grendia says, "this is everything you walked away from. You're really going to accept this?"

I shrug. "What choice do I have? The Authority is being merciful and in an unprecedented manner. It seems that cooler heads have prevailed here today. That, and maybe a little bit of coercive arm twisting from Leo here, has laid this path out in front of us."

I step toward Grendia and stand in front of her. "Grendia, I won't be able to do this without you. Are you with me?"

Grendia stands up straight and holds my gaze with a stern and serious composure. "I am, my Prince. Now, and always, no matter the planet or title you hold. You are my friend first, and that means more than any of the rest."

I nod and smile. "Then I think with you, Lyra, and Leo standing with me, I just might be able to do this."

I turn toward the council. "I am ready."

"Not that it was really a request," Gassy says, "but it appears that you are, yes."

I walk up to the center of the council table, directly in front of Gassy. A panel opens on the tabletop, and a small device on a robotic arm extends upward to meet my eye level. The device activates and takes my biometric scan data. Retinas, blood type, even my hand prints. This little thing is thorough. When it is done with the biometrics, text begins scrolling on the screen, explaining all about how the council has decreed that Prince Jarokin of Prentia shall hereafter be appointed to the stewardship of the planet known as Earth, acting as regent in place of a planetary ruler, until such time as…blah blah blah.

"Repeat after me," Gassy says once the formal decree finished its scrolling.

I drone my way through the Oath of Regency, and at the

end of it, I feel no different. I mean, I know that I'm in charge of a whole solar system now, but that's a long stretch to completely comprehend, even for me at this point. I started the weekend in charge of a forty-by-forty booth at a fandom convention. A planet is a bit of a difference. Wait. Is it? Yeah. It's got to be. Maybe. I think.

"This hereby closes the proceedings of this body as pertains to the Earth, Prince Jarokin, Grendia, and the humans Lyra and Leo," Blue Scales announces. "Any further matters are hereby canceled or postponed as per the edict laid down by this council today. Regent Jarokin, may you always prosper in your endeavors, and may Earth be the better for your leadership. You are free to go."

Hearing that we are free to go is the release my body must have been waiting for. I walk, more stumble, really, over to the others and practically fall onto a bench. I look back to the council bench to see the last images of them waver and fizzle out.

"Whoa," Leo says, seeing the same thing. "So they were never *really* here?"

"They were," I say, "in all the ways that count. I'm not surprised they were using hologram proxies. They're a paranoid lot. Even the better ones among them."

Lyra pushes past Leo and wraps me in a huge hug. I'm really getting used to these hugs. Like, as in getting used to the good feelings that they bring. Lyra is here, and that's all that matters. We are free. Well, they are in any case. I am insofar as my new position will allow. But the Council will always be watching, and I need a plan.

"I don't really get what just happened," Lyra says, pulling away and sitting next to me, taking my hand in hers. "I have this feeling that you're still being punished, and in our place, too."

I shrug. "It's not so bad, really. Being regent of a planetary system does have its advantages. At least, on a normal system it would. Earth is going to take some work. It's not like I can walk around and just tell people I'm in charge now."

"No, far from it," Grendia adds. "Being Regent of Earth is going to be a bit more like being the caretaker of one of those…what do you call them? The places where the burrowing insects live between two panels of glass so their honeycomb-like dens can be observed by all?"

"Ant farms," I say.

"Yes, that," Grendia says, nodding. "Being Regent of Earth will be like managing an ant farm. Only the ants can go anywhere, don't recognize you as their caretaker, and would sooner capture and dissect you than listen to what you have to say."

"Hey now," I say, standing up from the bench. "Don't go overselling how awesome it's going to be all at once. It sounds horrible, and I'm already considering committing a capital crime on my way out of here to make the council have to kill me."

"No you're not," Lyra says, punching my shoulder, "and don't talk like that. You're going to be great at this, Jack."

"I hope you're right," I say, "but there's a lot to do. And speaking of, that starts with how to get out of here. Anybody get a valet ticket?"

"Well, you didn't die!" Palle is standing next to his shuttle in the landing bay when we finally find it. "I can say on this side of things that I was rooting for you the whole time."

"You know, I had the feeling you were a decent fellow," I say, clapping Palle on the shoulder. "Are you our ride out of here?"

Palle nods. "I am. And what's more, I'm now your point of contact for official Authority communications, *Regent*."

"Ah, so they told you," I say.

"They did," Palle says.

"Exactly *when* did they tell you about how things turned out?" I ask, raising an inquisitive eyebrow and staring Palle down.

Palle chuckles and turns to walk into the shuttle. "Now that would spoil all the mystery of how the Authority does things, wouldn't it?"

The ride back to Earth is uneventful, and that in itself feels like a miracle. To have something go as intended and not blow up in our faces feels a bit odd after so much adrenaline has pumped through our bodies over the past few days.

Time works differently in the space where the *Unbeknownst* exists, and Palle returns us to Earth only about an hour after we left. It felt more like six hours to us, and Leo has a mini freakout over the time dilation needed to pull off what we just went through.

Though we're all very tired, we all go to my room and sit around the table for several hours, just talking about everything that has happened. Lyra and Leo have some blank spots about this or that, mostly having to do with parts of whatever happened that they missed or weren't a part of directly.

I get the story of what happened on Bossy's ship while I was out of it and plugged into the ships auto-med unit. Leo falls asleep first, crawling onto the couch and folding his tall and lanky frame into an impossibly small shape before losing consciousness. Fortunately, we had him deactivate his auto-posts on social media before he did so. Grendia nods off next. One moment she is laughing about a joke while I tell the story of one of my many fights from my perspective, and the next moment she is lightly snoring, her chin drooping onto her chest as sleep finally claims her. I don't think she's slept in a few days.

"You want to go for a walk?" I ask Lyra, who looks as awake as I do. She nods and takes my hand. We leave Grendia and

Leo in the room and head out of the hotel into the pre-dawn morning glow.

48

"How does it feel?" Lyra asks.

"It's kinda tough to feel anything but sore at the moment," I say.

We've been walking around for almost an hour now, spending most of the time in silence, just holding hands and enjoying the peace. The city is still asleep, but it will soon be starting a brand new Monday morning. The first Monday morning with me as regent, though none of them know it. I am purposely deciding to not think about what my first moves should be, at least not just yet. I'd like to take a selfish moment and enjoy this walk with Lyra. I have a feeling that things will get complicated soon, and I *know* she didn't sign on for this. I am scared she won't like the new situation once she realizes what it means for me.

"Drugs worn off?" she asks.

"Long ago," I say. "The last bit of emergency painkillers that Grendia still had in the hotel wore off about the time Palle collected us to take us to meet with the Authority."

"You hide it pretty well," Lyra says, looking me over. "I can tell your walk is a little stiff, but other than that you seem fine."

"It's the maccomp," I say. "It's doing a lot of work right now."

"Oh right, that thing," Lyra says. "Do you think that *I* could get one of those? It would make the morning routine so much easier."

I laugh softly. We are a few blocks from the hotel now, and a corner breakfast café has just opened up. I suggest that we get some coffee and a bagel, and Lyra agrees that it sounds like a great idea.

"So what I asked before," Lyra says after we order our coffees.

"Yeah," I say. "I'm trying to avoid that."

"But you can't," she says.

I look across the table into her deep brown eyes. I didn't want very much out of life a few days ago, and that part of me remains. I still don't want very much out of life. Not much, except for Lyra. So much of my old life has come back to haunt me, and Lyra has refused to let it drive her away.

"You're staring, Jack," Lyra says, giggling.

"Am I?" I ask. "I'm sorry."

"Don't be," Lyra says. "I just want to know what you were thinking about as you were getting lost in my eyes."

"Well," I say, "I was thinking about you."

"That's an easy answer," Lyra says. "But what *specifically*?"

"This weekend changed everything," I say.

"Even before I knew who you really are, that was true," Lyra says.

"Yeah…" I say. "We haven't really had a chance to talk about all of that change, have we?"

"No," Lyra says. "We haven't even successfully completed a date yet."

"What about right now?" I ask.

"This is breakfast," Lyra says, "not a date. And a well-earned We-Just-Saved-the-World breakfast at that."

"That's fair," I say. "Leo and you have been adapting to a new normal pretty well. I am very impressed."

"Well, our lives haven't exactly been a hallmark of stability anyway," Lyra says. "First our parents, then Leo becoming my responsibility. And life on the con circuit isn't the best thing for a teenager. I am afraid I've done it all wrong with Leo."

Our coffee and bagels arrive, and Lyra stares down into her cup, letting her last words hang until the server has departed.

"I don't think that's the case at all," I say. "Leo is a great kid, and he's about to be all grown up. Sure, maybe he's quirky, but I don't think I'm the one to judge that kind of thing. And you have given him the best life possible considering the circumstances."

Lyra smiles and appears to take my words of encouragement to heart. We sip on our coffees for a moment. There is a different dynamic to me and her now, though. I don't think either of us feels the need to fill empty air with something, and that's a brand new feeling. I think it's mostly the extreme fatigue of the weekend's adventures, but I like not feeling like I have to be "on" around Lyra. Not that I did previously, but before our date I know I would have said something here to keep the conversation going.

"You have still managed to avoid my question," Lyra says, breaking the silence.

I'm mid-bite into my bagel, so I make a gesture that communicates I should finish my bite before I start speaking.

"Mhmm," Lyra says. "Stall all you want, I'm not dropping it."

I take another sip of coffee to help the hastily chewed bagel go down before attempting to speak.

"I'm not trying to avoid it," I say. "I just want the time I spend with you to not have to be bogged down by the near future. There's a lot to do."

"Like what?" Lyra asks. "What really needs to change now that you're the regent?"

"Practically, on the surface, that humans will see in their daily lives? Almost nothing." I respond. "I *will* have to carry through with my promise to form a tech company that will develop a version of the maccomp, albeit a much downgraded version. We will likely have to work with Palle to make sure that I don't take things too far, but I'm not worried. Human technology is making breakthroughs all the time. I guess it's just time for another one."

"But what about actually getting Earth ready to join the intergalactic community?" Lyra asks. "Isn't that something you're supposed to do, too?"

"Technically, yes," I say. "In time, we could make progress on that front, I suppose. Earth is a very divided planet, though, and I will have to be careful. It will start with the shadow markets. By now I'm sure news has started to spread about the new situation the Authority has established on Earth, and I will have to figure out how to reorganize the shadow markets to best suit the needs of humanity first and the aliens who run it second."

"You're talking like you're one of us," Lyra says.

"Legally, I am now," I say. "As Regent of Earth, I'm human on paper, in a sense."

"I think I get that," Lyra says. "Our fate is your fate now, and vice versa."

"Yep," I say.

"You sure you don't regret tying yourself to us like that?" Lyra asks. "Humanity is a handful."

"Well, it includes you and your brother, so yes," I say playfully. Lyra tilts her head to the side and narrows her eyes in response to my dig.

"You weren't complaining about me being human last night on the elevator," Lyra says.

"And I hope that I can continue not complaining more in the future," I say.

"We'll see," Lyra says, raising an eyebrow as she raises her coffee cup to her lips.

We finish breakfast in no hurry at all. Checkout time at the hotel isn't until noon, so we can take our time getting Leo and Grendia and all of our stuff together before we figure out the next move. Lyra and Leo live in Cleveland, and I have an apartment in Los Angeles as well as apartments in Atlanta and Miami. I would like to head to LA next, as that is the location that is closest to the central import and export hubs for the shadow markets, but I am dubious about my chances of getting the other to agree to get onto a plane. Some of them might be a little burnt-out on flying at the moment.

Lyra and I walk back to the hotel as the city shows more signs of waking up. Cars drive by, workers needing to get to work. More of the shops are opening up now, and the sun is ready to crest over the distant trees and buildings and shine onto the east/west-oriented streets, one of which we are currently walking on.

"I guess we could go to Los Angeles," Lyra says. "I don't mind where we are right now, as long as I'm with you."

"You're really all in on us, huh?" I say.

Lyra pulls back from walking close to me, side eyeing me with an all too familiar look of skepticism. "Are you not? Cause if you don't think this is the real deal, then we best talk about that now, buddy."

She has me going for a moment, and the look of panic and confusion about what to say next must be excruciatingly hilarious. She holds her look for a moment more, waiting for me to say something.

"No, that's not what I…No, Lyra, I just meant that it's nice, and that I'm all in, too. And that I have been for a while now, like a long while. You're not just a passing fancy, if that's what you mean. I could never…and…but…" I am drowning. Like fast. And hard.

Lyra stops and pulls me to the side, into the shade of an awning next to a shop. I am still trying my best to stammer out a reasonable response that won't get me dumped by the love of my life, and she's just shaking her head and laughing at me.

Wait.

She's laughing at me? I stop talking.

"Some regent you are," Lyra says, pulling me close to her. "So easy to get you all tongue-tied."

Lyra grabs my jacket and pulls me the rest of the way into a kiss that shuts me up very handily. I wrap my arms around her as she slides her hands into my jacket and, gingerly, around my midsection. I appreciate her remembering how hurt I am in the middle of such a passionate kiss. I'm not sure I could have done the same, if I'm being honest.

After a solid minute, she pulls away just slightly and smiles.

"I knew you were all in," she says. "I've known for a while, Jack. You might have been able to keep some things a secret from me, but not that. You're pretty terrible at it, actually."

"Oh," is all I manage to say before she kisses me again for a long moment before stepping back and taking my hand to continue our walk back to the hotel.

As we walk into the hotel lobby, I catch a spot of color out of the corner of my eye. It is nothing, just a wisp, but it is there. By the time I look over toward it, it is gone. But I know what it means.

"Lyra," I say, "go on up and see if you can get the others up and organized."

"Where are you going?" Lyra asks, a moment of panic in her voice. She is probably afraid that there is a new danger, and I don't blame her for thinking that.

"I won't leave the hotel," I say. "There's just some business to take care of. Regent stuff."

"Ah, so it begins," she says.

Lyra squeezes my hand as we part ways, and I walk into the hotel restaurant. The hostess greets me, and I tell her that I am here to meet my party in the executive room. The hostess nods and leads me to the back of the restaurant, through a closed door made of frosted glass. I thank her for escorting me to my destination, and as she closes the door I sit down at the small table meant for an intimate dinner of no more than six guests. But there is only one other person at the table with me.

"Hello again, Mother," I say, looking across the table at the Queen of Prentia.

49

"Regent of Earth. How about that?" My mother somehow manages to convey more pleasantness in the title than she ever did in me personally.

"No thanks to you," I say.

"Oh, no, Jarokin," she says, raising a finger at me. "Shame on you. *Every* thanks to me."

"So you say," I respond.

I really have no idea how involved she has been in the background of all of this. She could have orchestrated the whole thing, or she could have stepped in at the last minute and changed the initial plan to one that suited her goals better somehow. I'll never know, and I don't care to know. She sent a guy to kill me. *That* I do know. And for that, she will never get a thank you from me for any of this.

"You really don't have to pretend with me, Jarokin," she says, dropping her hand to her side as if she has just let a butterfly that landed there fly off into the trees. I'm already at my limit with her air of flighty superiority.

"I'm not pretending, Mother," I say. "I don't want to see you. Ever, let alone sit here and talk to you about anything."

"But it is customary for the ruler of a planet to meet with a visiting dignitary," she says, her tone the kind of fake, nasal contrition that has driven me to near madness since I was very young.

"Oh, so this is a state visit, is it?" I ask.

"Of a sort, Jarokin," she says.

"Very well," I say. "Then what does the Queen of Prentia

want with Earth?"

"Oh, very little. Practically nothing at all," she says. "I just wanted to see if you were aware of the circumstances that put you into your new position of power and authority and make sure that you were grateful to the right person."

"That right person being the Authority Council, of course," I say.

"Of course," Mother says with a polite nod.

"Okay, drop it," I say. "What do you *really* want?"

"I want for you to be happy, son," she says.

"I won't ever believe that," I say. "Until I return to Prentia and am your obedient little puppet prince, one day your puppet king, if you can somehow manage it, you won't ever give up trying to make my life as terrible as you can."

"What a thing to say to your own mother," she says, recoiling from my statement.

"The scullery maid was more of a mother to me than you," I say. I chose my words carefully, too. The scullery maid in the palace where I grew up was a widow with no children, and she loved spoiling me with treats from the kitchen whenever she could spare any. She died two years before I left Prentia, leaving no one behind, save perhaps myself, with a kind memory of her. My mother cannot hurt her or anyone she loved.

That's how careful I have to be with the Queen of Prentia. As soon as I show her a weakness, she is likely to exploit it. She probably saw me walking into the hotel with Lyra, which means I need to give up the naive fantasy that my mother somehow is unaware of my affection for her.

"Now I think you're just trying to be mean," Mother says.

"Oh, I'm sorry," I say. "Perhaps if you told me why you're here, I could help you leave this planet and never return."

"I'm here to make sure you understand the weight of the

burden that has been placed on you," she says.

"I think I have a pretty good idea," I say.

"I do not believe that you *do*, Jarokin," she responds. Her face narrows as her tone gets serious. Oh good, we've moved past the repartee part of the conversation and are about to get to the serious part. The threats usually follow soon after.

"Then enlighten me," I say. "Not that I could stop you from saying whatever it is you're going to say."

"You're being set up to fail, you know," she says.

"Am I?" I ask.

I mean, yeah, probably. The Authority is going to be keeping one huge, hairy eyeball on Earth for a long while, maybe until I am no longer Regent and even after that. I know that none of them, even the ones who might somehow consider themselves the good guys, were doing me any kind of favor by making me Regent. Earth is a powder keg primed to blow. One more bad exposure that I can't get ahead of, a ship crashing in a place that can't be covered up, like a convention center or similar place, and it could be game over.

But the council, above all, wants to keep its power, and the more intelligent among them understand that if the situation on this planet goes badly, it likely means a turnover in the power structure of the Authority. And that's exactly why Mother is here. Her game is to make sure that happens. Why she's decided to sacrifice me in the balance of her power game, I don't know and don't really care, but the pieces are falling in for me now. No matter what, I can't fail on Earth. Not only because I love humanity and their planet, but if nothing else it means that my mother won't succeed in whatever scheme she is playing at.

"Of course you are," she says. "Even a novice at statecraft could see that, Jarokin. I am disappointed if this is truly news to you. Although, I suspect it is not. As much as I tried to influence your early development, I am afraid that your father's tutors may have won out on that one. Your statecraft comes from him. And your backbone."

The dig is not unexpected. She sees me as weak for leaving Prentia and fails to consider that I left because she is wrong. Well, mostly. The fact is that her way of looking at things *was* creeping into me. Her ways of managing a planet, the schemes, the assassinations, the payoffs that lead to more assassinations, the cover-ups of assassinations…actually, there were *a lot* of assassinations now that I think of it. I wonder if she's aware of the human historical figure Machiavelli?

All of her was becoming all of me, and I realized it before it was too late. That's why I left. Because the person sitting in front of me right now is everything I never wanted to be. I hope she never finds out how close she was to truly having her claws in me. I was almost the very thing she wanted, and she might not have even known it. Or worse, she did. And that's why she's being so vindictive now. In either case, I'm right back where I started, caught up in a web of her design. And right now, I'm the fly.

"Well, thanks for the warning, then, I guess," I say, getting up to leave.

"Just one last thing, Jarokin," she says. I turn back toward my mother to see what this last gem from her will be.

"And what's that?" I ask.

"I'm afraid that I can't release Grendia from my service at this time," she says. "She *is* a Prentian Royal Guard, after all, and that means that she will need to return to Prentia with me."

I am a real son of a bitch.

If Grendia stays with me on Earth, she will be in violation of her service to the Prentian Crown, something my mother knew would be the case all along. Of course. And *that* is the other reason why my mother convinced my father to withdraw from me the support of the Crown. As long as I had the protection of my station, Grendia's presence on Earth could be justified by being part of my royal guard detachment. But with my no-longer-legal status as Prince of Prentia, Grendia will be labeled a deserter if she does not return with my mother now. I wish she was here.

"I am with you, my Prince…"

That's what she said to me in the council chamber. I am choosing to trust in that now. It is the only option I have.

"No," I say.

"No?" Mother asks, both of her eyebrows raising at the question. "No what?"

"No, you won't be taking Grendia back with you," I say. "I won't have her continue to be a pawn in your games, at least not on Prentia where I cannot protect her."

"But, Jarokin—" Mother begins, but I cut her off.

"*Regent*," I correct her. "And as my first official act as Regent of Earth, I am formally granting Grendia political asylum and the full protection of the sovereign system of Sol, as established and upheld by the Authority."

Mother is silent for several seconds, looking at me with an expression devoid of any emotion. I am not so naive to believe that I have stunned her into silence. In fact, it's entirely possible that I've just done *exactly* what she wanted me to do. But I'm not going to let her dictate the fates of the people I care about. No longer, and never again.

"I hope you know what you're doing here, Jarokin," she says, rising from her seat and moving past me toward the door. "It would be a shame if your tenure as regent is shortened by mistakes that you make early on."

And like a wisp, she is gone. I get the feeling that I won't see her for a while, but that doesn't mean forever. She'll be keeping an eye on Earth, no doubt. And one of my new hobbies is figuring out exactly how she has been doing that. The game is on, Mother, and I'm not going to lose.

*   *   *

"You really didn't need to do that, Jarokin," Grendia protests as I tell her about the encounter with my mother.

"No, I did," I say.

"But you've just placed Earth in political opposition to Prentia," Grendia says. "I'm not worth that." She is not trying to hide the worry on her face.

"You most definitely are worth it," Lyra says. "And Jack was right to do whatever it is that he says he just did. I didn't follow most of it, but it sounded like the right thing, and that's that."

"It is done," I say, "and my vice regent is definitely worth any amount of trouble that she brings me. I wouldn't be here with her, after all."

"None of us would be!" Leo says. "Grendia is my hero. No offense, Jack."

"None taken," I say, "she's my pick for hero, too."

Grendia comes the closest to crying and blushing at the same time that I've seen someone get to, and she wraps me and Leo in a giant hug that causes me to wince, especially after she pulls in Lyra, too. Grendia is a hugger, that's for sure. And people keep forgetting that most of my ribs are broken. But hers are, too, so I'm sure Grendia is in as much pain as I am right now. But like her, I don't care.

"Well," Grendia says to the group after letting us all go. "Where to now?"

50

Earth.

Sure, it's native species can be a pain. But they're evolving just fine into what they are meant to be. And now that I call Earth my home, too, I am very excited to see where they are headed. I mean, there's nowhere else in the galaxy, or any other galaxy, that I'd rather be. And that's a good thing, too, because I'm in charge now.

I'm still figuring out what that looks like, but I have a team of dedicated friends to help. My girlfriend, who isn't afraid to speak her mind and let us aliens know what's what when it comes to humans. Her brother, who is all too eager to help out, even when the danger level is much too high for any human to sanely want to be involved. And a down-and-out ex-royal guard from my days as prince of another planet.

In the months following my installation as regent, Grendia and I found a tech company to buy. Based out of Los Angeles, it was already exploring a similar technology to the powered-down specs that we both came up with for the prototype version of Earth's maccomp. The technology still has a few decades to go before it begins to look anything near what alien tech can achieve, but the business is providing a great cover for our travels, which have become extensive.

We renamed the company Cos-Player. It was Leo's idea. He said that I'm not only a cosplayer, but that I'm also now a "Cosmic Player." We all rolled our eyes at the bad pun, none more so than Grendia, but the name stuck.

Meeting with all of the shadow market hubs, vendors, and

import and export individuals and companies is exhausting, and we're not done yet. Grendia is working hard to convince everyone that doing business on Earth is still as lucrative as ever, and while we do have to regulate things a bit more now, as regent I have a lot of leeway in how things are handled. I think the shadow market is on its way to becoming one of the best clandestine economic ventures in this part of the Milky Way, and that's all part of the grand plan.

Oh yeah, the grand plan. We have one, for the moment, but that's a lot to get into right now. Lyra and Leo moved to Los Angeles to work with us, too. Leo loves LA a little too much I think, and getting to work alongside Lyra every day makes it feel like one less thing has changed since the con circuit days. We're still planning on going to several every year, but not as vendors. Those days are, sadly, behind us.

"Hey, Jack!" Lyra calls out to me.

It's almost sunset, and I'm walking along the sidewalk on my way to meet Lyra for dinner at a little bistro along the beach that we've come to consider "our place." Even though it's been a few months now since QUASITASTICON 9, I am still checking my surroundings with a lot more vigilance than I used to. I'm not sure I will ever stop, especially now.

I wave to Lyra as I cross the street and join her at the table she has secured for us. My favorite drink is waiting for me, and Lyra gives me a quick kiss before sipping on her umbrella drink.

"Am I that late?" I ask.

"No," Lyra says, "I haven't been here very long."

"Grendia and I got…" I start.

"…caught up with some affairs of state," Lyra finishes for me.

I wince.

"Has that become my line?" I ask.

"You've said it a couple of times now," Lyra says, nodding along as she speaks.

"Well, I am running a company *and* a planet now," I say.

"And that's the only reason I forgive you for being late," she says. "You're protecting my favorite planet from being blown into space dust by the evil Authority, or the Prentian military, or whatever the danger of the week is now."

"Your favorite planet, huh?" I say, raising my eyebrows. "You know you've only ever been to the one, right?"

"Makes the decision of which one's my favorite that much easier!" Lyra says, raising her drink as we toast to Earth.

We spend the evening talking about what's next for Earth, for the company, and for us. And yeah, I'm definitely going to ask Lyra to marry me before too much longer. Not that I'm worried that she's going anywhere. I just feel like making our family official is important to her, for both her, and for Leo. Having a family again would make them feel whole, and if I'm being really honest with myself, it would make me feel the same, too.

We end the night looking out at the last embers of sunlight disappearing over the horizon of the Pacific Ocean. Earth is my favorite planet, too, and I'm not just saying that because I'm in charge of it. As homes go, I could have done a lot worse than Earth. I maybe could have done better, but on this side of all that's happened to get us to where we are, I seriously doubt it. It's the people I've met here that have made Earth that much better, and that's why I'll keep fighting for them, with every fiber of my being.

Earth has a bright future, and this alien is going to give all he has to make sure they see it.

Jack, Lyra, Leo, and Grendia will return in

The I, Player Series: Book Two
Role-Player

Hey there, Reader! Remember that part in the book you just read where Jack doesn't know what Grendia did for three hours?

Wanna know what happened?

Well now you can!

Scan the QR code below to download an exclusive, extra-length bonus chapter directly from my website!

Enjoy reading all about

Grendia's Three Hours!

About the Author

David G. Martin lives in Murfreesboro, TN with his wife and dog. An avid reader and fan of many science fiction and fantasy universes, David often plays games in many of these worlds and enjoys such hobbies as Lego kit building and musing on the finer points of Star Wars through ceaseless armchair commentary.